P9-DUG-853

"I want to kiss you so badly I can hardly stand it. But we can't let it happen like last time."

"We've never really talked about…that night," Jenny said. Maybe this was the moment to share her secret with him, when they were both aroused and incapable of denying what had happened.

T.J. shook his head. "Jenny, we're in a dangerous position. If we open all this up again…it might lead to something we can't handle."

It might lead to love, she thought. But who was she kidding? T.J. had bullied his way back into her life without asking permission or considering the cost.

She should be grateful for the distance he was putting between them now. A part of her *was* grateful. But the rest of her ached unbearably.

Dear Reader,

What better way to start off this month—or any month—
than with a new book by *New York Times* bestselling author
Nora Roberts? And when that book is the latest installment
in her popular Night Tales series, the good news gets even
better. I think you'll love every word of *Night Smoke* (which
is also this month's American Hero title), so all that remains
is for you to sit back and enjoy.

With *Left at the Altar,* award-winning author Justine Davis
continues our highly popular Romantic Traditions program—
and also brings back Sean Holt, a character many of you have
suggested should have his own book. *Annie and the Outlaw,*
by Sharon Sala, is another special book. This one boasts
the Spellbound flash to tell you it's a little bit unusual—
and as soon as you meet hero Gabriel Donner and discover
his predicament, you'll know exactly what I mean. Our
successful Premiere program continues this month, too,
introducing one new author in each line. Try Kia Cochrane's
Married by a Thread for a deeply emotional reading
experience. And don't forget Maggie Shayne—back with
Forgotten Vows...?— and Cathryn Clare, who checks in
with *The Angel and the Renegade*. All in all, it's another
wonderful month here at Intimate Moments.

I hope you enjoy all our books—this and every month—and
that you'll always feel free to write to me with your thoughts.

Enjoy!

Leslie J. Wainger
Senior Editor and Editorial Coordinator

Please address questions and book requests to:
Silhouette Reader Service
U.S.: 3010 Walden Ave., P.O. Box 1325, Buffalo, NY 14269
Canadian: P.O. Box 609, Fort Erie, Ont. L2A 5X3

THE ANGEL AND
THE RENEGADE

Cathryn Clare

INTIMATE™ MOMENTS®
Published by Silhouette Books
America's Publisher of Contemporary Romance

If you purchased this book without a cover you should be aware
that this book is stolen property. It was reported as "unsold and
destroyed" to the publisher, and neither the author nor the
publisher has received any payment for this "stripped book."

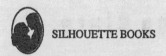

SILHOUETTE BOOKS

ISBN 0-373-07599-5

THE ANGEL AND THE RENEGADE

Copyright © 1994 by Cathy Stanton

All rights reserved. Except for use in any review, the reproduction
or utilization of this work in whole or in part in any form by any
electronic, mechanical or other means, now known or hereafter
invented, including xerography, photocopying and recording, or in
any information storage or retrieval system, is forbidden without
the written permission of the editorial office, Silhouette Books,
300 East 42nd Street, New York, NY 10017 U.S.A.

All characters in this book have no existence outside the imagination of
the author and have no relation whatsoever to anyone bearing the same
name or names. They are not even distantly inspired by any individual
known or unknown to the author, and all incidents are pure invention.

This edition published by arrangement with Harlequin Enterprises B. V.

® and TM are trademarks of Harlequin Enterprises B. V., used under
license. Trademarks indicated with ® are registered in the United States
Patent and Trademark Office, the Canadian Trade Marks Office and in
other countries.

Printed in U.S.A.

Books by Cathryn Clare

Silhouette Intimate Moments

Chasing Destiny #503
Sun and Shadow #558
The Angel and the Renegade #599

Silhouette Desire

To the Highest Bidder #399
Blind Justice #508
Lock, Stock and Barrel #550
Five by Ten #591
The Midas Touch #663
Hot Stuff #688

CATHRYN CLARE

had a dozen different part-time careers—from secretary to musician to arts administrator—before she finally gave in and admitted that writing was her full-time love. "No matter what I'm writing," she says, "the most important thing is that I care about my characters and what they're going through—and that I find a way to make my readers care, too."

Cathy lives with her trumpet-player husband and three cats in a small central Massachusetts town, where she divides her time between writing and renovation. "The cats and the view of the forest outside the window help with the writing part," she says.

To Annemarie,
and to Alice and Gemma,
who may be angels, or renegades,
or both, or anything at all

Prologue

*Pete Alvarez's Diary
1960s*

That night is still clear in my mind, clearer than a lot of things that have happened since then....

I didn't know what was happening at the time, and I still don't understand all of it now. I only know there was danger in it, danger and the devil....

I'd had a drink or two with some of my buddies in a bar. I was walking back alone. A beautiful night, I was thinking. I heard the shot—only one—and never thought about it. That was Saigon, it was wartime. You heard shooting and you never blinked.

Then I saw a door open and a man stumbled out, falling almost. He'd been shot in the thigh. I'd spent enough time in-country to know it was bad.

"For God's sake," he said to me. "For God's sake, help me."

You get a feeling sometimes. Like I was there at just that moment to help that man. An American, in uni-

form. I had another feeling, like he was still in danger, lying there in the street. I got him into an alleyway, him trying not to make a noise, and then I saw the other man.

He was standing in the doorway, with light behind him. Like a halo behind his head. Funny about the halo. I never knew a more evil human being.

I didn't know that then. I just knew he was looking around. The light from the doorway behind him caught something metal in his hand, a gun.

A bunch of people came along then, Americans, soldiers, in a jeep. The man stepped back inside and slammed the door. I was already tearing my shirt apart to make a tourniquet. I was a medic then. I was going to be a doctor once, but that was a long time ago.

I saved him, and it cost me. But he was a good man, and if I had to save one man and make an enemy of the other one again, I would still do the same thing.

And what does it matter, really . . . as long as she is safe?

Chapter 1

"Patricia, if you don't go home soon, I'm going to turn out your office lights and kick you out bodily."

Jenny Alvarez spoke lightly, but there was a firmness in her tone that Patricia Nesbitt didn't miss.

"I'm almost done," she said. "I just want to finish up these notes so you can have them over the weekend. Honestly, Jenny, I never knew you could be such a mother hen until I got pregnant."

Patricia was smiling, and Jenny smiled back. She had been very concerned about her friend and colleague ever since Patricia had announced she was going to have a baby. It wasn't just that Patricia was thirty-nine, or that this was her first child, or that she still tended to work late at the office even seven and a half months into her pregnancy.

"Five more minutes," Jenny said. "And then I'm pulling the plug on that computer."

Patricia laughed and promised she would do her best. Jenny went into her own office and started clearing off her desk, so she would have a fresh start when she came back on

Monday morning. The room was already neat and comfortable, with its upholstered sofa and chair and tastefully chosen flower posters on clean white walls. Jenny had decorated it with care, trying to create a place where her troubled clients would feel at ease.

She knew perfectly well why she was acting like a mother hen with Patricia, and sometimes she wondered whether she should share her secret reasons with her friend. Talking could be good medicine, as Jenny knew perfectly well from her four years as a therapist. But there were still some things in her own past that she didn't like to talk about.

"What are you doing for the weekend?" Patricia asked her, as the two women left the building. "Got anything special planned for your birthday?"

Jenny didn't like to make a fuss about her birthday, and Patricia knew that. She would be turning twenty-eight on Sunday, and in spite of her friends' hints that she should kick up her heels over the occasion one of these years, she was planning to keep it quiet, as usual.

"I'm going to be gardening, if the weather cooperates." Jenny cast an eye at the clouds. It had been drizzling all day, but there were gaps in the gray now, and she was hoping for the kind of warm early spring weekend that North Carolina sometimes provided in February.

"That's not a birthday celebration, Jenny. Why don't you come over for dinner on Sunday? Steven and I—"

"Deserve all the time to yourselves you can get. Don't worry, Patricia. I like spending my birthdays alone. You should know that by now." Patricia didn't know, and wouldn't, as far as Jenny was concerned, that she'd had a big blowout celebration for her birthday exactly once, the year she'd turned twenty-one. The experience had been directly responsible for the fact that she now preferred her birthdays to pass unnoticed, if possible.

"How about you and Steven?" she asked, as lightly as she could. "What have you got planned for the weekend?"

"Steven wants to wallpaper the baby's room. We picked out the paper when we went shopping last weekend, and he can't wait to get at it. And, since you're about to ask, no, he's not going to let me help. He's already informed me that I'm going to sit in a comfortable chair and tell him what a great job he's doing."

"And you call *me* a mother hen."

"You're each just as bad as the other. And I love it. I can't imagine doing this without all of you to rally round. Speaking of which, are you *sure* you don't mind taking on those three new clients?"

"Of course I don't mind. You know I've been wanting to do more with addictions counseling. And you've got to start lightening up your caseload, if you're going to be able to take a proper maternity leave."

"Sometimes I can't believe this is really happening." Patricia eased herself into the driver's seat of her car, grimacing a little. Her pregnancy, although welcome, had been unplanned, and Jenny knew she hadn't found it easy to adjust either physically or mentally to the sudden change in her life. "I mean, look at me. I already have to straighten my arms to reach the steering wheel. What am I going to look like in two more months?"

"Maybe your arms will have stretched by then," Jenny suggested. "Have a relaxing weekend, all right?"

"Don't worry. I will. And you have a happy birthday, even if it's a quiet one."

Jenny got into her own car, but she didn't turn the key in the ignition right away. It was hard to speak lightly to her friend these days, when every stray comment about Patricia's pregnancy cut deep into Jenny's own memories. And the memories conjured up by Patricia's birthday wishes weren't exactly happy ones, either.

Sometimes she felt haunted by the past, as though there were a part of her that had never escaped the uncertainties of her childhood, or the shadowy questions surrounding her father, or the loss of the one person who had ever really felt like family to her.

Usually she stopped her train of thought right there. What was the point of going over and over questions that had no answers? She acknowledged the pain she had been through, the feelings of loneliness and longing. All of that was real, but so was the fact that she had survived, and found strength in herself and her work. Why call up ghosts that had no place in her life now?

Jenny wondered afterward if her sudden thoughts about T.J. were some kind of premonition. Certainly it wasn't like her to be sitting in her car, eyes closed, picturing in intimate detail the man she'd once loved intensely, the man who had walked so completely out of her life. His unruly dark hair...that flashing smile, cynical, impossibly sexy...his thick, powerful hands...those tiger's eyes...most of all those eyes...

Usually these were images she fought against, and usually she won. But this evening they wouldn't go away. Whether it was second sight, or the memories her friend's pregnancy was stirring up, or sheer coincidence, Jenny was never sure. But she was still thinking inescapably about T.J. Madison twenty minutes later when she walked into the courtyard of her low-rise apartment complex and found him sitting on her front doorstep.

There had been sea gulls overhead, T.J. recalled. Sea gulls crying to each other, and a stiff breeze, and the tide had been coming in. He'd been about four, at the shore for the first time and completely in love with it, with the smells and the water and the sheer freedom of the sea. He'd been chasing a ball that someone had thrown him—it must have been an uncle he'd been playing with, he thought, because his mother was already dead and his father had never been one for playing children's games.

The ball had bounced off a big rock and disappeared out of sight. And T.J. had flung himself after it, wildly, happily, not caring what was around the corner until he found himself floundering in an unexpectedly deep pool of tidewater, unable to touch bottom or—at that early age—to swim.

He didn't remember who had fished him out—the same uncle, probably. That wasn't the point. He *did* remember, very clearly, the moment when he had first understood how much trouble his own recklessness could get him into. It hadn't taught him not to be reckless, but it had made him realize that sometimes it paid to think about where his next step might land him. It was a lesson he'd been thankful for many times in his eventful thirty-seven years.

He'd applied it only this morning. Confronting Jenny after all this time wasn't exactly going to be easy, but it would help to think in advance about what kind of situation he might be walking into. He was thinking about it again now, as he waited on her front doorstep for her to come home.

Her name—J. Alvarez—had been by itself on the label next to the doorbell. That probably meant she lived alone, and T.J. was amazed at how relieved he was by that. Sometimes, when he was too restless to sleep, he found himself tormented by images of Jenny lying next to some other man, perhaps snuggling close, perhaps wakened in the night by a child's cry. He'd gritted his teeth a lot over the past eight years, imagining that. He'd always thought Jenny would make a good mother—sensible, loving, warm.

But her name was definitely alone. And the low apartment complex looked like a place that would appeal more to single professional people than to families, anyway. So the prospect of walking in on some happy domestic scene, complete with children, was less probable than T.J. had been dreading.

Still, there was the possibility of a boyfriend. And it was Friday evening, a likely time to get together with her significant other, if she had one. So he was less worried about the family scenario, but still steeling himself for the sight of Jenny arriving with a companion. It made him crazy inside to think about it, but at least he'd prepared himself for the possibility.

No matter how she arrived, there was still the question of how she would react to the sight of him. On the positive side, she might say how good it was to see her former guardian after all this time, and how much she'd missed him.

On the other hand, she might throw him off the property.

T.J. had to admit that no matter how much thinking ahead he did, he had no idea what Jenny would say when she saw him. There were just too many things he didn't know about this woman who had once been closer to him than anyone in the world. He might find himself floundering again, as he had on that memorable day when he'd been four years old and unable to get his feet under him.

His thoughts about Jenny's possible reactions didn't include the notion that she might refuse even to talk to him.

He heard the light click of heels on the walk at about six-thirty and opened his eyes to the sight of Jenny Alvarez walking toward him. She got as far as the fountain in the center of the courtyard and then she stopped.

T.J. felt everything in him stop, too. She looked exactly—*exactly*—the way she did in his dreams. She was still slender, with just a hint of the coltishness she'd hated so much as a teenager. Her lips were the color of wild roses. Her eyes were brown, deep brown, seductively soft and dark. She'd always referred to her complexion as olive, but to T.J.'s way of thinking, her skin looked as though it had just been warmed by the sun's kiss.

It looked that way now. He could practically feel the smoothness of it under his mouth, under his fingertips. He hauled in a deep breath and felt something stirring inside him that had been missing from his life for a very long time.

He had to say something, he knew. But the opening lines he'd planned on seemed all wrong now. He'd been so busy wondering about Jenny's possible reactions that he hadn't given much thought to his own. This hunger down low in his belly at the very sight of her was something he hadn't bargained on.

He got to his feet slowly. Jenny still hadn't moved, and the sound of the gently tinkling fountain was starting to seem very loud in the quiet courtyard.

"I didn't call first because I thought it would be better to do this in person," T.J. said. His voice sounded rough, as though he hadn't used it in a while.

Jenny didn't answer.

"This isn't a social visit," T.J. added. "I came because I have some questions I need to ask you." He waited. She just stood there, looking at him. "About your father," he said. Damn it, when was she going to react, speak, give him some idea what was going on in her head?

Not yet, he realized. Her expression had changed slightly, from what looked like shock to something that looked more like disdain. Disdain didn't make any sense to T.J. Anger he would understand. But she was looking at him as though he wasn't worth taking notice of, and that puzzled him.

She hadn't even blinked at his mention of her father, which puzzled him even more. Well, he thought, when in doubt, plunge ahead. It was a philosophy that had gotten him into trouble more than once, but it had gotten results, too.

"You probably won't believe this, after all the complaining I did about the military when I was younger," he said, "but I'm working for them now. Sort of." He paused, until it became obvious she wasn't going to answer this, either. "I'm with the CID," he said. Jenny, like himself, had grown up in a military household, and she would know that CID stood for the army's Criminal Investigation Division.

If she remembered, she was giving no sign of it. T.J. wished the damned fountain would stop splashing. It was beginning to get on his nerves. He frowned, hooking his thumbs into the pockets of his jeans. It was a nervous gesture, one he hadn't used for years. But the sight of Jenny was bringing the past back in a disconcerting rush.

"I'm investigating a general who's being promoted as some kind of Asian specialist," he went on doggedly. "Guy's name is Ross, Gen. Haviland Ross. Your father's name turned up in his file. It looks as though your dad was involved in some kind of disciplinary hearing when he was in Vietnam. I want to check it out if I can."

And that was all he was going to say, damn it. It was Jenny's turn now.

So he waited. And she finally moved.

But it was only to pull a key ring out of the purse over her shoulder, and once she'd done that, she started up the front walk as though there wasn't a burly, nearly six-foot male standing between her and the door.

"Good idea," T.J. said. "We should talk about this inside."

He didn't like the slight frown that had puckered her forehead. As she mounted the steps, her eyes left his for a moment, and then, when she got to the top, she met his gaze again. She was standing slightly above him now, and their faces were on the same level.

And T.J. was rocked by a bolt of desire stronger than anything he'd experienced since the unforgettable night of Jenny's twenty-first birthday. Jenny's shoulder-length hair was pulled back by a single clip this evening, and T.J. felt his fingers trembling with the sudden temptation to reach up and let it loose. He had never forgotten the way those glossy black tresses had looked against the warm satin of her skin.

He wanted to take hold of her, to shake her into telling him what she was thinking, what she was feeling. They had been so close once. They'd been the best of friends, before sexual longing had flared up at the wrong place and time. Surely Jenny hadn't forgotten what they'd once meant to each other.

Her steady dark gaze was telling him he meant nothing now. As she stared silently at him from the top step, T.J. could practically feel that thought radiating from her. For a split second he thought she was going to speak, or to move—in fact, it didn't seem out of the question that she was about to raise a hand to slap him, hard—but then something in her face tightened a little more, and she seemed to decide it wasn't worth the effort.

Still without saying a word, she marched up to the front door. When she closed it behind her, T.J. got the very definite message that Jenny was refusing to admit that he was even there.

"Well, I'll be damned." He said the words out loud, wonderingly. People frequently reacted to him with annoyance or amazement. He'd been shouted at and argued with and even shot at, on occasion. He was used to all those things. But he had never simply been ignored before. Especially by Jenny.

It frustrated him, and T.J. Madison didn't like to be frustrated. "All right," he said, still speaking to the empty courtyard. "It you want to do it that way, that's the way we'll do it."

He unhooked his thumbs from his jean pocket, and sauntered around to the other side of the building.

Jenny turned off her kitchen tap with hands that were still shaking and drank down half a glass of cold water as though it could wash away everything that the sight of T.J. had brought back.

One glass of water wasn't going to be enough to do it, she knew. There were too many memories, too much hurt. And now he had the unbelievable nerve to show up at her apartment without warning, looking just as demanding and cocky as always. As though she should be glad to see him. As though he hadn't simply walked away from her life eight years ago, leaving her to face an exceptionally cold, hard piece of reality all by herself.

Jenny closed her eyes. She couldn't let herself be overwhelmed by all these old feelings now, not with T.J. Madison still lurking somewhere just outside. She had never known him simply to go away because he'd been told to go. She was virtually certain her doorbell was going to ring in a minute or two; her silent response to him had been a delaying tactic, nothing more.

It surprised her when five minutes had gone by and the doorbell stayed quiet. Another five minutes, and she started to be puzzled. T.J. had *looked* just the same—the same powerful body, the same brown eyes flecked with gold, even the same unruly hair misbehaving in exactly the same places, refusing to stay where he'd put it. But if he had actually gone away simply because she had refused to speak to him, then he had changed in some pretty fundamental ways.

It took another five minutes to discover that he hadn't changed at all. If anything, he'd gotten worse. It wasn't the doorbell that announced him, but a loud, almost jaunty knock at her door. *I'm back*, the sound said clearly. *Might as well open up*.

She did, but only because she was getting angry with him now, for making her wait, and for showing up in the first place. She pulled open the apartment door and stood firmly blocking the entrance to her living room. "This is as far as you get," she said, before he could speak. "How did you get into the building? And how did you find me, anyway?"

He was grinning at her. Those tiger eyes were dancing. He looked proud of himself, maybe because she had finally broken her silence.

"I'll tell you," he said, "if you'll invite me in."

"I have no intention of letting you in," she said crisply. "I have nothing to say to you, T.J."

"This doesn't have to be personal, Sugar. I told you, I just want to ask you about your father."

How could he tell her it wasn't personal, and then use his old nickname for her in the same breath? Jenny's own breath caught at the familiar sweetness of his voice, even while she felt her anger at him growing stronger.

"I didn't open the door because I wanted to talk," she informed him. "I just wanted to tell you you're wasting your time."

He didn't look bothered by that. "Hey, you asked me two questions," he said. "At least let me answer them before you shut the door in my face again."

"I take them back. I assume you got in by waiting for one of my neighbors to come home and getting them to let you into the hall. And if you're working for the CID, you probably have access to any number of ways to track me down. Am I right?"

"Partly."

"Partly will do."

Not for T.J., apparently. "I didn't get anybody to let me in," he said. "That's the part you're wrong about. I got in through the service entrance, at the back, near the Dumpster."

"That entrance is locked."

"I know. It's a pretty good lock, too. That's what took me so long. But I'm good at getting past locks. It's what I do for the CID."

He waited, as if he knew she would want to know more. The annoying part was that she did. She had never been able to feel neutral about anything T.J. did. Her emotions about him had ranged from mindless adoration to furious dislike, but she had never been indifferent about him since the day they'd met.

"All right," she said. "Tell me."

"Let me in first."

"Forget it, T.J. Why does the CID employ you to pick locks?"

"I'm a security enhancement specialist. That's the fancy way of putting it. Basically I'm the guy who tells the military whether their security systems are good enough. If I can't get through them, they figure nobody else will be able to, either."

"You must be a very good lock picker."

"I am." He said it as a simple fact, and Jenny tended to believe him. T.J. Madison could be wild and opinionated and plain old-fashioned bloody-minded, but he had never been one to boast about his own abilities. Pride was not one of his character flaws.

Stubbornness was. Jenny noticed he had put the toe of his boot between the door and the frame, without even bothering to be subtle about it. He was going to stay until she let him in, his stance told her.

He was telling her more, about his job. "I broke into a renovated wing at the FBI building this morning, at about four-thirty. Had a hell of a time, but I finally found a weak spot." He was wearing a scuffed brown leather jacket, and he pushed up the sleeves now, showing her the smooth brown skin she remembered so well and so intimately. He still had a sailor's tan, and her heart beat a little faster at the familiar strength of those sun-burnished arms.

It wasn't the tan or the muscles he was showing off. It was the series of scratches from his wrists to his elbows. "There was a heating duct nobody had secured," he said. "It was almost too small to fit somebody my size, but not quite. In my report to my boss I said I wanted them to issue me a rubber suit for the next time I had to wriggle through a two-by-two-foot opening.''

"T.J.—"

"Not to mention the fact that I don't mind the dark when I'm outside in it, but small enclosed spaces have always made me—"

"T.J., listen to me."

He finally stopped. Jenny knew what he was doing; it was typical of the way he did everything. He was blunt and forceful and uncompromising, and once he had an advantage—physical or conversational or any other kind—he never let up. He had her talking now—or at least listening to *him* talk—and he was using that to prolong this visit, until she would let him in and do what he wanted.

And she still had no intention of doing that. "I'm *not* letting you in," she told him. "I'm sure your job is fascinating—I never knew anybody like you for finding fascinating ways to spend your time—but I don't want to hear about it. And I don't want to get into a heart-to-heart with you. I just want you to go."

She felt a little less shaky, a little more in charge of things, while she was speaking. She didn't have to let T.J. bully his way back into her life again, she thought. The sight of him was churning up all kinds of old resentment, old memories of loss and bitterness—and old longings, too, to be honest about it. But that still didn't mean she had to go along with what he wanted.

"I'll go," he was saying, "as soon as I find out how to get in touch with your father."

"You can't get in touch with him."

"What makes you so sure? I got in touch with *you,* and you've been very careful for the past eight years to keep me from knowing where you were."

She *had* been careful, for very good reasons that she didn't want to get into. And she didn't like the faint challenge she heard in T.J.'s voice. The last thing she wanted was to get into a discussion about why she'd guarded her privacy so carefully.

Instead, she tilted her chin up slightly and said, "You can't get in touch with my father for the very good reason that he's dead. He died just a few months ago."

T.J. was actually silent. He hadn't been expecting that, Jenny realized. And her news had startled him enough that he shifted his stance, as if he knew he had to attack from a new angle next time.

She didn't want there to be a next time, or a new attack. T.J. had moved his foot away from the door, and before he could speak again, or move, or do anything else, she had closed the door in his face and slid the dead bolt into position.

It was an ordinary lock, not designed to keep out a man who had—apparently with the FBI's blessing—broken into FBI headquarters. But somehow she didn't think T.J. would push his point this far. She had made it clear that she had nothing to say to him, especially since her father was dead and couldn't be of use to T.J., anyway. She just hoped that would be enough to persuade him to leave.

For half an hour she thought it might be. She waited until she heard him head down the hall to the front door of her building. The front door shut, and Jenny let out a long breath.

"Goodbye, T.J.," she said. She intended the phrase to sound defiant, and it probably would have worked if her voice had been steadier.

She went into the kitchen and drank the other half of her glass of water. "I am *not* going to let this throw me," she said. She had sorted out her feelings about T.J. Madison years ago, after he'd disappeared, after she'd dropped out of college, after the whole unhappy time she'd spent longing for him and coping with the aftermath of their single night of love. That sorting-out process hadn't been easy, but it *was* finished. She had no intention of letting T.J. shake up the new life she had built for herself here in Charlotte.

She had a comfortable home and a job she loved. She had come to terms with the gaps in her own past, the ones left by her absent father and Colonel Madison and by T.J. himself. She had even—almost—gotten to the point where she didn't think about baby Joy every time she woke up in the night.

She didn't know why her father had given her up when she was four, or why Colonel Madison, T.J.'s father, had agreed to adopt her. She had never really figured out why T.J. had gone from companionable to distant when he had become her guardian after his father's death. They'd grown up as the best of friends, and Jenny's only guess about his abrupt change had been that being in sole charge of a teenaged girl had been more than the footloose T.J. Madison had wanted to handle.

She didn't understand these things, but at least they were safely in the past now. They were settled, and she needed them to stay that way. T.J.'s sudden appearance tonight wasn't going to change that.

She repeated that thought to herself as she put a pot of soup on to heat up for her dinner. It was just seven-thirty, and still light enough to work outside. She had bought seeds and bedding plants last weekend, and they were sitting on her balcony now, waiting for their chance to grow. Quickly, she changed into a pair of jeans and a white turtleneck, with a loose denim-blue sweater thrown over it for warmth.

Jenny loved gardening. It made her feel solid and stable and connected to the earth, even when the earth in question was just potting soil she'd bought to fill up her clay pots and wooden window boxes. Still, it was an activity she had always turned to when she needed to feel calm, to think things through. She ate her soup at the little table in her kitchen, and then headed to the balcony to start getting things in order for tomorrow's planting.

It was darker out than she had realized. She flicked on the outside switch and slid open the glass balcony door. T.J. Madison was sitting in her porch chair, grinning in the sudden light.

Chapter 2

Her attempt at composure disappeared instantly at the sight of him. Jenny gasped and glared at him.

"You're not getting the message, T.J.," she said.

"I was just going to say the same thing to *you*."

He got to his feet. His big shoulders and strong legs seemed to fill the small balcony. T.J. was as lean as always, but he was just as broad and powerful, too, and the sheer size of him could be overwhelming. And it wasn't just his size. It was the way he somehow forced one's attention, even when he wasn't speaking. He'd been doing it sitting on her front steps a little while ago, and he was doing it again now.

Jenny fought against that larger-than-life aura he had, and spoke as firmly as she could. "Thomas Jefferson Madison," she said, "you are without doubt the stubbornest man I've ever met." His grin only widened. "It *wasn't* a compliment," she added.

She could see the flecks of gold glittering in his eyes, and she felt herself responding to the sight in spite of her determination not to. A lot of years had passed since the last time she'd seen T.J.—a lot of years and a lot of hard lessons about living. So why was it that every time she looked into those tiger eyes of his, she felt as if they'd never been apart?

It was just the shock, she told herself. He'd startled her, that was all. She wasn't about to start softening up just because he was grinning at her in that old, heart-stopping way.

"Look, sugar," he was saying. "We can talk about this now, or I can keep showing up every time you turn around. You know I'll do it."

She did, too. But that didn't mean she was going to go along with him the way she had when she was young. "I've already told you, there's nothing to talk about," she said. "My father's dead. You're wasting your time, T.J."

His brows lowered, and Jenny remembered that T.J. had never bothered with disappointment when he ran into a dead end. He just accepted it as a challenge and started trying to find another way out.

"He must have left papers and things when he died," he said. "Were you the one who cleared out his stuff? Maybe I can find some reference to Haviland Ross, or to the disciplinary hearing your father was involved in. A lot of ex-military guys hang on to their documentation forever."

In fact, there *were* a few military documents in the mass of paper that Pete Alvarez had had with him when he died. But Jenny wasn't ready to tell T.J. that. There were other things to be cleared up first.

"Yes, I have his 'stuff,'" she said. "My father's 'stuff' consisted of one cheap suitcase full of paper. That was it."

His frown deepened. "I don't get it," he said.

"My father had apparently been living on the streets ever since he turned me over to *your* father when I was four. I know he was an alcoholic, and he may have had other addiction problems, too. He died at a homeless shelter down in New Orleans. By the time the shelter people finally tracked me down through my lawyer here, my father had already been buried. The shelter mailed me his personal effects, which meant the suitcase and nothing more."

She didn't go into any more detail. There were so many secrets in her past, she thought. Secrets that T.J.'s father, Colonel Madison, had never shared with her. Secrets she was keeping from T.J. at this very moment. Sometimes Jenny felt an almost physical longing to have everything out in the open, to clear away the shadows in her life.

"I'm sorry, Jenny," T.J. was saying now. "I didn't know. I remember you and I used to spend a lot of time speculating about why your father had given you up."

It hurt to be reminded of those days when she and T.J. had formed a unit that had seemed unbreakable. "My point is," she said quickly, "that my father can't be of any help to you in your investigation. Even if he'd been alive, I gather he was usually pretty incoherent."

Jenny was still standing in the balcony doorway. T.J. stepped toward her now, and she moved quickly back into the hall. He was crowding her, she thought. Trying physically to change her mind.

"What about the papers he left?" T.J. asked. "Maybe if I looked through them—"

Jenny didn't get a chance to tell him she had no intention of sharing her father's forlorn legacy with him. There was a knock on her door just then, and she half turned toward it.

"Are you expecting anybody?" T.J.'s voice was unexpectedly taut.

"No." Jenny shook her head. "Why?"

He didn't answer right away, but just stood there looking hard at her closed apartment door. Jenny could practically feel him thinking.

Finally he said, "I'm probably being overcautious, but I'd be happier if you didn't open it before you find out who it is."

"You're being a lot more than overcautious," she told him. "It's probably just a neighbor."

"Do you get a lot of neighbors knocking at your door in the evenings?"

"No, but—"

"Humor me, Jenny, all right? The timing feels funny to me, somebody showing up right after I did. Just tell them you'll be there in a minute and ask who it is."

She heard the knocking again, more insistent this time. She looked into T.J.'s face and remembered how completely she'd always trusted him when she'd been small. She knew now, of course, that she couldn't trust him at all, at least as far as her heart went. But something inside her still believed that he wouldn't have that intent look on his face if there wasn't a good reason for it.

She frowned and moved into the living room, then said loudly to whoever was on the other side of the apartment door, "I'll be there in a minute—I'm just getting changed. Who is it?"

There was no reply. Jenny repeated the question, a little louder this time, but still nothing came back from the hallway outside. She hadn't had time to do more than register how strange that seemed when she noticed T.J. moving into action. With a softly muttered oath, he took her elbow and pulled her back toward the balcony.

"I want you to get out there," he said, "and stay until I say it's okay."

"This is my apartment, T.J." Resentment warred with uneasiness inside her, making her voice sharper than she'd intended.

"I know it is." The heat of his fingertips made her intently aware of how tightly he was holding on to her. "And I want to make sure I haven't brought anything dangerous into it."

"Dangerous?" She repeated the word incredulously. Having T.J. here was disturbing, and challenging, and arousing in ways Jenny didn't really want to think about yet. But the idea that it might be dangerous—

The idea became terrifyingly real when the first bullet came through her apartment door. T.J. cursed again and propelled her onto the balcony as he demanded, "Where are your car keys?"

She didn't understand what was going on. Half an hour ago she'd been counting on a quiet evening with her petunias and her window boxes. Now T.J. Madison was barking orders at her like a drill sergeant and someone was shooting at them through her door. She saw another spurt of fire come through the wood, splintering it, shattering her dead-bolt lock. It wasn't until afterward that she realized the gun must have had a silencer on it and that whoever was out there was methodically shooting off the locks, trying to get in.

"Get the hell out there!" T.J.'s voice was harsh. "And where are those keys?"

"On the hook by the door. T.J.—"

She felt something clutch her throat as he headed into the living room, straight toward whatever the danger was. No, not quite straight, she noticed. She watched his big, agile form as he crouched over and took an indirect path to where her keys hung on the wall. She didn't like the idea that he'd been under fire like this before and knew exactly what to do.

She didn't like standing helplessly on the balcony watching him, either. She had a lot of reasons to be furious with T.J., but that didn't mean she wanted to stand here and watch him get himself killed. She was already back in the hallway, heading toward him, when she saw him spin around suddenly and clutch his left shoulder.

"T.J.!" She heard the fear in her own voice. "Oh, God—"

He was righting himself now, grabbing her car keys, heading toward her with a face like thunder. "I told you to stay out there, damn it," he said. "Come on!"

He had let go of his shoulder and was dragging her now. She could see a gash in the brown leather of his sleeve, and her stomach lurched slightly.

"T.J., your arm—"

"We'll worry about that after we get out of here." He pushed her ahead of him onto the balcony, and for the first time Jenny understood how he'd managed to get himself up to her second-floor balcony. He must have balanced on the railing of the balcony underneath hers and hauled himself up. Apparently they were going to reverse the process now.

"Grab hold of the railing," he was saying, "and you should be able to dangle over the edge until you get your feet on the balcony below. I'll hang on to you until you reach it."

"How are you going to—"

"Never mind about *me,* damn it. We haven't got much time."

She knew he was right. She could hear the sound of her apartment door being kicked in now. There was a stranger in her living room, she thought. A stranger with a loaded gun at the ready. It was enough to get her over the edge of her balcony railing faster than she would have thought possible.

T.J. followed her, but his left shoulder was obviously causing him trouble. Jenny let herself drop to the ground just as he maneuvered his big frame over the railing. Without a hand from above to help, as she'd had, and with one arm not in working condition, all T.J. could do was dangle briefly from the edge of the balcony and then plunge directly to the ground.

Jenny heard him give one muffled curse, and then he was up again. His eyes looked more than ever like a tiger's, she thought. They were glittering with concentration under the unruly brown hair that had fallen across his forehead.

"The Dumpster," he said tersely. "Let's go."

She saw instantly what he meant. If they crouched behind the Dumpster at the rear of her building, they would be safely hidden from the gaze of anyone standing on her balcony. They made it with only seconds to spare. Jenny dropped to her knees next to T.J., her heart pounding wildly, just as she heard a voice from her apartment.

The words weren't clear, but it was male, and it seemed to be asking a question. Another voice from inside said something in answer. The first voice spoke again, more clearly. "I don't see them out here," it said.

"Damn!" T.J.'s back was up against the Dumpster, and he was holding his shoulder again. "I wish I could get a glimpse of them."

"It's too dangerous," Jenny said immediately. She reached out for him, instinctively afraid that he would stick his head out, anyway. She could feel the hard muscle under the forearm of his leather coat. Then she took her hand away again, realizing that he was going to do the common-sense thing for once.

"I know it's too dangerous," he said. "God, Jenny, I'm sorry. If I'd had any idea there was going to be a chance of this—"

He didn't finish the sentence. They both heard the glass balcony door sliding shut and being locked from the inside. "What are they doing in there?" Jenny wondered out loud.

"Same thing I was, with a little less finesse. Looking for anything your father might have left behind."

Jenny was halfway to her feet herself when T.J. seized her arm and pulled her back down. "Don't even think about it," he said curtly. "These guys are serious about what they're doing."

"Who are they? Do you know?"

"I've got some ideas."

"Care to share them with me?"

He seemed to be debating with himself. Finally he said, "Yeah, but not here. We've got to get clear of Charlotte, if we can."

"T.J., that's my apartment up there, in case you'd forgotten. Everything I own is in those four rooms. I can't just walk away from—"

"We won't be walking. We're taking your car, because it's a pretty good bet those guys are keeping an eye on mine. Where are you parked?"

She knew he was right, that staying around while there were men with guns in her apartment was craziness. But the idea of turning tail and leaving didn't appeal to Jenny, either. Her apartment was her refuge, her own place, the nest she'd made for herself in a life that had all too frequently left her feeling uprooted and uncertain. She hated to run away knowing there were people searching through her belongings at this very moment.

They were heading around the corner of the building now, toward Jenny's little car in the side parking lot. T.J. took a long look around before they stepped out into the open, checking, Jenny thought, to see if anyone was watching for them. He seemed to decide the coast was clear, which cheered her only marginally.

"We're going straight to the police," she said firmly.

He shook his head, just as firmly. "We're not going anywhere near the police," he said. "Or near anybody in any kind of a uniform."

"The police are the good guys, T.J."

"It's not that simple, sugar."

"Would you mind telling me why it's not?"

He pulled her car keys out of his jacket pocket. She could see that his right palm was sticky with blood, and she felt her insides turn over again. When they'd been younger, T.J. had managed to scrape or gash or bruise nearly every part of himself, apparently without minding it too much. But Jenny had always hated to see him hurt, and she didn't like it any more now than she ever had.

He tossed her the keys and didn't answer her question until they were both in the car and she was pulling cautiously out of the lot and into the street. "People in uniforms have to put things into official reports," he said. "And that means other people can trace those reports. I'd just as soon not have anybody knowing where we are, until I can figure out what's going on and get it stopped somehow. Head for the closest expressway, all right?"

"I'm heading for the closest hospital, and I don't want to argue about it."

"Neither do I. I'm not going to a hospital."

"T.J., you've been shot!"

"Not badly. Believe me, I've been through this before."

If she hadn't known him so well years ago, she'd have wondered if she was dealing with a crazy person here. But T.J.'s bravado and his physical courage were characteristics she remembered only too well.

It was too bad that courage didn't extend into the realm of emotion, she thought grimly. If T.J. Madison had been able to face his own feelings eight years ago, maybe they wouldn't be in this situation now, and she wouldn't be battling her own wildly conflicting needs to both patch him up and kick him where he most deserved it.

She couldn't do either of those things while she was concentrating on getting them safely out of harm's way. So she just gritted her teeth and said, "You know, T.J., it's only in movies that heroes get to say, 'It's only a scratch' and carry on with the plot."

"It *is* only a scratch. You can trust me on that, sugar."

The moment the words were out of his mouth, he seemed to regret them. Once, they both knew, Jenny would have trusted him with her life. Now it seemed she was being forced to do just that, long years after he'd proven she couldn't really trust him at all.

"At least let me pick up some first aid supplies," she said.

He nodded. "All right," he said. "Not this close to your apartment building, though. Pick someplace across town."

They stopped at a convenience store that T.J. pronounced sufficiently distant from the threat that had chased them out of Jenny's apartment. T.J. waited in the car while Jenny bought some gauze, adhesive tape and disinfectant, but vetoed her suggestion that she should take a look at his wound then and there.

"Under all these lights?" It was early evening now, and in spite of her worry, Jenny shared his feeling of not wanting to stay in the brightly lit parking lot. She put the car back in gear and headed for the expressway again, telling him she was planning to take the first available exit again and pull over into the first quiet spot she could find.

He didn't argue this time, and that only increased her concern. "Are you all right?" she asked him sharply. "I mean, *really* all right?"

He shot her a grin. It wasn't nearly as exuberant as the ones she'd seen earlier this evening. "I'll be fine," he told her, "just as soon as we've put some miles between here and there."

Jenny turned her mind to doing just that. Her little Volkswagen was hardly a high-speed vehicle, but she covered the distance between suburban Charlotte and the main westbound expressway in respectable time. She waited until they were clear of Charlotte, and of Gastonia to the west, and then she did as she'd promised and pulled off at the first exit.

She'd noticed T.J. checking behind them from time to time as she drove. Was he watching to see if they were being followed? *Were* they being followed? After a while he seemed satisfied that they weren't, although as far as Jenny was concerned that was cold comfort. She'd gone along with his insistence that calling the police would increase their danger, because something in his gold-flecked eyes had told her he was deadly serious about it. But that only gave whoever was in her apartment free rein to take or destroy anything they wanted to. The thought of it tightened her fingers around the steering wheel, until her knuckles were white.

T.J. hadn't said much of anything since they'd stopped at the convenience store. Jenny was not inclined to take that as a good sign. Normally T.J. hated leaving gaps in the conversation. Now, though, he sat slouched over in the passenger seat, right hand clamped to his left shoulder, not speaking.

"All right, T.J.," she said, as she slowed at the end of the exit ramp. "Time to look at the damage."

"Not here." His voice sounded suspiciously faint. "Find a side street."

Jenny could see a quiet residential street up ahead, at the end of a strip of gas stations, and decided it wouldn't hurt to be a little bit more out of the way. But she was churning with impatience by the time they got there and increasingly worried about the sound of T.J.'s voice.

"Not that I should care about this," she muttered, as she parked the car and undid her seatbelt, "but I'd appreciate it if you didn't fade out on me, all right?"

"Why—shouldn't you care?" He was shrugging awkwardly out of his brown leather jacket now, and it made his speech uneven. "We used to be—good friends."

We were a lot more than that, she wanted to say. But the whole subject—her feelings for T.J., and their single night of love together, and what had happened afterward—was too big and too precarious to get into at the moment. Cleaning T.J. up was going to take a lot of concentration.

She'd already moved close enough to him to get a good look at the angry blaze across his left shoulder. His navy sweatshirt was hanging open, and there was blood on his smooth, tanned skin. But she could see immediately that he'd been right about it not being deep. The wound wasn't life-threatening, although there was always a danger of infection, but she was pretty sure it had to hurt like hell.

She hadn't realized quite how frightened she'd been for T.J. until she felt a great wave of relief wash through her. She helped him pull the sweatshirt over his head and got busy with disinfectant and gauze, wishing her fingers weren't shaking.

"Even in your wildest days," she told him, "I don't remember anybody ever shooting at you. T.J., what's going on?"

"I don't exactly know yet."

They seemed very close in the small car all of a sudden. T.J. had turned his face slightly away from her; otherwise, their foreheads would have touched. Even with that slight distance between them, though, Jenny was acutely aware of the pounding pulse at the base of T.J.'s throat and the raw power of his neck and shoulders.

He had a golden tan—he'd always had a tan, ever since he'd taken up sailing in high school. The skin under her fingertips felt hard and warm, as if he'd just stepped out of the sun a moment ago. That skin was scratched from elbows to wrists, and she recalled him telling her that he'd been up at dawn breaking into a wing of the FBI building. She felt herself wanting to smooth a gentle hand over his scraped arms, and fought hard to chase the impulse away.

This wasn't the first time Jenny had had to struggle with her own feelings for T.J. They had been the best of friends when she'd been little, and had thought T.J., nine years her senior, could do no wrong. When he'd taken over her guardianship after his father's death, he'd changed toward her, and although they'd never discussed it, even then Jenny had had a vague idea that it had something to do with the new feelings he was stirring up in her fifteen-year-old heart.

T.J. had been twenty-four then, a restless wanderer with a heart-stopping smile and a masculine frame that had been the talk of Jenny's boarding school on the rare occasions when he visited her there. Jenny had laughed at the talk at first, then started to wonder about it more seriously. And finally she had realized that somehow, T.J. Madison had changed from a familiar presence in her world to the sexiest man she had ever met. From the moment she admitted how she really felt about him, all her resistance to his renegade charms had utterly disappeared.

Now, being this close to him in the interior of her little car, it was easy to remember why she'd loved him. And all too easy to remember the disaster that had resulted. The two sets of memories battled inside her, shaking her deeply. Jenny frowned, reached for the adhesive tape and reminded herself that she'd already known this wouldn't be easy.

"I thought you were a psychologist, not a nurse."

T.J.'s voice sounded distant. She looked sharply over at him, but he didn't seem to be in any danger of fainting. He was speaking to the roof of the car, almost as if she wasn't there.

"I took a few nursing courses in college, before I decided to switch to psychology," she told him. "Hold still, all right? This might hurt."

She could tell that it did, but beyond a growl that he buried deep in his throat, and a sudden tightening of his muscles, he stayed still as she'd told him to. The man was so strong, she thought, so fearless, as long as he wasn't dealing with love.

"Speaking of college—" He seemed to reconsider the question, and then plunged ahead with it. "You pulled a pretty fast fade in your senior year, once you turned twenty-one. I always wondered why you did that."

"You disappeared first, in case you'd forgotten." The words were out before she'd planned to say them.

"I had a good reason to disappear."

"So you told me." The wound seemed clean enough now. Jenny pulled the tape out of its packaging and dug in her glove compartment for the Swiss army knife she kept there. She had to lean past T.J. to reach it, and she felt wrapped in

the clean male scent of him. It had always reminded her of
sea and waves, of blue water and freedom.

That didn't make it any easier to stick to the subject. She
knew her voice sounded tight as she added, "You made it
sound like you were breaking up with me for my own good."

"That's exactly what I was doing. You were too young to
fall in love with the wrong man, sugar."

"And you were the wrong man."

"Of course I was. I was the wrong age, I was never
around, I wasn't ready to settle down with anybody. Hell,
I'm *still* not ready to settle down. And I was your legal
guardian, for God's sake—"

"Not that night, you weren't." It had been the night of
her twenty-first birthday that she had given in to everything she felt for T.J. Madison. She'd been her own woman
at that moment. And it had left her more completely alone
than she'd been before or since.

"I still don't understand why you dropped out of school.
Or why you told your lawyer not to let me know where you
were."

Jenny was wrestling with a stubborn length of adhesive
tape that seemed to be trying to stick to itself in three different places. T.J.'s voice sounded puzzled and uncomfortable. But it *didn't* sound as though her disappearance had
created a major gap in his life.

And that made her angry, on top of everything else she
was feeling at the moment. When she thought of all the pain
and upheaval she'd gone through after dropping out of
school and severing her ties with T.J. . . .

When she thought about it, she was half tempted to do
something to this wound of his that would make it hurt
more, not less. And that would be counterproductive at the
moment. So she said, "Some other time, all right, T.J.? I've
got enough to think about right now."

She glanced up and saw him looking curiously at her,
dark eyebrows raised. The mouth that had once kissed her

into near-delirium was far too close to hers for comfort, and she ducked her head away again, forcing her attention to his injured shoulder.

"Tell me about this suitcase full of papers that your father left behind," T.J. said.

Jenny repressed a sigh. So they were back to business. Well, she shouldn't have expected anything more. T.J. had always been handy at escaping from situations that threatened to turn emotional on him.

"It's kind of a diary," she said. "A very loose one, and there's no way at this point to put things into any kind of order. But he seems to have wanted to keep some record of his life, however incoherent it was."

"Did he write anything about his experiences in Vietnam?"

"Some. A lot of it reads like somebody recording their dreams. It's hard to tell how much of it really happened and how much was drug- or alcohol-induced, or made-up altogether."

Her voice quivered when she thought about the two men in her apartment. T.J. seemed to be thinking the same thing. "How easy would it be to find the suitcase?" he asked her.

"Very easy. It's next to my desk in my spare room."

"I'm sorry, sugar." She felt him looking at her and resisted the temptation to gaze back into those seductive eyes of his. "If I'd had any idea this might happen, I'd have handled things a different way."

"What *is* happening?" She applied the final piece of tape and started to put her first aid supplies back in the bag. "Why are people shooting at us, T.J.? Why should anybody care what's in my father's diary?"

"I told you I was checking out a general who's getting a new and very fancy posting as an Asian-affairs expert. I was doing a routine computer search on the guy's background, and your father's name kind of jumped out at me." T.J. winced as he pulled his torn sweatshirt back over his head.

"So you think there's something in the general's past that my father knew about, and that the general wants to hide?"

"Well, I thought it was worth checking out. That's why—well, that's most of why I came down here from D.C." She wondered about the pause in the middle of his sentence, but he went on quickly, "What worries me is that the only people who knew what I was working on are military personnel, in the CID. And that seems to mean—"

"That there *is* something worth covering up, and this General Ross is trying to make sure that it stays that way." Jenny let out her breath as she shook her head. "Honestly, T.J., I thought all these years might have cured you of jumping into things without thinking twice, but—"

"I know." He held up both his hands. "I *am* sorry, Jenny. Sorry about your father's diary, I mean. And about getting you involved in this. I probably just should have called you on the phone, but I—well, I had the feeling you might not want to talk to me. It seemed better to show up in person."

It was as close as he'd gotten to admitting the unresolved emotions that lay between them. But it wasn't nearly close enough to suit Jenny's taste. She wasn't about to open herself up to him any more than she'd already done, without some evidence that her heart wouldn't be broken a second time. And she wasn't about to tell him there was a second copy of her father's "diary," either. Not until she knew more about what was going on.

"So," she said crisply, "you don't want to go to the police or to a hospital because you're worried that military intelligence would be able to trace you that way."

T.J. nodded. "That's about the size of it," he said.

She was about to ask him what next step he could conceivably take, when a sound from behind the car caught her attention. She jumped a little, realizing she still felt far from safe, and turned at the same moment as T.J. did.

A police cruiser was pulling into the parking space behind them. "Ah, hell," T.J. said. "That's what we get for sitting around looking suspicious in a nice quiet neighborhood. Nothing personal, sugar, but I think I'd better kiss you, all right?"

Chapter 3

She didn't have time to decide whether it was all right or not. With one big hand T.J. was already stowing the bag of first aid supplies under his seat. With the other, he was gathering her closer to him, pulling her against his broad chest, and then—before Jenny could speak or protest—his mouth was covering hers, urgently, intensely.

She waited for herself to feel outraged, but the outrage wouldn't happen. A lot of other things did. Every conflicting emotion she'd been battling since she'd seen T.J. sitting on her front steps uncoiled inside her at the first touch of his lips, and she felt herself reeling with the sudden power of it.

T.J. still seemed to know her with maddening intimacy. He commandeered her mouth like a high-seas pirate taking over another vessel carrying treasure he wanted. Jenny moaned slightly at the sudden force of his kiss and felt herself grasping at defenses that suddenly weren't there anymore.

She felt surrounded by him, swept into an unpredictable current where she was no longer the one in charge. The scent of his skin, the strength of his arms, were enough to make the world outside disappear for as long as his lips were touching hers.

Nothing personal, he'd said. She remembered it vaguely, as though he'd spoken the words a year ago instead of a few seconds ago. And at first, the kiss *was* almost impersonal, as if his only concern was to make it look convincing in the eyes of the police officer who was getting out of the cruiser that had pulled up behind them.

And then something changed. There was a single, still moment, a moment when Jenny sensed T.J. hesitating, holding back. *Why?* she asked him with her eyes, and his own eyes darkened suddenly, looking startled and almost angry.

And then, when he lowered his lips to hers again, his attempts at being impersonal had clearly vanished. She heard a faint groan from deep in his throat and felt him lift a hand to smooth back her hair. Her eyes closed, but the image of his strong, assertive features still swirled behind her lids.

He was kissing *her* now, she thought, not just a woman who happened to be handy when he needed to fool an approaching cop. And the deeper he probed, the more Jenny felt herself responding, her thoughts turning as erotic as any dream she'd ever had.

He still knew exactly what it did to her when he just teased her mouth with his own. In an instant Jenny was transported out of the little car and back eight years, to the night when he'd awakened her in exactly this way. She'd always thought of him as the most demanding of men. But when he'd touched her that night, he'd been achingly slow, infinitely patient. It had been like tapping into a hidden well of sensuality in Jenny's body and soul, and she'd responded with a wildness that had astonished and electrified both of them.

She was responding the same way now. T.J.'s mouth was intimate, inviting, aware. Jenny heard another small, ach-

ing moan from her own throat. The sound was full of open
desire, and T.J. seemed to recognize it, too. He probed
deeper, hungrier now, surrounding her more seductively
with his strong arms. She melted against him, suddenly
wanting more, wanting everything he'd once offered and
then taken away.

"T.J.—" Her voice was the merest whisper—urgent,
questioning.

"Shh." He smoothed her hair back again, and then his
hold on her shifted. At the very edge of her awareness,
Jenny heard a brisk tapping on the window next to her. "Let
me do the talking, okay?" T.J. was saying.

For a second she couldn't imagine what he meant. And
then she saw him squint in the sudden brightness of a flash-
light beam and remembered the reason he'd been kissing her
in the first place.

That erotic exchange had been nothing but window
dressing, a convenient excuse for their presence on this quiet
street. And the only reason T.J. was still holding her so
tightly was that he didn't want the torn shoulder of his
sweatshirt to show.

Jenny's heart was still pounding, nearly out of control.
All she could think about was the heat of his skin and the
way his arm circled her, so familiar and so close. But to T.J.,
it had meant nothing. How could she have forgotten her
own rules about keeping this sexy, unruly, utterly infuriating man at arm's length?

She fought to get her breathing back to normal. The
sound of bullets ripping through her apartment door still
echoed in her ears, underscoring the fact that T.J. could be
dangerous to her heart *and* her body this time around.

The hell of it was that she still couldn't stand the idea of
watching somebody else kill him, much as she occasionally
wanted to do it herself. And that meant going along with the
story T.J. was getting ready to tell this policeman. Well, if

Jenny looked anywhere near as aroused as she felt, she knew there wouldn't be much need for her to put on an act.

The policeman turned out to be a woman. Jenny accepted that as good luck: T.J. was a strikingly attractive man, and women had always been fascinated by his flashing smile and the glint in his gold-flecked eyes. Once the police officer had dispensed with the formalities of looking at Jenny's license and registration, she seemed to have no difficulty believing the story T.J. was telling.

"We were on our way out of town for the weekend," he was saying frankly, with a smile. "And—well, we got a little carried away. I guess we picked the wrong neighborhood for it."

He gave Jenny's shoulder a squeeze, and she managed a faint smile up at him. The officer nodded. "Folks around here tend to get a little edgy about strange people sitting around in vehicles," she said. "Been more break-ins this year than last. I suggest you folks go on and get where you're going, and then you can go back to doing what you were doing."

Her smile was indulgent as she went back to the cruiser behind them. When Jenny turned her car around and drove past a moment later, she could see the officer telling her partner all about it. The two cops both had grins on their faces.

"Thanks." T.J.'s lightly amused tone of a moment ago had gone now. He sounded serious, and a little shaken. "It seemed like the best way to get out of things."

"No need to apologize." Jenny's voice was shaking, too. "After all, it isn't the first time you've kissed me without meaning anything by it."

"*Damn* it, Jenny—"

She waited for the rest of the sentence, but it never came. When she glanced over at him, he was looking fiercely out at the road. He didn't speak again until they were nearly back to the main highway.

"I should have stayed away," he said flatly.

The old hurt flared up inside Jenny again. She could still hear the echo of his words from years before—that she was wrong in thinking they meant anything to each other, that she should just put him out of her mind and get on with her own life. And so she had, but not by choice.

"It's too late to wish that now, isn't it?" she asked. "I don't exactly feel confident about going back to my apartment at this point."

"I know. I'm sorry. I need a little time to figure out what to do about that."

"The first thing you can do, T.J., is to stop telling me you're sorry." He had more to be sorry for than he knew, Jenny thought. But *she* needed a little time to figure out how—or if—she should break that news to him. "And the second thing is to start thinking of somewhere safe we can stay for the night. You need to rest and give that shoulder a chance to heal."

"I know." The fact that he didn't argue made Jenny think he was in more pain than he was admitting to. "Let's get back on the highway going west. I'd like to put some more distance between us and Charlotte before we stop for the night. And, Jenny—"

She looked over at him and was surprised by the restless uncertainty in his eyes. It was like seeing her own expression in a mirror, and the sudden moment of connection between them startled her almost as much as T.J.'s kiss had done a few minutes earlier.

T.J.'s next words killed the moment dead. "As soon as I can, I'll put things right again, I promise you."

Her response was immediate and gut-deep. "Don't make promises, T.J.," she said sharply. "We can't go back to the good old days when I thought you could fix anything in the world. Let's just get some rest and figure out where to go from here."

She felt, rather than saw, his frown, and knew he was looking curiously at her. But she didn't look back at him, and they lapsed into silence again as she pulled the car back onto the westbound highway and headed into the night.

It was after midnight before they stopped. They'd reached Asheville, up in the Blue Ridge Mountains, and T.J. hadn't seen another car on the road behind them for ages. Jenny was smothering one yawn after another, trying to hide how tired she was, and T.J. himself felt as though he'd been run over a week ago and nobody had bothered to scrape him up off the road yet.

"Here," he said, as they drove past a sign advertising Night o' Rest Motel And Cabins, 2 Miles. "Turn here."

"'Rustic simplicity'?" Jenny had been reading the sign, too. "I just know I'm going to want a hot shower in the morning, T.J. 'Rustic simplicity' sounds a bit too close to nature to me."

"If it's a motel, it'll have showers," T.J. said. "And it's off the main road, which is what we want."

The Night o' Rest was undeniably rustic. The motel was six units long, faced in imitation log-cabin style. And there were several log cabins scattered over the grounds, each with its own little chimney and a front porch complete with a rocking chair. To T.J.'s exhausted eyes, it looked like heaven.

Once they'd roused the sleepy owner from the back office, where he'd been dozing in front of the TV set, it only took a few minutes to find themselves the proud temporary owners of the cabin farthest from the road. Each cabin, it turned out, had a shower with hot running water. Maybe it really *was* heaven, T.J. thought.

"How much cash are you carrying on you?" Jenny asked, as T.J. unlocked the door. He'd pulled out his wallet to prepay for the room, and she'd seen a wad of bills that had surprised her.

"Enough to buy us a little time. I don't like carrying credit cards—they're too easy to trace."

"Are people usually trying to trace you?"

He fought off a yawn of his own. "It happens," he said. "There are times when I just feel better knowing I can operate completely alone, that's all."

He couldn't interpret the look on her face, and he was too tired to try. He clicked on the light switch, and warm light filled the small cabin. The single room was cozy and inviting, with a sofa, chair and table in front of the window and a big bed covered with a red-and-blue-patterned quilt.

"There's only one bed." Jenny's voice behind him was suddenly wary.

"So I'll sleep on the sofa. I don't care." He turned to face her and saw that same troubled expression in her brown eyes—the one that had been eating at him since he'd first seen her at her apartment. "Believe me, sugar, I'm so tired I could sleep standing up in the doorway." He hesitated, and then said almost roughly, "I didn't plan on kissing you back on that street—it was just the only thing I could think of to do on the spur of the—"

"It's all right, T.J. You don't have to explain. And *I'll* sleep on the sofa. You should be worrying about that shoulder healing, and I can't imagine it'll do it any good to be cramped up on a couch all night long."

"'All night long' is wishful thinking." T.J. spoke around a yawn that he couldn't repress. "I want to get as early a start as we can."

"Where are we going?"

"I'm working on that. Good night, sugar."

Jenny had done a creditable job of cleaning and bandaging his shoulder, he knew. But the thing still throbbed like an overheated engine, and he'd had a hard time all evening hiding the fact that he was in a lot of pain.

His anger at himself for getting Jenny into this mess had helped take his mind off his wound. And in the heady moment when he'd kissed her, his throbbing shoulder might not have existed at all. But he was too tired to summon up the energy for anger now, and kissing her again was out of the question. It was simply too dangerous to let himself remember the thousand different ways Jenny Alvarez aroused him.

So without anger or passion to distract him, he knew he could be in for a miserable night. The thought of Jenny sleeping just across the room wasn't going to make things any easier.

"Serves you right, Madison," he growled at himself as he shed his jeans and shoes and pulled the covers back. He couldn't help thinking about the one night he'd spent in the same bed with Jenny, and he growled again at the thought of it. He couldn't guess the reason for her sudden tension whenever the subject of that night had threatened to come up. Hell, it had been more than eight years, hadn't it? Surely she'd had more than enough time to get over whatever disappointment she'd felt. And he was still sure he'd done the right thing, telling her they just weren't right for each other in the long run.

If there was something else behind that troubled look in her eyes, he was far too tired to puzzle it out tonight. T.J. had no clear recollection of collapsing into the big double bed, or of crossing the line between waking exhaustion and the all-too-real dreams that were waiting for him when he finally fell asleep.

She was so soft. Impossibly soft....

T.J. groaned and tried to turn over. Something was hurting him, rolling him back onto his right side, to where Jenny was waiting for him. Her hair was loose on her shoulders, and she was looking into his eyes. Warily, he thought. Searchingly. All he could think of was the unimaginable softness of her olive-hued skin. And her mouth, that full bottom lip, rose-petal pink, rose-petal smooth...

A small part of him knew this wasn't real. He'd had this dream before, for years now. But it had never seemed so vivid, so urgent. His head had never felt so hot, so detached from the rest of him. The dream had never made the edges of his vision shimmer before, so that Jenny's face was haloed in a light that moved and danced and refused to keep still.

"Jenny..."

He reached for her. How many times had he done this in his dreams? How many times had he felt his empty palm clutching nothing but air, leaving him frustrated and alone?

Tonight, though, his fingers connected with warm skin, and the shock of it made his head spin. Was she here with him, in his dream? He gripped her hand convulsively, unwilling to let the moment slip away.

"Shh, T.J...."

He heard her voice, murmuring to him, and he shook his head. The room swayed when he did it. That had never happened in his dreams before, either.

"God, Jenny..." His voice was hoarse, as though he hadn't spoken in a very long time. "Don't go away again, Jenny."

She wasn't moving away. But she wasn't moving toward him, either. And suddenly T.J. couldn't stand it. He pulled her hand closer and felt her shifting her position. Moving nearer, finally, joining him on the bed.

"Just let me hold you." He meant the words to sound strong, but they were barely more than a whisper. "Just once, let me hold you again."

Dreams had their own logic. He knew that, dizzily, even while he was in the middle of this one. He'd been dreaming about Jenny Alvarez for years, but he'd always seen her disappearing, retreating, occasionally looking back at him over her shoulder with that wide-eyed look that had always driven him crazy. But mostly she'd been just about at the vanishing point.

Now, for some reason known only to his semiconscious brain, she wasn't going anywhere. She was staying, saying soothing words he couldn't quite understand. The sound of her voice was like the musical murmur of a shallow brook, warmed by the sun, and it soothed T.J.'s overheated mind.

He'd never been able to touch her like this. To feel that she was really here, with him. He felt himself moan and fought against the slight resistance that he sensed in her.

"Please, Jenny." He'd wakened feeling too hot, and now, strangely, he was cold. Jenny could warm him, he knew. She could make the room stop swaying, and make him feel whole, too. He was sure she could do those things. If he could just hold her in his arms...

She was moving again, toward him. T.J. clamped his teeth down against their sudden chattering—and felt something warm enfolding him. The source of the extreme heat—and the cold, too, now that he thought about it—seemed to be in his own body. He moved and felt the left side of him light up.

"Be still, T.J." Jenny's soft voice wrapped him like a blanket. "You've got to stay still."

"No." He got the word out through clenched teeth. He couldn't be still while she was so close to him, so close and so soft. "I'm cold, damn it...."

He kept his grip on her hand, and finally, slowly, she eased down against him. T.J. wanted to cry out with the exquisite rightness of her body snuggling against his, but he was afraid to shatter the dream. He let go a long breath and wrapped both arms around her, not caring if it hurt.

He knew he would wake up all too soon. He had to savor this fantasy while it lasted. He closed his eyes and drank in the faint perfume of her dark hair, of her skin. She fit against him as if they were made to be together, exactly like this.

"Sweet Jenny," he whispered. Was that her heart beating, or his own? He didn't care. He was warming up again now, and the swirling movement in his head was slowing down. He said Jenny's name again, or tried to, and felt himself easing into a deep and dreamless sleep.

His shoulder still throbbed, but the bright lights and dizziness had gone. T.J. opened his eyes and blinked.

The light looked all wrong. He raised himself enough to look around the one-room cabin and saw what seemed to be the soft light of late afternoon illuminating the blue carpet, and the beige sofa with the red-and-blue-patterned quilt thrown carelessly across its back.

He could hear Jenny's voice, speaking softly. T.J. frowned, struggling to sit up. He felt strangely drained, and his muscles weren't cooperating with him. Finally he managed to get to one elbow, prompted by the uneasy thought that Jenny shouldn't be talking to anyone, because no one was supposed to know they were here.

She was at the door of the cabin, still wearing yesterday's jeans and light blue sweatshirt. Was it tomorrow already? T.J. wished he was clearer on just what was happening. Surely Jenny wouldn't have announced their presence here to the world, when T.J. had made it so plain that it would be a dangerous thing to do.

The smell of food reached him, and he realized suddenly that he was hungry. He realized, too, what Jenny was doing at the cabin door. He saw her hand a bill to a young man outside and take a large white bag in exchange for it.

T.J. lay back down again, cursing the pain in his shoulder. He turned his head to the bedside table. The clock read 4:30 p.m. Was it possible he'd slept through the whole night and most of the day?

He saw the rolls of gauze and adhesive tape that Jenny had bought, too, and wondered if she'd changed his bandage without him realizing it. There were a couple of bottles on the table that he didn't remember, too—painkillers, from the look of them.

What *else* had been happening while he'd been fighting off the fever his bullet wound must have brought on? T.J. recalled his dream, and the hazily erotic thoughts that had accompanied him into sleep, and actually felt his face flush at the memory of it. Was it possible that it had been real, and no dream?

His heart was beating a little faster as he heard the cabin door closing and Jenny's soft footsteps heading toward the bed. T.J. cleared his throat and said huskily, "I don't suppose there's a decent Chinese restaurant within ten miles of this place."

He'd startled her, he could tell. *Good,* he thought. He was startled, too, by his own physical reaction when her curving hips came into his field of vision. Had those hips been nestled up against him in the night, the way he half remembered? In spite of his exhaustion, he could feel the stirring of desire all over again.

"If you're healthy enough to be insisting on Chinese, I'm going to stop worrying about you," Jenny said. She sat down on the edge of the bed, setting the bag on the table next to T.J.'s head. "And as it happens, we're having chicken and biscuits. I thought it would be better not to challenge your stomach until I knew you were going to be all right."

"What do you mean *challenge?* I'm fine." He tried to sit up, to prove it to her, and was assailed by that sudden weakness in all his muscles again. He put his head down on the pillow again and muttered, "Well, give me a couple of minutes and I *will* be fine."

"Sure you will, T.J." There was some asperity in Jenny's tone, but T.J. couldn't spare the energy to figure out what it meant. She was leaning toward the table now, and he could see a couple of crumpled-up washcloths in the midst of the bottles and bandages. More surprising yet, he noticed a thermometer, which Jenny was shaking down with a practiced hand.

"Where did that come from?" he asked suspiciously.

"I got the front desk to find me a drugstore that delivered," she said. "Don't worry, T.J. I just told them you'd come down with a flu bug. And I paid in cash. I hope you don't mind that I helped myself to what was in your pockets."

He waved away her words. "What, exactly, has been going on for the last twelve hours?" he demanded.

She glanced at the clock. "More like fourteen," she said. There were circles under her eyes, T.J. noticed, and the expression on her face made him think she'd found those hours very, very long. "And what's been going on is that you had a fever hot enough to fry griddle cakes on, courtesy of that bullet wound. Just about the time I'd decided to hell with it and was about to call an ambulance to get you to a hospital, the fever finally started to go down, and you actually got some real sleep."

"When did that happen?"

"About nine this morning."

And she'd been sitting with him the whole time, T.J. suddenly realized. Soothing his forehead with damp washcloths, sending out for painkillers, crawling into bed with him when he'd pleaded with her to keep him warm.

"Jenny." His voice was rough, betraying his own need to say these words. "I seem to remember . . . pulling you into this bed. Did I really do that?"

She nodded. That troubled look was back in her eyes again, and she wasn't quite meeting his gaze.

"I thought I was dreaming it." T.J. turned over on his back, ignoring the shooting pain from his left shoulder. "Damn it, Jenny—I thought it was a dream. There really wasn't anything more to it than that."

This was even worse than that moment in her car last night, when he'd pulled her into his arms to kiss her and realized, in one shattering second, that everything he'd ever felt for Jenny Alvarez was still there, rocketing around inside him, just as confused and untamed as it had ever been. The force of his feelings had shaken him then, and he still hadn't figured out what he was going to do about it.

Jenny's voice was clipped and precise. T.J. didn't know if he found that reassuring or not.

"Don't worry, T.J.," she was telling him. "If I'd thought you had some kind of agenda for getting me into bed with you, you can bet I would have stayed well away."

That blissful moment of union, of warmth, swam into T.J.'s bloodstream again, and then it was gone. Jenny was telling him that it might as well have been a dream, and that was for the best, of course. Then why did T.J. feel so oddly disappointed? He wished he had a better handle on all the things he was suddenly feeling.

"I paid for another night here," she was saying now, "since I don't think you're in shape to travel yet."

His protest was automatic. "I've traveled under a lot worse circumstances than this," he said.

"I'm sure you have. But there's no reason to think anybody knows we're here. And surely even someone as stubborn as you knows that you'll stand a better chance if you feel stronger."

Something was nagging at T.J.—something he knew wouldn't have slipped by him if he'd been in better shape. But whatever it was, he couldn't dredge it up right now. That seemed to prove Jenny's point that he needed to rest, at least a little while longer.

But that didn't mean he had to be happy about it. "You've gotten very bossy over the last few years," he grumbled.

"I've learned to do a lot of things over the last few years," she said. The crispness in her voice seemed to be designed to tell T.J. that sitting next to him on the bed meant nothing to her. "I suggest we spend another night here and try to come up with something sensible to do about this mess."

"It's a hell of a shame we can't get to that diary of your father's." T.J. was already forcing his mind back to his investigation, because it was preferable to thinking about how close Jenny was to him and how easy it would be to reach out and wrap his arms around her as he'd done last night.

Jenny gave the thermometer a final efficient flick. "As it turns out," she said, "we *can* get a copy of it. I'll tell you about it after we've eaten."

He didn't have time to protest this time. She had popped the thermometer into his mouth before he could speak, and he was pretty sure she'd done it that way on purpose.

Bossy, he'd called her, but there was something in Jenny's manner this afternoon that was a whole lot more appealing than bossiness, and a whole lot more unsettling, too. There was an independence and resolve in her that she'd never had as a girl, and it was throwing him for a loop whenever he met that serious, determined look in her brown eyes.

"Did you remember how much I like gravy with my biscuits?" he asked around the thermometer.

"Of course." She was on her feet again, straightening the things on the bedside table, all brisk efficiency with that unexplained note of tension running through it. "There's very little I've forgotten about you, T.J., although heaven knows I've had good reason to try."

T.J.'s muscles still felt maddeningly weak, and his shoulder still ached. He was hungry—ravenously hungry. And he couldn't keep his mind off the way Jenny's hips swayed as she moved around the room, tidying things up. *And* he had a damn thermometer stuck in his mouth. When he'd taken care of all those things, he told himself, he was going to have to ask her just what she thought she'd meant by that last remark. There had been a definite challenge in it, and a challenge was the one thing T.J. Madison found it impossible to resist.

No, that was wrong. He couldn't resist Jenny Alvarez, either. He hadn't decided what he was going to do about that, but he knew for certain that it wasn't going to make his life any easier for the next little while.

Chapter 4

Pete Alvarez's Diary

That whole time was like a dream, like a bad dream you can't get out of.

Mostly what I remember is trying to get home. Like being caught in a web and I couldn't pull free. But I knew home was out there somewhere. And I had to get to it.

She was there, the little one. Growing so fast, the letters said. Walking, talking. Asking where her daddy was.

Daddy was in hell. Couldn't see, couldn't think, couldn't cry out for help. And the devil was there, laughing at me.

You can't cheat the devil, *he said.*

And when I said justice, *he laughed and said* There is no justice here. *Maybe no justice anywhere.*

I wanted to go home. I wanted to see my little girl. I wanted him to stop laughing. God, I can still hear it. I hear it when I try to sleep, sometimes. I didn't sleep then, not at all. Not for weeks, maybe more than that, even. I don't sleep now, not much. But when I do, I hear him laughing.

Nobody will believe you. You're just like all the rest of them.

And I said No. You did this to me.

Yes, *he said.* I did it to you. But it's done, just the same.

I came home like that, with a needle in my arm and not wanting to face my little girl anymore. Caught in the web, this time for good.

"I think," T.J. said, "that you just saved my life."

Jenny watched his big hands, strong and purposeful as ever as he mopped up the last of the gravy with the final bite of biscuit. He'd eaten like a man who hadn't seen food in ages, and when she'd commented on it, he'd said that was about right. His last meal had been a quick snack he'd grabbed before starting the drive from Washington to Charlotte, early yesterday afternoon.

Those broad, powerful hands affected her the way they always had. They weren't made for fussy gestures or precise shadings. They were designed for movement, for action.

And for caressing a woman's hair. A woman's body....

Jenny closed her eyes, assailed by the memory of how he'd pulled her against him last night. He had held her tightly to him, as if he thought she could ward off the feverish dreams that were gripping him. Those hands had been achingly intimate then, closing over her breasts, her belly, binding the two of them together for a few brief, astonishing hours.

When she opened her eyes again, Jenny knew her breathing had quickened slightly. And T.J.'s grin had faded.

"It hardly seems right for you to save my life, when I put yours in so much danger," he was saying, much more seriously now.

"Do you really think those two guys would have killed us?" She had to ask it.

"Anybody who comes armed with silenced weapons and is prepared to shoot through doors in an occupied building isn't going to hesitate over anything—or anybody—in their way," he said.

Jenny shivered slightly, in spite of the warmth in the cabin. She had lit the fire that was already laid in the fireplace grate and had closed the drapes against the growing darkness outside. She'd been hoping to create an atmosphere that would dispel her feelings of being cut off from the world, on the run, unprotected. But T.J.'s words were cutting deeply into the fragile sense of safety she'd managed to come up with.

"The problem with military intelligence is that it can reach everywhere," he was saying. "Hell, I've been working for the CID for five years now, and I'm still constantly amazed by the resources those guys have."

"So you don't want to call your boss, in case those calls can be traced," Jenny said.

"Right." T.J. threw his napkin onto his empty paper plate with a gesture of annoyance. "I never went up against somebody high up in the military establishment before. I don't know what the rules are here."

"I would imagine the odds are stacked against you." Jenny spoke slowly, hating the thought of the danger that T.J. was in—that both of them were in.

"You could say that. That's why your father's diary could be so important, sugar. If we stand a chance of shaking off these guys, I'm going to need some kind of hard evidence on Gen. Haviland Ross. About this second copy—"

Jenny had debated with herself over whether to tell him about the second copy of the diary. But at dawn this morning, when she'd been most afraid that T.J.'s wound was more serious than she'd thought, she had decided that she couldn't very well hold out on him. He was in serious danger, and if her father's diary could help, T.J. needed to know about it.

"My father was involved in a lawsuit against a crooked doctor in Memphis a few years ago," she said. "I got intrigued by the story, and spent some time in Memphis last fall trying to tie up some of the loose ends in the case. It was...a way of feeling some connection with my father, I suppose."

T.J. was nodding. "So you'd had no communication with him at all," he said.

"None. Not since that day when I was four, and he took me on the train to Washington, D.C., and told me I was going to live with you and your father from then on."

She paused, remembering the confusion and loss she'd felt on that memorable day. Her mother had died only the year before; now her father was telling her she was going to have a new family, one she'd never met. Colonel Madison, T.J.'s father, had been serious and kind, but not at his ease with small children. It had been T.J. himself, a brash thirteen-year-old at that point, who'd taken it on himself to make her laugh, to play with her, to welcome her as family.

She swallowed, willing the stubborn memories away. She would deal with them later, when the present wasn't so threatening. For once, she was glad that T.J. had a habit of sticking fiercely to the business at hand.

He was already a jump ahead, as usual. "So you had a copy made of the diary while you were looking into the lawsuit in Memphis," he was saying. "Who has the copy?"

"A private detective and a lawyer who wrapped up the case for me."

"Think they'll ship a copy to us?"

"I've already called about it." She saw the surprise on his face. "I went up to the lobby to call after you were finally

sleeping this morning. It turns out that Sunny and Creed—
that's the lawyer and the detective—are away for the weekend. But the friend who was house-sitting told me she'd
leave the message. I figured we could call them as soon as
they're back tomorrow evening.''

The house-sitting friend had told Jenny more than that.
She'd said that Sunny had just announced that she was
pregnant, and this weekend trip away was a celebration for
Sunny and Creed. Jenny had grown to like the two of them
in the brief time she'd spent in Memphis, and she was honestly happy that they'd overcome tragedy and separation
and managed to find each other again.

But it only underscored all the unspoken things that lay
between herself and T.J. Madison. They were stuck together for the moment, until T.J. figured out a way to get rid
of the threat to their lives. But beyond that, Jenny thought
unhappily, there was nothing left of the powerful bond that
had once held them.

Nothing, that is, but a memory of passion and the lingering sensation of T.J.'s body against hers, hours after
she'd moved away from him on the big bed. Jenny cleared
her throat and added, ''I suppose we can stay here until tomorrow night.''

He was shaking his dark head even as she said the words.
''Too risky,'' he said. ''It's better to keep moving. First
thing tomorrow morning we'll head for a place I know, on
the coast. But there's no way we can get there tonight. And
much as I hate to admit it, I'm still pretty whacked. Some
more sleep won't do me any harm.''

''Shock and fever can be exhausting,'' Jenny said, as she
started to clear away the remains of their dinner. They'd
been eating picnic-style, sitting across from each other on
the bed, but now T.J. showed signs of getting up. ''Where
are you going?'' she asked him.

''I just want to check this place out. I wasn't in any shape
to do it last night.''

She watched as he moved around the cabin, shaky at first, and then seeming to limber up a little. He was looking at all the windows, she realized. "If there were armed desperadoes out there trying to get in, I think they would have made their move by now," she said, as he headed into the adjoining bathroom and rattled the catch on the window in there.

"It's just habit," he said. "I'll sleep better knowing I've done it."

"What kind of life is that, T.J.?" She couldn't help asking the question. "Poking around looking for holes in things, putting yourself at risk—"

"It's not such a bad life." He sounded more defensive than she'd expected. "I'm good at what I do. There's a challenge in it. I get to take more time off to go sailing than I would in an ordinary job. And the danger is the exception, not the rule."

"You never did want to do anything ordinary, did you?"

"No." His answer was blunt, his eyes serious. "I still don't. Why?"

Settling down with one person was ordinary, Jenny thought. Having babies was ordinary. T.J. had bolted out of her life the one time they had seemed to be heading anywhere near that direction, telling her she was mistaken to think he could ever be the man for her. And she knew he was probably right.

Except that her heart still ached for him whenever she saw his thick brown hair tumbling down over his forehead the way it was at the moment. And in the dark of the early morning hours, gripped by fever, he hadn't been the tough, strong male he was trying to be now. There *were* other, softer sides to T.J. Madison. Jenny had always known that. She knew, too, that she was one of the few people on earth—maybe even the only one—who knew those gentler places in him existed. It was one of the reasons she had found it impossible to forget him.

They spent what was left of the evening watching the TV news on the Charlotte channel and arguing about who would sleep in the bed tonight. T.J. insisted he felt fully recovered, and that he was planning to take the couch this time.

"If you feel so good, why do you keep tensing up whenever you move too fast?" Jenny demanded.

"Who says I tense up?"

"I do. I've been watching you."

It had been impossible not to watch him, when every move he made reminded her so achingly of how she'd felt wrapped in his arms. With luck he wouldn't notice the faint blush on her face when she thought about it.

"Bed's big enough for both of us," he was saying. "I promise to stay on my side if you promise to stay on yours."

"The couch is fine with me. And since I didn't get a lot of sleep last night, either—" She yawned, moving toward the quilt she had neatly refolded and draped over the arm of the couch. "I think I'm going to turn in now. Good night, T.J."

His answering "Good night" sounded reluctant, as though he had more to say but wasn't sure how to do it. Jenny kicked her sneakers off and settled herself on the couch, hoping her own unsettled thoughts would let her sleep.

They probably would have, if it hadn't been for two interruptions. The first one occurred not long after T.J. had turned out the bedside lamp, plunging the cabin into darkness. Jenny heard his quiet breathing and the rustle of the covers as he tried to settle himself in some position that would suit his shoulder. And then she heard his voice, deep and surprisingly smooth in the shadows.

"Why *did* you drop out of college in your senior year?" He tossed the question at her without warning. "And why did you disappear so suddenly after that?"

"I already told you I don't want to talk about it."

"You said you'd talk about it some other time. What's wrong with now?"

"I'm tired, for one thing. We're both tired."

"Haven't you ever been tired, but too tied up with thinking to sleep?"

She knew exactly what he meant. She sighed and said, "You hurt me very badly when you walked out on me, T.J. It took me a while to come to terms with the idea of splitting up. Can't we just leave it at that?"

There was a very long silence from the other side of the room. When T.J. finally spoke, there was an uncharacteristic caution in his voice, as if he were picking his way around a subject that made him uneasy.

"'Splitting up' is the wrong term, sugar," he said. "We couldn't really split up, because we weren't ever really together. Not . . . that way."

"Not romantically." She spoke bluntly.

"Right. Not romantically." She heard him pause again, and then he charged on, sounding a little more confident now. "We were so close, when we were growing up. You were the only person in the world I could really open up to. I assume . . . you felt the same way about me."

"You know I did." The words came out almost angrily.

"Well, what we did that night—the night you turned twenty-one—"

Once again, she refused to let him skirt around it. "The night we made love," she said.

"Yeah. That night. That wasn't real life, sugar. That wasn't really you and me. That was too much champagne, and you feeling like a grown-up, and me celebrating because I wasn't your guardian any more and—well, damn it, you *looked* like a grown-up. You looked so beautiful, and so happy, that I lost my head. I thought—"

She'd heard this all before. He'd used almost the same phrases the morning after that one night together, and hearing them again now filled her with a fury she'd been too young and too hurt to feel at the time.

"You make it sound as though you'd taken advantage of me somehow," she said.

"That was how I felt. How I still feel."

"I was a willing partner, if you cast your mind back."

"I know you were. Oh, God, Jenny..."

The sudden hoarseness in his voice made her realize he must be recalling that night of love in the same erotic detail as she was. It didn't do anything to slow her pounding heartbeat. But his next words were about rejection, not passion.

"I know how you felt about me," he said roughly. "It was infatuation, sugar, nothing more."

"You have no right to assume—"

"Jenny, you were twenty-one. You'd never had a boyfriend. You'd never lived on your own. You were at boarding school, then at college. I was thirty, with no intention of staying in one place for more than a few weeks and no fixed address other than my boat. I didn't have what you needed."

He sounded so certain, so sure of himself. For a moment Jenny was tempted to tell him everything, to see what would happen to that self-confidence if she let him know he had left behind a lot more than just a heartbroken young woman who had always adored him.

She fought off the temptation. If there was any chance that T.J. was going to have a place in her life in the future, she would have done it, to clear the air and ease the burden of carrying these painful secrets over the years. But T.J. had already made it plain that as soon as they were safe, he was going to go back to his own life again. Jenny didn't dare open up to him too much, because she already knew how it felt to pick up the pieces after he'd walked away.

And, anyway, he hadn't come up with any concrete way to keep them safe, not yet. For the moment, Jenny knew they should both be concentrating on the present, not the past.

"Since you're so certain what's best for me, I'm sure you'll realize how much I need to get some sleep," she told him. "You did say you wanted to get an early start in the morning."

The only answer from the big bed was a surprised snort. Jenny lay without moving for a few minutes, until she heard T.J. turning over again, settling in for the night. She let out a long breath and let herself sink a little deeper into the soft cushions of the couch. Sleep was the answer, she thought. After a solid night's rest, she'd be able to see all this in perspective.

But for the second night in a row, she was robbed of sleep. This time it was T.J. who awakened her.

She couldn't see the clock across the room, but it was still pitch-dark outside. She'd been sleeping deeply, dreaming about sailing and sunshine, and it seemed strange to open her eyes to darkness.

She could feel T.J.'s big hand against her shoulder, shaking her gently but urgently.

"What—"

The single word was all she got out. Then T.J.'s other hand was covering her lips, cutting off the rest of the question.

"We've got to get out of here," he said. "There's somebody outside."

She struggled against him. The masculine scent of his skin was far too close and too provocative, swirling itself around her and suggesting tantalizing images to her still-sleepy brain. T.J. was cradling her against his chest, trying to keep her silent, and for a disoriented moment Jenny *wanted* to be there. She wanted to stay close to him and revel in the strength and sensuality she knew he could offer her.

And then she heard the noise.

It wasn't loud, but the suddenness of it in the nighttime silence startled her. It was a scraping sound, coming from the cabin's front door.

"What if it's just an animal?" She whispered the words almost soundlessly.

"Picking the lock? I doubt it." T.J. was pulling back the quilt now, urging her to her feet. She still hadn't quite grasped what was going on, but she could feel the tension in him, and some of it seeped into her own body.

"The bathroom window." He spoke almost directly at her ear. Jenny could feel his warm breath against her skin. "And we have to be absolutely silent."

She was already groping for her shoes in the dark. There was something to be said for traveling without luggage, she thought. Her car keys were in the pocket of her jeans. T.J. had that impressive roll of cash in *his* jeans. They were both carrying their shoes, which T.J. dropped out the bathroom window before giving Jenny a boost to reach its sill. And that was all they needed, all they had, except each other.

She wanted to ask whether he was going to be able to manage the climb, with his shoulder still far from functional. But she knew there wasn't time. She turned her full attention to scrambling as silently as she could out the window, and did what she could to break T.J.'s fall when he came out after her.

He cut off her expressions of concern with a quick chop of his hand in the night air. "Give me the keys," he whispered.

"Are you sure—"

"Damn it, Jenny—"

Jenny hesitated for only a second. He seemed completely alert, completely in control. And he'd heard the tiny sound at their door, after all, when she'd slept right through it. This was T.J.'s game, and although the thought of it made the pit of her stomach feel hollow, she knew she would be wise to do as he told her.

Her little Volkswagen was parked beside the cabin. Quietly, T.J. opened the driver's door and urged Jenny in ahead of him. He followed immediately, just barely latching the door closed. And then, after their frantic burst of activity, he didn't move.

"What are we waiting for?" She mouthed the words at him, looking sharply at his handsome face in the faint light from the motel's main entrance.

"The door." T.J. was stock-still, listening intently. Jenny waited, too, and finally heard the barely audible sound of their cabin door swinging open. T.J. had been waiting until their pursuers were inside, she realized. Whoever it was would be busy searching for them for the next few seconds, and that would give T.J. and Jenny a better chance to get away.

Fortunately, the car was parked on a slight incline, leading down to the front gate. T.J. depressed the clutch, and it started to roll down the smooth pavement of the driveway. The tires made a very slight hissing sound as they moved, but the light nighttime breeze nearly covered the small noise.

Jenny felt as though she'd been holding her breath ever since T.J. had wakened her. Her chest was tight with tension as they backed onto the deserted road in front of the motel, and she didn't haul in a fresh lungful of air until T.J. finally turned the key in the ignition and started the engine with a sound that seemed to split the night.

She looked back at the cabin they'd just fled, and saw two dark figures appear in its doorway. "There they are, T.J.," she said tightly.

"I know. Hang on, sugar."

The Volkswagen's tires screeched against the pavement, and the car shot forward just as a spurt of flame came from one of the shadowy figures at the cabin.

"They're shooting at us." It was so outlandish that Jenny couldn't quite believe it was happening. No one had ever shot at her in her life. And now, twice in two days—

"Not for long, they won't be." T.J. was concentrating grimly on the road.

"They'll follow us, won't they?" Jenny asked.

"Yeah. But they won't be able to find us. It's all right, Sugar. We're in the clear, for the moment." She heard him curse softly as they rounded a sharp corner and he had to wrench the steering wheel around. "I wish I knew this road," he muttered. "But since I don't, we'll just have to improvise."

Improvise seemed to mean driving at a speed that had Jenny clinging to the dashboard every time they rounded a bend. It was just after five o'clock a.m.—she could see the time on the instrument panel—and there was, mercifully, no other traffic around. But they were high up in the mountains here, and the road was both hilly and winding. And it was clear from T.J.'s muffled profanities that none of this was doing his shoulder any good.

His concentration never wavered, though. Jenny couldn't tell what he was looking for, and they were going far too fast for her to want to demand his attention, so she just hung on and waited for his next move, whatever it was going to be.

Chapter 5

It happened without warning. One minute they were hurtling along at a speed she didn't even want to think about, and the next moment T.J. had slammed on the brakes and cranked the steering wheel hard to the left. Jenny hadn't even seen the little dirt road, but that was clearly what T.J. was aiming for, fighting hard to keep all the wheels on the ground as they screeched into the turn and off the pavement.

"This isn't—exactly—an off-road vehicle." Jenny's teeth clicked together as she spoke around the bumping and jolting of the car.

"It doesn't have to get us *far* off the road. Just far enough that we can't be seen."

Jenny had been counting on a few seconds to catch her breath once the Volkswagen had come to a halt. But after their bone-jarring ride through overhanging branches and over very uneven ground, T.J. finally stopped the car, only to urge her out of it in a hurry.

"But if they can't see us—"

"They can't see us *easily*. That's not the same as being really safe."

She could hear the sound of a car approaching on the main road, and it was enough to make her pick up her pace as she followed T.J. into the woods away from the Volkswagen. He stopped in the shelter of a group of trees, reaching out an arm for her, pulling her against his right shoulder as he listened for the pursuing car.

It was moving fast, and Jenny couldn't repress a slight shudder at the realization of how close behind them their pursuers must have been. The vehicle whooshed by in a split second, it seemed, but even after it had gone, T.J.'s rigid muscles didn't relax. He was still waiting for something, she thought, although she couldn't imagine what it was.

"How long until they figure they've lost us?" she asked softly.

His lips were moving slightly, as though he were counting out loud. He shook his head, not answering her question, focused completely on the car that had whipped past them. Jenny could feel the heat of his body through her sweater, but there was nothing amorous about the way he was holding her at the moment. The tension in his stance told her he was thinking only of safety, not of desire. It still made her heart beat faster, just being this close to him.

It wasn't long before she heard a car engine coming their way again, from the opposite direction this time. It was moving much more deliberately. "Is it the same people coming back?" she whispered.

T.J. nodded tersely. "I'd bet on it," he said.

"Won't they notice this dirt road?"

"I hope not. I went past at least half a dozen others before I took this one. From the sound of things, they're not bothering to detour onto every side road."

The car *was* driving slowly enough that it was easy to picture the gunmen peering off into the woods whenever they saw a track. Now Jenny understood why T.J. had driven her car so deeply into the forest.

"The good news," T.J. said, "is that there's probably a crossroad up ahead. Within a couple of miles, I'd say."

Suddenly she realized why he'd been listening so hard. "So they turned back after they came to a crossroad and had no way of guessing which way we might have taken," she said.

"Right. They're probably doing a cursory check of the available dirt roads, but it doesn't sound like they really think that's what we did."

He seemed to be right. She felt his muscles tighten again as the car got closer, and wondered what would happen if, by some awful chance, the gunmen decided to check out this one dirt road. But they didn't; the engine cruised slowly past, and as it did, T.J.'s body finally relaxed, and he let go his grip on Jenny's shoulders. She suddenly realized how hard she'd been breathing, and how cold she felt without T.J.'s arm around her.

She half expected him to move back to the Volkswagen, but he was turning in the other direction now, back toward the main road. "Come on, sugar," he said. "We don't have a lot of time. I want to get moving."

"T.J." His name came out almost pleadingly. "We don't know where we are. We don't have any idea where we're going. And we're supposed to get there on *foot?*"

He grabbed her hand and started walking. They were heading back along the dirt road, and T.J. was already moving fast.

"All roads lead somewhere eventually," he was telling her. "And it's quiet enough that we'll have plenty of notice when anybody's coming. Believe me, it's safer than staying with your car."

"Wait a minute." She pulled against him now, forcing him to a halt. "I'm not wild about just leaving my car out here in the woods."

"We have to. Don't you get it? That's how they traced us—by the licence-plate number. If I'd been even half-awake when we checked in, I would have thought of that. Your car is a liability now, not an asset. Fortunately, though, these guys aren't quite as slick as I'd been thinking."

"They were slick enough." Jenny shuddered, thinking of the quiet scraping noises that had been so close to the couch where she'd been sound asleep. If T.J.'s hearing hadn't been so acute, the two gunmen might have been inside the cabin before Jenny had known what was happening.

"They're good, granted. They ought to be, with the backup they've got." He was walking again, gripping her hand hard, giving her no choice but to follow. "But if they'd been *really* good, they would have disabled your car before they broke into the cabin. That's what I would have done. They left us an escape route, and that makes me think they're not quite as cagey as they might be."

"Why do I not feel completely reassured about that?"

"Because you're smart, sugar. We're in a mess—there's no way around it."

They were almost back to the main road now. T.J. paused and listened. In the distance Jenny could hear another car— or was it the same one, patrolling this stretch of road, hoping to catch a glimpse of T.J. and Jenny?

"This is the hard part of walking out of here," T.J. said. "We're going to have to stay out of sight, and that means getting down every time somebody drives by."

There was a little hollow to one side of the dirt road, and T.J. was heading into it, urging Jenny along with him. The car was getting closer in a big hurry, and Jenny had barely settled into the dip in the ground next to T.J. when it whizzed past them.

T.J. had his right arm around her again, holding her close. Jenny could feel the solid warmth of him and feel his quickened breathing at her ear. For a moment she felt as she had when he'd wakened her: drowsy and disoriented and longing for more of his touch. And then she reminded herself where they were, and what was happening.

"You don't have to hold me so tight, T.J.," she told him. "I may not be thrilled about being with you, but I'm hardly likely to take off into the night at this point—not by myself."

She knew her voice sounded breathless, but with luck he would put that down to fear, and the way they'd been hurrying a moment ago. When he answered, Jenny thought she heard a huskiness that hadn't been there before.

"I'm not letting you go," he said. "Not this time. Not until I'm sure it's safe."

His words struck her as odd. She met his gaze and felt something tighten low down in her belly at the familiar gleam of those gold flecks against the brown depths of his eyes.

"Not this time?" she echoed. "You didn't *let* me go last time, T.J. You took off—you disappeared."

"Damn it, Jenny!" T.J. sat up suddenly, and Jenny moved with him. They were staring at each other from dangerously close range, and Jenny wondered if her expression was as wild and hungry as T.J.'s. "I took off because I knew it couldn't work between us. I knew you deserved better. I'm sorry if I was abrupt about it—hell, you know that's just the way I am. But if you think for one moment that it wasn't just as hard on me as it was on you—"

"Listen to yourself!" Jenny was suddenly angry with him again, the way she had been last night. "You sound as though you thought you did something noble in leaving me."

He scowled at her. The effect of it was like being at close range with a big and very angry wildcat. "I didn't say it was noble," he said. "I *did* think it was the right thing to do."

"Maybe you should have consulted with me about that, before you took off on your sailboat for a two-year cruise around the world."

"Wait a minute." His eyes narrowed slightly. "How do you know that's what I did?"

Something caught in Jenny's throat. Here it was again, she thought. She could tell him the whole story now and make him understand what he'd really done to her by leaving. She could describe her search for him when she'd discovered she was pregnant, and the despair she'd felt when his lawyer had told her T.J. was planning to be gone for at least two years and would be all but unreachable.

And once again, it seemed crazy to get into it when they were so hemmed in by danger in the present. She shook her head at him and said, "I looked for you. That's all."

He seemed to sense that it wasn't all, but he didn't pursue it. "What was I supposed to do?" he growled. "Haul you out of your last year of college and take you with me on my boat?"

She didn't have a good answer to that. But she knew that T.J.'s response—to run to the other end of the earth—hadn't been the answer, either. "If you'd really loved me," she said, "we could have found a way."

That was the crux of it—the part that had always hurt most when she'd thought about it. She'd loved T.J. with her heart and soul, and finally with her body, as well. And she'd believed—once—that he loved her in return. She suspected that he had left because deep down, he didn't know what to do with love and commitment and stability—and passion, too. She suspected he'd really run because he was scared of all that, and scared to admit it to himself, too.

But the bottom line was still the same: he hadn't loved her enough to stay. She heard the tremor in her own voice as she finally said it out loud to him.

It was very clear that he didn't see it that way. His eyes darkened at her words.

"If I'd loved you..." He sounded amazed that she would even question it.

Jenny was suddenly aware of how quiet it was, and how dark. The leaves hadn't come out this high up in the mountains yet, and she could hear the faint clicking of bare branches touching each other as a slight breeze passed overhead. Other than that, the world was silent, except for T.J.'s ragged breathing and her own.

She shifted her position slightly, feeling crowded by his oversize anger. She was still half sitting, and last year's dried leaves rustled as she moved. The sound seemed to shake T.J. out of his astonishment.

He had reached for her before she was aware of it. She felt him pulling her close and gave a wordless cry that might have been a protest or an invitation, she couldn't be sure. At the moment she was only sure that T.J. Madison did things to her, inside and out, that no man had ever come close to doing. She knew him so well—knew there were depths to him that even he had never really faced. She knew the strength he was capable of, and the tenderness, too.

She met his kiss willingly and tasted some of her own frustration on T.J.'s lips as his mouth crushed against hers, hard and uncompromising. *Damn you, T.J.*, she was thinking. And the force of her thoughts went into the kiss. *Damn you for making things so difficult for both of us, when it should have been so simple.*

The desire that sizzled between them was simple enough. They were half kneeling in a bed of last year's fallen leaves, and T.J.'s furious grip had pulled Jenny agonizingly close to him. She could feel the power of his thighs against hers, and his hands on her back were broad and possessive.

All of her came to life as he held her. Every part of her body remembered in exquisite detail what his hands and his mouth could to do her. Her breasts under her loose sweater felt taut against his hard chest, begging to be touched. Her lips rediscovered a thousand sensitive places as they met his with a hunger that was almost violent.

And deep inside her, it was as if a silent pool had been shaken by a tremor, ruffling its still surface with the promise of passion. Jenny felt that tremor in all her limbs, as she matched T.J.'s kiss in ferocity and wove her fingers into his thick, dark hair.

"Jenny..." T.J. sounded stunned, caught completely by surprise at the force of the embrace he had initiated. "God, Jenny... this is crazy. We can't do this. Not here."

He seemed to be trying to convince himself, as well as her. And it didn't work, not for either of them.

"If you try to deny this doesn't mean anything..." She didn't finish the sentence. She was breathing too hard, and her lips were only inches from T.J.'s. She could still feel the touch of his mouth against hers. She wanted it—wanted everything he had been trying to deny, everything he had walked away from all those years ago.

He gave a startled half laugh at her words. "Deny it..." He shook his head. "My God, who in their right mind could deny it? That doesn't mean—"

She couldn't stand to hear any more rationalizing, not now. She reached up quickly and put her fingers over his mouth, stifling what he'd been going to say.

"Just don't tell me it wasn't real, all right?" She could feel his pulse beating against her fingertips, steady and strong. She didn't know where any of this was leading. She didn't have any idea how T.J. thought he could shake off the men who were following them, or how she was going to deal with his sudden intrusion into her life after all this time.

But it somehow seemed important that T.J. at least acknowledge the strength of what was happening between them. He'd been afraid of it years ago, and it had scared him out of her life. It might still scare him now, but she'd be damned if she was going to listen to him talk himself out of it again.

His mouth felt heated and enticing under her hand. She heard T.J. bite back a groan in his throat and gave a soft cry herself as he parted his lips, caressing her soft fingertips with his tongue. The gesture tantalized him as much as it did her; she could feel every inch of his torso pressed against her, and the hard outline of arousal was impossible to miss.

She moved her fingers over his face, outlining that familiar strong jaw, pushing his hair back from his forehead. She moved closer, meeting his lips with her own again, loving the sensuous swirl of his tongue against hers, feeling all of herself begin to dissolve into liquid as she recognized the depth of her need for this man.

"We have to stop." T.J.'s voice was a rasp, a plea. "We've got to get out of here."

"I know we do. Oh, God . . ."

Jenny pulled in a long breath as they separated. He was right, she knew that. This isolated woody hollow in the middle of nowhere, in the predawn darkness, with armed gunmen searching for them, was hardly the place to give rein to the passion they aroused in each other.

The point was, T.J. wasn't denying that passion anymore. Jenny had no clear idea where it might lead them, but at least they were agreed on that single thing. After the sizzling moment they'd just shared, and the ravenous way they were still looking at each other, T.J. wasn't going to be able to write this off as mere infatuation, or anything other than what it really was: a blood-deep longing that had the power to shake both of them to the core.

"What are we going to do?" She pushed her own hair back with shaking fingers and took a cautionary step away from him. Having pulled the lid off that mutual longing, coping with it while they were on the run wasn't exactly going to be easy.

"We're going to walk, until we get to someplace I can wangle some kind of vehicle out of someone." T.J. got to his feet and reached a hand down to help Jenny up.

"Sounds like it could be a long walk."

"Could be."

"Do you feel up to it? Crawling out that window couldn't have done your shoulder any good."

He stared at her for a second, and then, to her surprise, he gave a short laugh. Even in the dim light she could see his eyes glinting at her, sexy and amused. "You know," he said, "nobody but you ever really worried about me. I'd forgotten how it feels."

"Your father worried about you. All the time."

He shook his head, and the hair she'd just smoothed back from his face came tumbling back down again. "My father worried that I was going to get myself into some mess that he'd have to scrape me out of," he said.

Jenny had to admit it was true: Colonel Madison had been a stiff and strict father, and was often exasperated with his rebellious son. "Your bosses must worry about you," she said. "Especially if they send you on risky missions."

"As long as you don't screw up, the military assumes you know what you're doing," he said. "No, the only person who ever really gave a damn about how I was feeling was you, Jenny." He paused. His face looked very serious in the faint light. "Thanks," he said finally. "For giving a damn, I mean."

"You have the most romantic way of phrasing things, T.J."

His quick grin sliced through the dimness of the early morning, making Jenny's breath quicken all over again. "I try," he said, reaching for her hand. "Come on, sugar. It's time to hit the road."

T.J. had no clear idea how many miles they had covered by the time the sun came up. As he'd suspected, they reached a crossroad within an hour, and in the gray predawn light he flipped a coin to decide which way they should go. He hated leaving things to chance this way, but the truth was that he was on completely alien territory here, and one direction was as unknown as the other.

"Heads we go left, tails we go right," he said, watching the coin turn over against the still-hazy sky.

The coin came down heads. And chance, it seemed, was on their side at last. Just as the first rays of sunshine were appearing over the top of the mountains behind them, he saw a farm ahead, with a very rusty pickup truck parked in its yard with what seemed to be a For Sale sign in the front window.

T.J. felt it was no more than they deserved. They'd had to hustle off the road more than a dozen times already, whenever a car had driven past them, and he ached all over from clambering in and out of hollows in the landscape. He was wearing only his jeans, sneakers and his torn sweat-shirt, and Jenny wasn't any more warmly dressed than he was. Both of them were cold, grubby and worn-out from the fear and passion that the night had held.

"Good timing," he said, as they caught sight of the farm. "It's too risky to keep hiking, now that it's getting light."

"Wait a minute." Jenny seemed to have figured out what he was planning to do. "You can't just buy a truck and drive away in it. What about registration and insurance and—"

"We don't have time for that stuff. And I'm only planning to drive it a few hours, anyway. Desperate times call for desperate measures, sugar."

"It'll be desperate, all right, if we get stopped in a stolen vehicle. I thought you were worried about not getting into police records, T.J."

"We'll just make sure we don't do anything the police will take exception to. And we're not really stealing it. The thing has current plates, and the owner obviously doesn't want it. Think of it as an unorthodox rental car."

Jenny rolled her eyes at him. "I can't believe you're doing this," she said.

What he was doing was quietly opening the driver's door of the old pickup so it didn't make any noise. Luckily, the owner had left it unlocked; either this wasn't a high-crime district or he considered the truck barely worth stealing. Most likely both, T.J. thought, as he pulled a wire off one terminal on the ignition switch and jammed it onto the other one.

His shoulder started to throb again as he extricated himself from under the dashboard and popped the hood of the truck open. Even when he was traveling as light as this, he always had a folding knife in his back pocket, and he used it now to touch the terminal of the starter motor and the frame of the truck, until the motor made a grinding sound and began to run.

"All right," he said, dropping the hood gently back down. The sign in the window said, on closer inspection, $400 or Best Offer, and T.J. quickly peeled five hundred dollars' worth of bills out of his pocket. "There," he said, folding the sign around the bills and weighting them down with a rock in the oil-spattered place where the truck had been sitting. "The owner'll be happy, we're happy, everybody's happy. Now let's get the hell out of here."

Jenny didn't look *completely* happy, he noticed, but she got into the cab with him quickly enough. Once it was warmed up, the old truck motored along efficiently. And the gas tank was a quarter full. The heating system didn't seem to be delivering any warm air to the cab, but hell, it was an imperfect world, T.J. figured, and at least they were moving again.

"This sure beats crawling around in the trees, in my book," he said out loud.

"Won't the owner report what happened to his truck?" Jenny wanted to know.

"He might. But I doubt he'll be in any rush about it. After all, we paid him for it, didn't we?"

"And those two men in the car? What if they noticed the truck for sale? If they come back this way, they'll probably notice it's gone."

T.J. had already considered that. "It's an outside chance," he said. "I don't think they got as far as that farm when they were looking for us. Remember, once they reached the crossroad they probably turned back. I think we're home-free, sugar."

T.J. himself would have noticed the truck *and* taken down the number. But he was banking on these two guys not being quite as on top of things as T.J. tried to be. If they could just get to the coast in one piece....

If they were going to do that, he needed coffee. And food. When the gas gage started dipping down into Empty, he pulled over at a gas station and filled the tank, picking up two large coffees and a box of doughnuts while paying for the gasoline.

When he got back, Jenny was out of the truck, standing in the ever-growing morning light. T.J. had caught a glimpse of himself in the mirror over the service station door, and he knew he looked terrible: his shirt was torn, his face haggard and his eyes hollow from three nights with precious little sleep. But Jenny...

Jenny looked like a dream. She was flexing her muscles, arms above her head, and looking into the rising sun that now lay ahead of them. T.J. had been muttering unfriendly things about the sun, which was getting into his eyes and making it hard to concentrate on the road. But he took all those comments back when he watched Jenny's curving body stretching in the warm light, and saw the sun bathing her skin with its rays.

God, she was beautiful. More beautiful than she'd ever been, because there was a mature strength and purpose to her face now that hadn't been there before. He looked at her slender waist and felt his palms ache with the need to wrap themselves around her again and hold her tightly against him.

"Jenny…" He'd intended to say her name firmly, letting her know it was time to get back on the road. But it came out softly, a whispered caress.

She was running her fingers through her hair now, untangling its dark disarray. It fell thick and glossy to her shoulders, and when she turned her upper body in one direction and then the other, T.J. had to smother a groan. He felt himself trembling inside with the memory of the night she had moved in his arms with that same sexy grace.

She'd been right, in the predawn stillness this morning, to tell him that they shouldn't—couldn't—deny the potency of the attraction between them. He'd done that, years ago, by running away from her because he hadn't seen any way for him to fit into her life.

But that hadn't solved anything, not really. He'd never gotten over Jenny Alvarez, and his reaction to the sight of her now only proved it. She was stretching like a sun-warmed cat, and T.J. had never seen anything so sensuous. The need to touch her again filled him completely and intimately.

Not now, T.J., he told himself. *Not until you're sure she's safe.* He cleared his throat, and Jenny turned at the sound. To his surprise, she was smiling—that spicy, inviting smile he had never been able to resist.

"Isn't it beautiful?" she said. "I've been living in North Carolina for years, and I've never made it to the mountains. I had no idea they were so beautiful."

To T.J., the landscape had been just a factor to be added into the problem of getting away. He'd seen the mountains as obstacles, and the sun as a driving hazard.

Jenny was pointing out to him that there were other, gentler ways of looking at the world around him. She was holding her open palms out toward the sun, fingers outstretched, and in spite of her obvious tiredness, there was joy on her face, and it was simple and heartfelt.

T.J. looked at the long view, the blue ridges succeeding each other into the morning mist, and felt the sun's warmth on his face. It was crazy, he thought, but his eyes suddenly seemed less tired. Was it the morning light or Jenny's smile that had performed that magic trick?

When he looked back at her, she was on her way into the truck cab. "I remembered about you and gravy and biscuits," she was saying to him. "I hope that means you remember about me and doughnuts."

"Absolutely plain, no jelly, no sugar, no sprinkles, no nothing." He flipped open the top of the box. "I still say it's deviant."

"Say what you like. I don't suppose—" Her smile dimmed. Damn it, it was the smile that had been affecting him, he thought. He could almost feel the temperature in the cab cooling as she said more seriously, "I don't suppose the gas station store had gauze or tape."

"Even if they had, I don't want to take the time to do anything about my shoulder until we get to where we're going."

"And that is . . . ?"

"East." T.J. ripped a small triangle out of the lid of his coffee-cup lid and balanced it on the dashboard. "Sorry we have to eat and run, sugar, but I don't want to sit around the neighborhood any longer than we have to. You ready?"

He was stonewalling her, and she knew he was doing it. But T.J. just couldn't shake the feeling that they wouldn't be safe until they'd left the Blue Ridge Mountains far behind. He'd been caught napping twice already, and he was damned if he was going to let it happen a third time.

Jenny was silent, but he could feel her eyes on him as he put the truck in gear and got back on the road. Her uncomplicated joy in the beauty of the morning was gone, and her dark brown eyes, he felt sure, looked troubled again, asking him wordless questions he didn't have the answers to yet.

Chapter 6

Pete Alvarez's Diary

How can you have your day in court when you don't know if it's day or night? If you're awake or asleep?

They came and got me in the middle of the night. Didn't even know I was in jail. It was a joke, a bad joke.

It's no joke, soldier.

Get him to his feet.

Man, he's in a bad way.

Court ain't gonna think much of this.

What did he do, anyway?

Smuggling. Caught him with the stuff on him.

Trying to get to my feet. Don't let them say that. I never did it, I hated to see those boys go that way.

I was going to be a doctor, a long time ago.

I was going to help people. I wouldn't do it, not what they said I did.

Couldn't talk, though. Couldn't think straight. Two guys propping me up, guys in uniforms. My own uni-

*form hardly fit me. Hanging on me, like I was already
dead.*

*They didn't see who I really was. They didn't see
what happened to me. The one man who would have
said something, he was already home. Where I wanted
to be. Home with his family, like I wanted to be home
with mine.*

*The devil was clever. Not enough evidence to con-
vict. Just enough to stamp me with "Dishonorable
Discharge" and send me home like this. Like I am now.*

*Sometimes I wonder why I write these things down.
Who is there who would understand? Who even cares?
No names, no dates—I made myself promise that when
I started. I don't think he can find me, after all this
time. I don't think he's even looking anymore. Who
would listen to me, even if I wanted to talk? But just in
case, no names, no dates.*

*Maybe I write it just for me. Sometimes I think these
things didn't happen the way I remember them. But
they did happen. When I die, the devil will still be alive.
But at least it will be written down. And that's all I can
do now.*

Jenny knew she had been dozing toward the end of the trip.
They had stopped twice more for gas and had gotten sandwiches at the second stop, but otherwise T.J. had insisted
that they keep moving. He had turned down her offer to
drive for a while, too, and had been remarkably silent most
of the way. So after three or four hours of heading east on
the same highway, she'd given in to drowsiness and slept,
arms wrapped around herself to ward off the chill.

They'd had only one real conversation, when they had
passed a convoy of military vehicles. Jenny had sensed T.J.
becoming more watchful, although her common sense told
her no one could possibly be shadowing them at this point.

When the green trucks had receded into the distance behind them, she said, "When you first showed up at my place on Friday evening, you commented on how strange it was that you should be working for the military."

It seemed even stranger that it had only been two days ago that she'd seen him sitting on her front steps. T.J.'s swaggering, oversize presence had taken over her life again in a hurry, she thought. Or maybe the gap he'd left had been even bigger than she'd realized.

"And?" The single syllable was uncommunicative.

"So how did it happen? Did you suddenly get an urge to follow in your father's footsteps? Or did they come looking for you?"

In his youth, T.J. had hated the way his father had insisted on a strict military-style upbringing for his only son. When Jenny had arrived on the scene, at age four, the junior and senior Madisons were in the middle of an epic battle over whether T.J. would continue going to the military boarding school that he loathed. It had been Jenny's arrival, in fact, that had enabled T.J. to lobby successfully to live at home again. *She's just a little girl,* she could clearly recall him saying to his father. *She should have some family around her.*

He hadn't seemed cut out for the military world, she thought. T.J.'s devil-may-care way of barging through life simply didn't jibe with the military establishment's more by-the-book approach. And he'd never dealt well with discipline, either.

So his choice of career now was a surprising one. She saw him considering the question before he finally answered it.

"In a way, they came looking for me," he said. "One of Dad's old friends—maybe you remember him, James Wilder?—invited me to see a new ship being launched in Annapolis about five years ago. He knew I was nuts about sailing and thought it might interest me. And it did—but not as much as the fact that I spotted what turned out to be a very tricky little hiding place right next to the podium where the secretary of defense was going to be making a speech."

"And the security people hadn't noticed it?"

"It hadn't been there when they'd secured the area. Wilder mentioned it to somebody, and when they'd checked out the spot, they found a disgruntled ex-serviceman hiding there with a loaded weapon."

It was typical of T.J. not just to have plugged a security leak, but to have saved the life of a major national leader at the same time, Jenny thought. Other men did things gradually. T.J. did them all the way, or not at all.

"So they were pretty impressed by you," she said.

"So they said. They interviewed me for what felt like about a solid month and finally offered me a position sniffing out other security problems. When I found out I wouldn't have to wear a uniform or keep regular office hours, I figured it wouldn't be so bad. And when it turned out I still had time off to go sailing, I started warming up to it."

Jenny knew he was being deliberately understated. She'd seen him last night, checking over every inch of their cabin, and again at the wheel of her car this morning, calculating every risk, staying at least two jumps ahead of their attackers. He loved this job, she thought. He loved the spice of danger, and the adrenaline of being out on the edge.

"You know," she said suddenly, "I remember going sailing with you. Do you still like to have the boat going absolutely as fast as it can, all the time?"

He gave her a startled glance. "That's what sailing's all about, sugar," he said.

She shook her head. "No," she said. "That's what *you're* all about, T.J. There are lots of people who go sailing to enjoy the breeze, or the fresh air, or the scenery. You go because it's a challenge—T.J. Madison versus the elements."

"What's wrong with that?"

What, indeed, was wrong with it? Jenny grappled with her own thoughts for a long moment, and finally had to admit to herself that one of the things she'd loved about T.J. was his passion for freedom, his courageous heart, his skill at negotiating life on the edge.

It was also the thing that made it impossible for him to think of settling down. This time it was Jenny who hesitated before answering, because she didn't want to raise that particular issue.

"At least you're consistent," she told him, and saw his eyebrows raise slightly. "You take everything in life as a personal challenge. Even this job with the military. Did it ever occur to you that maybe you're trying to get back at them for the way your father tried to mold you into a good little soldier when you were young?"

He snorted. "You're talking like a shrink," he said.

"That's because I *am* one, remember? You're the one who points out to the military that they're about to screw up, right? Maybe that's your way of proving that you know best, after all."

There was a very long silence. Jenny waited, but T.J. still didn't speak, so she added, "You know, the only time I've known you *not* to welcome a challenge is the time you walked out on me."

It wasn't precisely a question, or precisely anything else. Jenny had said the words because something in T.J.'s silence made her think she had startled him into seeing things in a new light. She didn't know what he was thinking at the moment, but at least he *was* thinking. That was enough for now.

His thoughts apparently kept him busy and silent, long after they'd put miles between them and the military vehicles that had sparked the conversation. And Jenny had dozed, at first fitfully, then for quite a long time, waking only when the truck came to a stop.

Her muscles felt stiff. She'd been holding herself tightly, seeking at least a little bit of warmth in the unheated cab. She felt disoriented and gradually realized it was the sounds and smells around her that seemed strange.

High overhead there were sea gulls crying, their voices wild and free. She breathed in deeply, and the sharp tang of salt air caught at her nostrils. When she opened her eyes, she was half blinded by the glare of the sun on the endless blue expanse of the ocean.

They were on a pier, she noticed. She could hear the waves lapping at the pilings under the wooden structure. The clean air cleared the sleep from her mind quickly, and she reached for the door handle, wondering where T.J. had gotten to.

She could hear his big laugh the moment she got out of the truck cab. The familiar sound of it tugged at her, drawing her toward it. She had always loved the way T.J. laughed. The sound had the same reckless edge as the cries of the circling gulls in the sky over her head, the same free-wheeling abandon.

She still couldn't see him, until he stepped off the deck of a big white sailboat moored alongside the pier. He was laughing again, waving a hand to someone in the boat's cabin. Jenny couldn't hear what they were saying—the fresh ocean breeze whipped their words away from her—but T.J. seemed invigorated, hopeful, more confident than he'd been while they'd been escaping from the mountains earlier today. Then his face had been grim and taut. Now he looked different.

Jenny still felt chilled, and the crisp sea air didn't do anything to warm her, in spite of the sunshine. But T.J. looked completely comfortable as he jumped easily from the deck of the boat to the pier. He'd always been this way when he was on the water, she recalled. He seemed made for the wide-open challenge of the ocean and the freedom of the salt air.

He was waving to her now, and she could see the white flash of his grin against his tanned face. "I thought I'd let you sleep," he said. "Feel rested?"

"A little. T.J., where are we?"

"Just north of Cape Hatteras. I have friends here."

Cape Hatteras was off the North Carolina coast, Jenny knew, toward the state's northern border with Virginia. She took a closer look around her and decided that they seemed to be in a little coastal town, dominated by piers and boathouses. The blue water was crisscrossed by the tall masts of sailboats of all sizes, bobbing in the lively breeze.

The breeze seemed to cut right through her loose sweater, and she wrapped her arms around herself again for warmth. T.J.'s eyes picked up the gesture, and he nodded.

"I'm chilled, too," he said, although he showed no sign of it. "And those doughnuts wore off about two hours ago. Let's go get warmed up and fed, all right?"

"All right."

She didn't ask him what he was planning after that. It was Saturday afternoon, and there was no way they could contact Sunny and Creed about getting a copy of her father's diary until tomorrow evening. That meant they had twenty-four hours to spend together, and she knew T.J. wouldn't be looking so supremely confident if this weren't a completely safe place for them to spend it.

She was still too tired to think beyond that. She got back in the truck with T.J. and they drove to the edge of the small village, where a low wood-sided building stretched out along the sandy shore. A discreet sign in front said Wanderers' Rest Inn.

"This is where your friends live?" she asked.

"Yeah. They own the place."

"Who was the man on the boat?"

T.J. hesitated for a fraction of a second before replying. "He's another buddy of mine. He and I and the owner of this inn used to race together."

His manner sounded very slightly defensive, although Jenny couldn't imagine why. And once they were inside the Wanderers' Rest, she stopped thinking about it. The place was a true haven after the alarms and anxieties of the past forty-eight hours. Everything, from the big double-glazed windows facing the ocean to the soft carpets underfoot, seemed designed to soothe the weary traveler, to provide the ultimate comfort while offering a spectacular view of the seaside world outside.

The man in the office had greeted T.J. with enthusiasm, and Jenny with pleasure. Jenny saw his gaze taking in T.J.'s ripped shirt and the white bandage that showed underneath, but he didn't comment on their obvious dishevelment. He just nodded at the rusty pickup outside the inn's front door as he said, "Snazzy vehicle you've got there, T.J."

T.J. grinned. "Best we could do at short notice," he said. "Think I can have the usual room?"

"Since it's off-season, sure."

Jenny had a feeling that even during the height of the season, T.J. would find his usual room available whenever he chose to drop in. There was something in the owner's manner that hinted at a long-standing and very close friendship between the two men.

She was used to thinking of T.J. as a complete loner, but she could also imagine him forming a few very deep attachments. She was glad for him—the image of him as a lonely sailor had sometimes haunted her in the moments when she hadn't been able to stop thinking about him.

T.J.'s "usual room" was at the far end of the low complex, and it featured a bank of oceanfront windows that made Jenny understand immediately why he favored it. The room was airy and expansive, and when T.J. had pulled the drapes all the way back, it was almost like looking out to sea from the bow of a ship.

"Next best thing to being on the water." T.J.'s words confirmed what Jenny was thinking. His friend had withdrawn discreetly, and T.J. was standing next to her, looking out the windows.

"You're sure we're safe here, aren't you?" She phrased it more as a statement than a question.

"Absolutely sure. I was a highly unofficial member of the racing crew down here, so my name isn't on anything that anyone could trace. And I'm sure we weren't followed this afternoon. So yes, we're safe. And about time, I might add."

"Amen to that. And it's about time to take a look at your shoulder again, too."

"I know. There are a few stores not far from here. I'm assuming you want a hot shower about as desperately as I do, so why don't you have the first shot at it while I take a shopping run and pick up some bandages and some food?"

Jenny had already cast a longing eye at the big bathroom. Even her bones felt tired, and the idea of being clean all over was seductive. It was too bad she didn't have some clean clothes to step into, but she supposed she couldn't ask for everything when she was running for her life.

The thought of the threat still hanging over them made her voice somber as she said to T.J., "Are you sure you feel up to it?"

He gave her that grin again, the one that always made her blood race. "You know me, Sugar," he said. "Get me within a mile of the ocean, and I feel fine. Go on and take all the time you want."

She was already shedding her grubby jeans and sweater in the bathroom as T.J. let himself out the sliding glass doors onto the beach.

The rush of hot water over her tired body was like a benediction straight out of heaven. She hadn't realized how dirty she'd gotten while they'd been hiding from passing cars in the woods this morning, or how badly her muscles ached from the tension of wondering where the next danger would come from.

She hadn't been intending to take a long shower, because she wanted to be safely dressed again by the time T.J. got back. But the water felt too good, and even after she had finally stepped out of the glass enclosure, she took her time, wrapping herself in thick peach-colored towels, turning on the heat lamp in the ceiling and basking in the welcome sensation of being warm and clean and safe.

She was still basking when she heard the sliding door open in the main room. She jumped a little and realized she didn't feel as completely safe as she'd thought.

"T.J.?" She could hear the edge of anxiety in her own voice.

"It's me." The smooth rumble of his reply made her ease back down on the upholstered divan where she'd been relaxing. But his next words got her sitting up straighter again. "You're still a size eight, right?"

Jenny frowned. "Right," she said, "but—"

The bathroom door opened slightly. "Don't worry," T.J.'s voice said. "I'm not invading. I just thought this might feel better than getting back into what you were wearing."

His hand and arm came into the bathroom, holding a large paper shopping bag. He dropped it on the carpeted floor, and the door closed again.

Jenny gave a startled laugh. "You were reading my mind," she said to him through the door.

"It wasn't hard to do. I feel like these clothes grew on me myself. I picked up some new ones for both of us."

Jenny opened the bag to find a new pair of blue jeans, a soft tan sweater that had the heft of linen or perhaps silk, a matching tan turtleneck and a pair of comfortable-looking brown pumps. She checked the inside label of the shoes. They were her size.

How much money *did* he have in the pocket of those jeans? she couldn't help wondering again. The clothes were understated but expensive looking.

She didn't have to wonder how he'd gotten the shoe size right. He knew for the same reason he knew her dress size: he had once bought her a complete formal outfit, right down to a pair of dancing shoes, to celebrate her twenty-first birthday. The dress had been deep blue velvet, the color of midnight and romance, with a white shawl and shoes.

She still remembered his exact words when he'd called her at college to find out what size to buy. *I'm not used to buying clothes for women, sugar,* he'd said. *But just this once I'd like to buy something really special for you.*

She realized that she was standing very still now, remembering it. Had there been any echo of that old memory in T.J.'s voice when he'd handed her the bag of clothes a few minutes ago? She didn't think there was; he'd been extremely matter-of-fact.

But she knew he must be thinking about it, just as she was. And that made her fingers tremble slightly as she unwrapped the towels around her and began to get dressed.

He'd bought underwear, she noticed as she came to the bottom of the bag. But there wasn't a new brassiere, as though he'd hesitated to trust his memory when it came to such an intimate matter of sizing. Jenny closed her eyes and felt her now-warmed body responding to the thought of T.J.'s big hands closing around her breasts.

Was there any way she would ever stop longing to feel that again? It was beginning to seem less and less likely, the more time they spent with each other. And an enforced twenty-four hours together in very comfortable surroundings—even though there was plenty of space between the two double beds in the room—wasn't going to make it any easier for Jenny to remember all the reasons why she should keep her distance.

T.J. was leaning back in an armchair when she went back out to the main room. He still wore his dirty clothes, and he had his head back, his eyes closed. He might be feeling confident and glad they were here, Jenny thought, but he also looked close to exhaustion. She walked over to the chair and ran a gentle hand over his cheek.

"Your turn," she said.

His eyes opened slowly, and she was startled at their darkness. She had gotten dressed quickly, because it had been unsettling to think of being this close to T.J. without any clothes on, with her body warmed and languid from the hot shower. Had he been having similar thoughts? Something in the abrupt way he stood up made her think he might have.

"Thanks," he said, seizing the pile of clothes he'd bought for himself. "I'll take you up on that offer to check my shoulder after I'm clean."

With that, he almost fled into the steamy warmth of the bathroom. Jenny heard the shower taps being turned on to full force a moment later.

She explored the room while he showered, and tried to keep her mind off the picture of T.J.'s gloriously male body standing under a hot cascade of water. The Wanderers' Rest obviously went in for luxury, she thought, inspecting the comfortable armchairs, the fine wool blankets, the elegant stemware in the cupboard above the small built-in kitchenette. It seemed odd to associate a rough-and-tumble male like T.J. Madison with a place like this.

His friend the innkeeper hadn't seemed surprised to have T.J. show up out of the blue with a woman, she recalled. Something tightened in her chest as she wondered whether this was a regular occurrence, or whether the friend was just being low-key.

She had always pushed aside the unwelcome idea of T.J. having other women in his life, but now she forced herself to confront it. He had had a couple of casual sweethearts when he'd been a teenager, when Jenny was too young to see them as anything more than minor intrusions into her treasured time with T.J. But ever since she'd grown to be a teenager herself, she couldn't recall him spending much time with any one woman.

Maybe he had just been discreet about it, she thought now. Maybe this favorite room of his at the Wanderers' Rest was his romantic hideaway. Would he tell her the truth if she asked him about it?

She was still trying to decide how much of T.J.'s private life she really wanted to know about when the bathroom door opened and he came out. His dark hair was smooth for once, wet and slicked back. It made his gold-flecked eyes even more arresting. He'd bought new jeans for himself, too, and they rode a little low on his hips, accenting the sexy tilt of his stance. He was bare-chested and holding a roll of gauze.

"I was trying to do it myself," he said, "but I can't quite see the damn thing to make sure it's clean. Could you—?"

He held out the gauze, and Jenny moved to take it from him. He hadn't been intending to change the bandage himself when he'd gone into the bathroom, she thought. Why had he changed his mind?

She knew the answer the moment they sat down together on the edge of one of the double beds. T.J. had stripped off the old bandage, and the moment Jenny put her hands on his skin to examine the gunshot wound, she felt him tense up in a way that she felt certain had nothing to do with pain. She hadn't done anything that might hurt yet; T.J.'s reaction was that of a man who had nerved himself up to resist a temptation he wasn't sure he could overcome.

"It *feels* fine," he said tightly.

"It looks a lot better," she confirmed.

The heat of his skin under her fingertips was doing crazy things to her. She took the scissors and tape out of the bag he'd handed her, and started working quickly, hoping to have the new bandage in place before either of them could do anything foolish.

"You always did heal fast," she said. "I remember that time you fell off the roof of the garage—"

"I didn't fall. I jumped. And I would have been fine if it hadn't been for that damned rosebush."

Colonel Madison had had a passion for landscaping, and the grounds of the house just outside Washington, D.C., where T.J. and Jenny had both grown up had been a miracle of color and design. Jenny tried to concentrate on that as she worked, and not on T.J.'s increasingly unsteady breathing.

"Who's living in the old house now, do you know?" she asked.

"I am. Sort of."

"You don't still live on your boat, then?"

"Some of the time. You know me, Jenny—I like to have lots of room to move."

She knew it, all right. "You must have to travel a lot, in your job," she speculated.

"Yeah." He didn't elaborate.

"Do you like it? Not really having a home base, I mean?"

He looked up at her suddenly, and she saw that his eyes were still very dark, disturbingly so. He looked as though he wanted to say something but couldn't find the words, or didn't want to commit himself to speech. For a long moment he just looked at her, while she felt her pulse hammering in her veins.

When he finally looked away again, Jenny felt as though she'd just run a speedy half mile. T.J.'s deep voice wasn't quite as even as before as he said, "I've been living this way for a long time now. I don't know if I could change."

The words were clear. He was telling her that the basic situation between them was still the same. But the pounding of Jenny's heart, and the hungry look in T.J.'s eyes when he swung them to meet hers again, were saying something very different.

Her hands had stopped moving now. She was holding the roll of tape and the small pair of scissors uncertainly in her lap, knowing that if she touched her fingertips to T.J.'s warm skin again, something might ignite in both of them that could very easily rage out of control.

He seemed to be realizing the same thing. "I can finish this," he said. His usually mellifluous voice sounded unsteady. "Thanks."

He reached to take the tape from her, and their fingers brushed against each other. Even that small contact was enough to make Jenny ache all over, and when she heard T.J. groan softly she knew he was sharing her hunger, and her indecision, too.

His fingers grasped hers, and the roll of tape fell to the bedspread as T.J. wrapped her hands in his own. "God, Jenny," he said, raggedly now. "Part of me wants to kiss you so badly I can hardly stand it."

"T.J.—"

There was protest in her tone, along with need. T.J. nodded tightly. "I know," he said. "It's crazy. We can't let it happen, not like it did last time. Neither one of us was thinking straight that night—hell, I know I'm not thinking straight right now."

His reference to "that night" did something to restore sanity to Jenny's thoughts. But the heat and strength of his hands holding hers still made her half-liquid inside, wanting him to touch and hold all of her, to love her as she knew he could.

"We've never really talked about...that night," she said.

"Sure we have."

"Not really. T.J.—"

She should do it, she knew. Maybe this was the moment to share her secret with him, when they were both agitated and aroused and incapable of denying that what had happened between them eight years ago was happening all over again now—that it probably would happen anytime they were together. Maybe it was time to try to make T.J. understand that this kind of passion had its consequences—that it had already had consequences he wasn't even aware of.

He was shaking his head, though. "Jenny, we're both worn-out. And we're in the middle of something that's going to get a lot more dangerous before it's over. If we open all this up again—"

"It might clear the air," she said.

"Or it might lead to something we can't handle, on top of everything else."

"What might it lead to, T.J.?" She was gripping his hands tightly now, feeling the escalating rhythm of his pulse. The forceful tempo of it seemed to have found its way into her own body, her own bloodstream.

It might lead to love, she knew. The answer was obvious to her, and it seemed important to know whether T.J. would acknowledge it or not.

He wouldn't. "It could distract us from the business at hand, which is to see that both of us get out of this safely," he said. "Getting—involved—is a luxury we can't afford yet."

Involved sounded so impersonal, Jenny thought. The word *yet* seemed to offer some hope, but not much.

On the other hand, she knew he was right that admitting to their longing for each other wouldn't do them much good if they weren't alive to explore it. And there were still things she had to tell him, and reassurances she needed in return, before she could bear to think of letting him back into her life on any terms.

Jenny loosened her grip on T.J.'s fingers, and they moved slightly apart on the bed. Who was she kidding? she asked herself. T.J. was already back in her life. He'd pushed his way in just as he always did, without asking permission or considering the cost. That only made it more important not to let things move too quickly, the way they had last time. She was an adult now, Jenny reminded herself. She should be grateful for the distance T.J. was putting between them now.

And a part of her *was* grateful. But the rest of her ached unbearably when he turned away from her and finished taping the new bandage over his wound. It was only when he was done, and reaching for the new T-shirt and dark green pullover he'd bought, that he let her know she wasn't the only one suffering.

"If I touched you again right now," he said, pausing before getting to his feet, "I would be incapable of letting you go until I'd pulled you back on that bed and made love to you until neither of us can walk. And I'm just not sure that's the wisest thing we could do right now."

His voice was rough with hunger, and Jenny felt herself wanting to move closer to him. But she knew he was right, and she appreciated the way he was—for once—looking before he leapt into something unknown. Their feelings for each other were as unexplored as an uncharted ocean, and neither of them was quite ready to set sail yet.

"And, anyway," T.J. added, standing up with sudden decision, "I'm ravenous, and you probably are, too. It's too early in the season for most of the restaurants to be open, but there's a place just down the road that makes crabmeat rolls that'll knock your socks off."

He gestured to the coatrack near the door, and Jenny saw two all-weather jackets hanging there, further products of his shopping spree. T.J.'s change in manner was deliberate, she thought, and his sudden heartiness was at odds with the dark hunger she could still see in his eyes.

Don't push this, his words were telling her. But his eyes were saying something quite different.

For the moment, she decided to stay on the side of caution. And besides, T.J. was right. She *was* ravenous. She let herself fall in with his new mood as he said, "Grab your coat, sugar, and let's go eat."

Chapter 7

There were trees in T.J.'s way.

He didn't like trees. He liked wide-open spaces, like the ocean, where he could see to maneuver. He didn't like being hemmed in, not sure what his next move should be.

There was some damn shrub or other tangling up his elbows. T.J. thrashed at it, trying to get clear. He knew vaguely that someone was behind him, or maybe they'd overtaken him by now. And he knew, too, that he had to get to Jenny before the other guy did. She was up there, somewhere, through the trees, waiting for him.

"Jenny..." He said her name softly, or so he'd thought. There was a sudden rustle off to his left, and he suddenly knew he'd spoken too loudly and given his position away.

He turned, reaching for the gun he carried with him when things got bad. But the gun wasn't there, and neither was the holster. Damn it, T.J. thought, he'd been *sure* he'd strapped the thing on before coming out tonight.

But he found himself grasping his own left shoulder instead, and a sudden bolt of pain rocked through him as he did it. He was wounded, he remembered with sickening suddenness. And Jenny was in danger, counting on him to save her.

He had to warn her, to make her run. Whoever was chasing them was closing in on him now, and his only chance was to make her understand she had to get out of here, without him.

"Jenny!" He put all the force he could into the name this time. Where the hell was she, anyway? He couldn't see a thing past these trees. "Jenny, get out of here! Jenny..."

Suddenly she was right there, with him. He pushed her away, trying to make her understand that it wasn't safe to be so close to him, but she held on, gently, unyieldingly, and kept murmuring words to him that he didn't quite comprehend.

And then, finally, he did. "T.J., it's all right," she was saying. "You're dreaming. But it's all right."

Dreaming? T.J. kept tussling with her, because it might be a trick and he couldn't stand the thought of screwing up when Jenny's life was at stake. But gradually, the dark mists started to clear, and he realized he was in his bed at the Wanderers' Rest, and Jenny was sitting next to him, her arms around his thrashing shoulders.

She'd turned on the lamp next to her own bed, and at first the light seemed very bright. As his eyes adjusted, though, T.J. realized that far from being trapped in the undergrowth of some unspecified and dangerous place, he was safe in the big room at the inn, bathed in the soft light of the single lamp.

And Jenny was safe, too. The last of the nightmare wouldn't quite let him go, and he grasped her convulsively, just as—he now recalled—he'd done two nights ago. She was wearing the virginal white T-shirt he'd bought as a makeshift nightgown, and her skin was even softer and warmer than the fabric. He heard her voice telling him it was all right, and he moved toward her without being able to stop himself. She was so close, and so gentle, and her arms seemed to be welcoming him, surrounding him.

He buried his face in the velvety refuge of her lap and felt her hands smoothing his hair. T.J. gasped, his mouth moving against her thigh under the thin white shirt. His heart was still pounding after the nightmare, but all it took was the thought of those impossibly white thighs so close to his lips to slam his pulse into high gear.

"Jenny..." He pushed himself up, shoving his hair out of his eyes and looking into her face. He had to pull back from this right now, he told himself, or it was going to be too late. He had to stick to the high-minded principles he'd spelled out earlier today, for both their sakes. And as soon as his pounding heart would let him speak, he was going to tell her that.

The problem was that she looked so adorably sleepy, so tousled and warm and young. In the dim light, her eyes were huge and dark, her lips moist and inviting. And there was a yearning in her face that shot all those high-minded instincts of his straight to hell.

"God, Jenny, we've got to stop meeting like this." His words weren't exactly the ones he'd intended to say. "I'm sorry if I woke you up again."

"I figure I owe it to you." Her voice sounded very slightly husky. "It used to be me that had the nightmares, and you who came in and calmed me down. Remember?"

Remember... As if there was one single thing about Jenny Alvarez he had forgotten. T.J. gave a short laugh and managed to sit up.

But she was still too close, and too lovely. T.J. couldn't stop himself. He swept an arm around her and pulled her against his good shoulder, so that they were both sitting leaning against the headboard. He dragged the disarranged covers up over their knees and tried to tell himself it was a comradely pose, not an erotic one, even while his thudding heart was informing him he was a liar.

"Do you still have nightmares?" he asked her.

She seemed to wait a very long time before replying, but maybe it only seemed long to T.J. because he was so lost in the exquisite rightness of the way she was tucked against him. As if she belonged there. As if this was real, not just a stolen moment in a dangerous time. He rested his chin on her glossy black hair and tried to slow his breathing down. It didn't work, and after a moment T.J. didn't care.

When she finally spoke, her voice seemed thoughtful. "I wouldn't call them nightmares, not anymore," she said. "I've come to terms with a lot of the ghosts in my past, these last few years."

"Do those ghosts . . . include me?" For the first time T.J. found himself wondering exactly how she was reacting to having him disrupt her existence this way.

"They include everyone I've ever loved who disappeared from my life."

T.J. didn't want to get back into the awkward subject of why *he'd* disappeared on her. He'd already made his position clear, he thought. He couldn't do better than that.

But he couldn't ignore what she'd said, either. "It can't have been easy," he said slowly. "Losing your mother so young, I mean, and then having your father turn you over to someone else. And then when my own father died so suddenly . . ."

His own father had had a heart attack when T.J. was twenty-four and Jenny fifteen, while on a rare evening out with fellow Marine officers. His death had left T.J. acting as Jenny's legal guardian until she turned twenty-one. And if that hadn't been the most awkward and difficult role he'd ever played—

Jenny seemed to know what he was thinking. "You never really wanted to be my guardian, did you?" she asked.

"Hey, I wasn't the steadiest person in the world at that point," he hedged. "All I wanted to do was sail, and explore the world. And I didn't exactly have a lot of experience being responsible for a teenage girl. And—"

"T.J." She turned slightly to look at him, and T.J. nearly groaned again as he felt the soft weight of her shifting against his thigh. The sight of a buried smile in her dark brown eyes caught him further off guard. "You don't have to sugarcoat it, T.J. I know it was awkward for you. We'd been the best of friends, and all of a sudden you were legally in charge of me. I hated you for sending me away to school at the time, but I've come to see why you did it."

"Thank you." He was too startled to know what else to say. He'd fallen back into the habit of seeing Jenny as always needing his protection, he thought, recalling the anguish he'd been feeling in his dream when he thought she was in danger. What the gleam in her eyes was telling him now was that she was long since grown-up.

"What about your father?" Only half of T.J.'s mind was on the question. The other half was fixated on the way they were touching under the covers now, with her long, slender leg against his sturdier one. He cleared his throat and added, "Have you come to terms with the way *he* treated you?"

She was silent again, thinking it over, he realized. God, he loved that gentle silence of hers, the way she weighed everything with such intelligence and spirit. He glanced down at her face, at the fullness in her lower lip that was almost a pout, almost an invitation to kiss her there.

But the question he had raised was a serious one, and she was giving it serious consideration. "I haven't really come to terms with my father giving me away, because I still don't understand exactly what happened," she said finally. "His diary isn't really clear on the subject, except to say over and over again that he hoped I would be safe, and that he wasn't in any condition to be a good parent to me. But I don't know why he chose your father as my guardian, or why your father agreed to take me."

T.J. could hear the vulnerability beneath her words. And it affected him just as it had done when they were both young. He wanted to make things right for her, to make her smile, to make her happy.

He cleared his throat again. "It's possible that clearing up this investigation with General Ross might shed some light on that," he said. "Your father met mine when they were both in Vietnam, after all. And your father was discharged right after the disciplinary hearing that Haviland Ross instigated. There may be some answers in this case for you, as well as for me."

She turned her face toward him again. There was a slight pucker in her forehead, as though she was bemused by something. "I keep forgetting that this is part of your work," she said. "I feel as though we're…on some kind of quest, just the two of us."

He knew exactly what she meant. He'd been having the same feelings himself. And he knew they were dangerous.

"It *is* just work, really," he said definitely, "and I can't let myself forget that." And then he added quickly, because he didn't like the disappointment that flooded her brown eyes at his words, "But it isn't work at the moment. We can't make another move until we get a copy of your father's diary, so we might as well put it out of our minds until tomorrow night."

"I guess you're right." She was still looking up at him, as if she wondered where this unlikely conversation might lead next. "T.J.?" she said finally, softly.

"Yes, sugar?"

"Do you ever get tired of not having a home?"

It was T.J.'s turn to consider, to take time over answering. "I'm not exactly sure that I understand what people mean when they talk about 'home,'" he said. "My father and I lived in half a dozen different places before I was ten, always in military housing. I was in boarding school while he was in Vietnam, and I took off on my own right after

high school. The only time I ever really felt settled was after my father adopted you, and the three of us lived in the
place in Washington. And after he died—''

T.J. stopped. He didn't want to talk about the things he'd
felt after his father had died, especially about his sense of
panic at being left in charge of Jenny. It had been bad
enough knowing that he had to take care of her, to find her
a decent boarding school and make sure she was happy
there. It had been much, much worse recognizing his own
growing feelings for her, feelings that had nothing to do with
being a responsible guardian and everything to with the
beautiful and vivacious young woman she had been growing into.

He shook his head, and finished what he had been trying
to say. "Home is where I find myself, I guess," he said.
"Home is right here, at the moment."

He didn't want to get into it any more deeply than that.
And the idea of his current momentary home being this
spacious, comfortable room at the Wanderers' Rest, with
Jenny close beside him and the darkness outside kept at bay
for now, was undeniably seductive.

She nodded, as if that suited her, too. "Are you ready to
go back to sleep, T.J.?" she asked.

He couldn't tell if her question was as straightforward as
it sounded. He only knew he was tired of second-guessing
his feelings, clamping down on urges that were quickly outrunning him. Damn it, he thought suddenly, why not just be
honest?

"No," he said bluntly. "I'm not ready to go back to
sleep."

She seemed to give his words a second's startled thought.
"Me, neither," she said. "And it's only four o'clock a.m.
Too early to go for a walk on the beach."

"Even if we *wanted* to go for a walk on the beach."

T.J. could feel his whole body stirring now, tantalized by
the idea that Jenny was staying beside him because she

wanted to be there, perhaps because she, too, was tired of fighting off the powerful impulses that kept drawing them together.

"Well." There was a definite throaty undertone in her voice now. T.J. drew in a long breath, and felt his whole body trembling slightly. "I suppose we could play Twenty Questions."

They had played countless thousands of rounds of Twenty Questions together, T.J. remembered. And Monopoly. And gin rummy, until it had occurred to him that Jenny won every single hand. T.J. didn't like being beaten.

He didn't like feeling unsure what was going on, either. He frowned down at her, at the hidden laughter in her face. "Jenny," he said seriously, "do you know how much effort it's costing me to sit here behaving like a gentleman? Because if you don't—"

"Oh, I do." Her smile, spicy and infinitely feminine, flowered across her face. "In the first place, I can feel your heart beating, and it seems to be in a race with mine."

She half turned and put her palm directly over his heart. Her hair was still disordered from sleep, and one strand fell flirtatiously down over her face as she moved.

"See?" Her touch went to the core of T.J.'s body, and he shuddered with the sudden pleasure of her open caress. "I don't know whose is outrunning the other."

She reached for his hand and put it over her own heart. T.J. felt an insistent rhythm there that echoed what he was feeling in his own blood. "God, Jenny," he rasped. "If you knew—"

"You're not listening, T.J." Her words were still teasing, but her eyes told him she was taking this far from lightly. "I *do* know. We feel the same things for each other—some of the same things, anyway."

T.J. didn't know what was behind the qualification, and he didn't ask. His palm ached with the need to push past the soft T-shirt she wore, and to feel the satiny flesh he knew was underneath.

He still couldn't quite trust himself to let go completely. He'd spent too long telling himself that he shouldn't be doing exactly this, and he had to say, hoarsely, "I seem to recall both of us agreeing that there were reasons why we shouldn't be letting this happen."

"You're right. We did."

"Then why—"

"It was what you said a few minutes ago. About this being home for the moment, as far as you were concerned."

It took a gargantuan effort for T.J. to cast his mind as far back as a few minutes ago. He couldn't bear to leave the present, even in thought, when being in the present meant holding Jenny like this, touching her, feeling her eager response to his caresses.

Her eyes had darkened now, to a velvety near-black. And the beating pulse at the base of her throat, when he touched his fingertips to the spot, told him her senses were running as wild as his own. But she spoke around the huskiness in her throat, seeming to feel a need to make T.J. understand.

"Maybe this is as close as either of us can really get to feeling that we're home," she said. "Maybe—maybe we should just seize the moment, even if it *is* only a moment. Oh, T.J.—"

Her sudden cry was in answer to the way he leaned forward and kissed that tantalizing pulse point. He gathered her to him, haunted by the expression he had just seen in her eyes, the troubled look that seemed to be grasping after some kind of happiness, no matter how fleeting.

It *was* fleeting, T.J. told himself. Had to be. And tomorrow might bring new dangers—in fact, it seemed more than likely. But for now, just for this moment—.

He had never known the kind of satisfaction that making love with Jenny Alvarez had brought him. He'd never known the kind of remorse that had followed it, either, but that was because she'd been so young, he told himself. She was a woman now—strong, independent, more than willing. With one final mental shrug, T.J. abandoned everything for the moment except the sheer pleasure of giving himself up to Jenny.

The T-shirt he'd bought her was extralarge; on her slender frame, it reached halfway to her knees. T.J. grasped the bottom edges of it now and pulled it over her head. She reacted with a startled laugh, a throaty, female sound that made him want her more desperately than ever.

Naked, she was even lovelier than he'd remembered. He'd always wondered if he had idealized his image of her, creating a dream woman far more perfect than flesh and blood. But nothing could be more perfect than her gentle curves and alabaster-pure skin. Her lips were slightly parted, and she was watching him as he worshipped her with his gaze. Her chest rose and fell as her breathing quickened even more.

"You are the most beautiful thing I've ever seen." T.J. whispered the words, as though the spell might break if he spoke them out loud. "Sweet Jenny..."

He dispatched his own T-shirt in one swift motion and took hold of Jenny's arms, still half-afraid to do more than just look at her, in case she disappeared again and he had to live on this memory, as he had before.

But then she let her head fall back, and he couldn't stop himself from leaning forward and kissing the smooth column of her throat, up to her delicate chin, back down again to the hollow between her breasts. The faint perfume of her skin was driving him out of his mind. The need to feel all of her against him was even more maddeningly insistent.

She was entwining herself with him now, seeming as eager as he was for the meeting of their two bodies. T.J. moaned as they wrapped themselves around each other, suddenly sharing a wild impatience to taste and possess and touch all that they could in the brief time they had.

Memories slammed into T.J.'s consciousness now, memories he'd tried his damnedest to block out. Jenny had astonished him in exactly this way once before, when he'd taken her in his arms expecting to find a shy and inexperienced girl, and had felt her turning to a woman under his touch.

She was astonishing him all over again, with the openness of her caresses, the eroticism of her hands and lips, the warmth and abandon of her loving. "I've never met a woman like you," he said hoarsely. "Jenny, do you know what that does to me?"

He heard her laugh, delightedly, wantonly. "I have a very good idea what it does to you," she told him. And she went on doing it, wrapping her palms around him in the most intimate way possible.

T.J. felt his head spinning, or maybe it was the room. He clung to Jenny as though he was drowning in an unfamiliar ocean and only she could save him. They were floating together, he thought, locked in each other's arms, exploring each other in ways that seemed both familiar and startlingly new.

T.J. thought he'd known what freedom felt like. But now, delving into the warm, soft center of Jenny Alvarez, he knew he'd only experienced a pale shadow of the real thing. Real freedom meant giving himself up to this mutual pleasure. Real freedom was being able to kiss Jenny all over, to swirl his tongue erotically over her breast, to let the feeling of that hardened bud against his mouth rocket through him, intensifying his own arousal.

He'd thought freedom had to do with open spaces. He discovered he was wrong. Freedom meant abandoning himself to his own long-buried hopes and dreams about this woman, about Jenny. It meant putting away his fears and letting the simple, primitive rhythm of their longing for each other tell him what to do.

It was telling him now that he needed to lose himself completely in her soft, willing body. And her eyes were telling him that was what she wanted, too. T.J. kissed her long and deeply, loving the sensual sweep of her tongue against his. And then, with an effort that took all the strength he had, he moved slightly away from her and reached into the drawer of the table beside his bed.

He felt Jenny go still against him and kept one hand firmly around her waist. Her skin was impossibly silky, supple and yielding all at the same time.

"T.J.?" He heard the hesitation in her voice, around the breathlessness.

"It's all right, Jenny." He was leaning over, opening the drawer, pulling out the package he'd bought at the drugstore when he had gone out for first-aid supplies yesterday afternoon. When he sat up again, there was something almost hesitant in Jenny's expression.

He raised his hand from her waist and smoothed it over her hair, wishing he could erase the sudden uncertainty he saw in her eyes, wishing he knew where it had come from. He nodded at the package and said, "I didn't exactly plan for this to happen, sugar. But it would have been crazy to deny that it was a possibility."

It was protection he was offering her, and consideration. Why, then, was she looking so startled? T.J. frowned, wishing his breathing was steadier. He sounded as though he'd been running a race.

And maybe he had, he thought. He was trying outrace his own desires, his own fears about what giving in to his feelings could do to him. Damn it, what did Jenny's silent stare mean? Was she having second thoughts when they'd already come this far?

He had to know. He gripped her shoulder, gently but insistently, and said, "I wasn't thinking clearly last time we did this, Jenny. Not about anything. I don't want things to be that way again. That's all."

He saw her swallow, and she half nodded, as if she understood what he meant but was wrestling with silent memories of her own. He couldn't imagine what they were. He only knew that her second nod was firmer, more decisive, and that the effort of waiting, of letting her consider his words, was nearly costing him more strength and self-control than he had in him.

"I know, T.J.," she said. The buried sadness in her voice caught at him, but she didn't explain it. "I don't want things to be the way they were the last time, either."

And with that she seemed to push away whatever private doubts had forced themselves to the surface. Her hands were already gliding over him again, helping him sheath himself in one of the condoms he'd bought, making that simple act more erotic than T.J. had thought possible.

The gentle, urging sounds she was making took away what was left of his self-control. He needed to be inside her now, to chase away the shadows that kept coming between the two of them, to follow that heart-stopping sense of freedom he'd felt only a few moments before.

When he had buried himself deep inside her, and heard her cry of welcome and passion, it was impossible to remember that anything had ever been wrong between them. He felt Jenny's smooth legs slide against his again, and then move to encircle him, pulling them closer together and beginning to rock them in a rhythm that emanated from deep inside her body.

"Wait, Jenny... not so fast."

He wanted this moment to go on forever, and he wanted to chase it to its inevitable end. He entertained a few fleeting ideas about spinning this out all night and then felt his own ability to make any kind of decision at all getting away on him, drawn out onto the shimmering sea that suddenly seemed to be washing all his senses.

Jenny was heat and light... she was the soothing lapping of waves and the uncoiled strength of a storm at sea. She was holding him, buoying him up, and both of them were floating on the surface of a passion that was all-enveloping, all-fulfilling.

And T.J. had never wanted to be anywhere else. They clung to each other, murmuring wordless truths, unspoken promises that this was right, that they belonged together. There had been other women in his life besides Jenny Alvarez; there hadn't been anyone who had offered him anything close to this sense of completion, of wholeness.

He felt his mind and body draw together at a single shining point as he recognized how badly he had missed that feeling of being strong and whole.

"Jenny—" His own voice sounded urgent, almost desperate. Did she understand, did she share what he was feeling inside? Her answering cry haunted him long after their two bodies had been gripped by a sudden spasm, gripping each other with convulsive need.

That physical release was sweet beyond anything T.J. could remember. But the sound of wild longing that had torn from Jenny's throat as they reached that shimmering moment together was one that T.J. heard with a sudden shock of recognition.

It sounded like everything he'd felt when he'd set sail on the open sea, heading for a new world to explore. It was the sound of every questing adventurer, uncertain where the wind and the tide would lead, but certain that it was time to find out.

The idea that Jenny shared that bone-deep longing was one he had never considered. What was she longing for? he wondered, as he cradled her in his arms and both of them edged slowly back toward sleep. He kissed her closed eyelids, ran his fingers through her glossy hair one more time, eased himself down beside her under the covers. They were at rest, he thought, safe and untroubled for the moment.

But it was the sound of Jenny's wordless cry, not the steady ebb and flow of her breathing now, that T.J. took with him as he slipped back into the shadowy world of dreams and desires.

Chapter 8

Jenny could smell the ocean when she woke up again. The tide must be low, she thought. She turned languidly under the warm covers and heard the distant sound of waves on the beach and sea gulls overhead. The fresh tang of salt and sand reminded her immediately of where she was.

She didn't need to be reminded what had happened during the night. Her whole body was still humming with it, satiated and yet longing for more. She stretched out an arm, expecting to encounter T.J.'s solid body in the bed next to her.

He wasn't there. Jenny frowned, her eyes still closed. That was when she smelled the coffee. And the roses.

She rubbed her eyelids and finally opened her eyes. Her gaze met an enormous bouquet of pink roses on the table next to the bed. "T.J.?" she said out loud. There was no answer. The big room felt empty and still.

Jenny raised herself to her elbows. There was a coffee-maker on the small counter of the kitchenette in the corner of the room, and it was filled with hot coffee; she could see steam rising from the surface of the pot. She frowned again and reached for the white T-shirt that was lying in a crumpled pile on the carpet next to the bed.

She should be feeling on top of the world, she thought, as she pulled the shirt over her head. A few seconds ago, she *had* been. But this was too much like what had happened the only other time she and T.J. had made love. There had been that same wild passion and need, that same bone-deep satisfaction, and then, without warning, T.J. had been gone. Surely, Jenny thought, he wouldn't do this to her again.

The last time, he hadn't sent roses. He hadn't sent anything—not a note, not a single word—until he had arrived at her door last week. What if he'd found their experience last night too overwhelming, too threatening to that loner's heart of his? What if he was even now heading fast in some other direction? Was she going to be stranded here, longing for him, trying to remember how it felt to hate him? Was this the reason why—

Half a dozen conflicting and very unsettling emotions had already gripped her by the time she finally noticed the note. It was propped up against the base of the vase that held the roses, and it said simply, "Happy birthday, sugar. I'll be back with breakfast."

Jenny sank back onto the bed with a sigh of exasperation and relief. And at the same moment the door to the room opened, and T.J. came in, immediately filling the place with his ebullience, his size, his flashing grin. The smells coming from the white bag he carried made Jenny think of bakeries and fresh bread.

"You know," she said, "I'd completely forgotten it was my birthday."

His grin widened. "Good thing I was around, then, wasn't it?" He deposited the bag on the round table next to the window and pulled the drapes open. Their room was slightly above beach level; they could see out to the wide sweep of the sand and the ocean beyond, but there was no danger of anyone seeing in. "I ordered up a particularly nice day for you," T.J. was saying. "Want to come and look at it?"

"What I want is some of whatever you've got in that bag," Jenny said. "I'm very hungry, for some reason."

"Well, I thought you might be. I woke up kind of hungry myself."

The glint in his eye was one she remembered from her very earliest days. It meant T.J. was feeling pleased with himself, and confident. It also meant he had something up his sleeve, frequently something that was going to get him into trouble. He shrugged out of his jacket and brought the white bag over to the bed, where he kicked off his shoes and offered Jenny her choice of croissants, rolls or cinnamon Danish.

"This is a nice little retreat you've found for yourself," she commented, as she helped herself to breakfast.

"Well, I like it." T.J. bit into a Danish with enthusiasm.

Jenny was tempted to give in to the magic of the moment, to the golden gleam in T.J.'s eyes and the physical pleasure that was still lapping her body like a gentle wave. It would be so easy to pretend that this was real, she thought. That it might last.

But one night of passion was not the same as real life, as she knew only too well. One bouquet of pink roses, however beautiful, didn't mean a commitment that went anywhere beyond this one day. And she knew, too, that the dancing glitter in T.J.'s eyes could spell danger as well as delight.

So she fought against the part of her that wanted to believe this moment could last, and said, as she finished a bite of her roll, "Have you used this as a romantic hideaway before?"

He seemed honestly startled by the question. "I don't go in much for romance, sugar," he said.

"You did this time." She nodded at the expensive-looking roses.

T.J. shrugged and picked up a croissant. "It's your birthday," he said. "I thought you deserved to have a fuss made about it."

"Why?" She knew the question sounded blunt, but she had to ask it. "There was never any big deal about my birthday when I was younger, as I recall. And to be honest, I've tended to ignore it, these last few years. So why did you feel you needed to make a fuss today?"

She suspected that she knew the answer already, but somehow it seemed important to hear it from T.J. Jenny nibbled her roll and waited.

He looked at the croissant he'd just picked up, and seemed to decide he wasn't quite as hungry as he'd thought. He put it back down and got off the bed, moving toward the coffeepot. He had filled two mugs with steaming coffee and was on his way back to the bed by the time he spoke again.

He set the mugs on the table next to the roses, but stayed standing this time. "I made a big deal out of your birthday exactly once," he said.

"The year I turned twenty-one," Jenny said.

"Yeah. I thought—hell, you were officially a grown-up that day, and you didn't need a guardian anymore, and you could do what you liked with your trust-fund income from my father. It seemed worth celebrating."

Again she waited while he looked for the words he wanted. Finally he sighed and shook his head. His hair was tousled this morning, in the way that Jenny found completely irresistible. One dark curl dipped down over his forehead and made him look exactly like the reckless adventurer he was. How was she supposed to keep her heart unentangled, Jenny wondered, when just the sight of him made her want to be back in his arms?

"That celebration didn't turn out the way I'd planned it," he said, shoving his hands into his jeans pockets. "I've been kicking myself about it ever since. I guess I wanted to do something today that might make up for what happened—the first time."

Nothing could ever make up for that. Jenny almost said the words out loud, until she remembered that she'd already decided not to tell him about the child they'd created together, not until she had some sign that he wasn't going to disappear again. So far, that hadn't happened.

"It's funny." T.J. was speaking quickly now, as if trying to get past this awkward moment as fast as he could. "You asking me if this was my romantic retreat, I mean. When I showed up at your place the other night, I was scared to death I was going to find *you* with a boyfriend or a lover."

His choice of words startled her. Scared to death? T.J. Madison? She'd never known him to be scared of anything. She was still puzzling over what this meant when he went on, "So *do* you have anyone else in your life, Jenny? Or are you alone right now?"

The truth was that she had never felt about any other man the way she felt about T.J., but admitting that fact, even to herself, had always made her feel more vulnerable than she liked. So she said simply, "I'm alone right now."

Slowly, T.J. eased back down onto the bed and picked up the croissant he'd abandoned a few minutes ago. "How about in the past eight years? Anybody really serious?"

"Does it matter, T.J.?"

"Yes, it matters." Once again he put the croissant back down. He sounded almost angry now, but she couldn't tell why. "I already told you, I wasn't planning for last night to happen. But now that it has—" He bit the words off, looked out the open window toward the sea and then met her eyes again. "I don't exactly know why it matters, but it does," he said. "That's all."

"Well, if it really does matter, then I can tell you I've had a few casual dates and a couple of relationships that just didn't seem to catch fire. Mostly they were colleagues, and

I finally decided that romance and work just don't mix for me.''

"What about where you work now? Any close friends there?''

Something about the conversation was beginning to bother Jenny. She couldn't help thinking of her senior year of college, before she'd dropped out, when T.J. had been simultaneously very removed from her life and very interested in who she was seeing and what she was up to. It had been as though he were trying his best to give her lots of room, but something in himself had found it impossible just to let her go.

He sounded that way again now—as if he were reluctant to pry into her life, but somehow he couldn't stop himself. Jenny frowned at him. "My only colleagues at the moment are female," she said. "Or isn't that what you meant?''

The sweeping way he waved his hand made her think she was right: he'd found himself asking questions he'd told himself he should keep a lid on. "Forget I asked," he said. "I guess maybe that old habit of looking after you went deeper than I thought.''

That wasn't the whole truth, and both of them knew it, but once again T.J. had jumped to a new subject before Jenny could comment on it.

"Speaking of where you work now," he said, "you might want to start thinking about calling them up and letting them know you won't be in tomorrow.''

"Who says I won't be?''

"Sugar, there's no way you'll be safe in Charlotte until after this business with General Ross is settled.''

"How long will that take? I've got clients, T.J., and they depend on me.''

"So call a colleague and get her to cover for you. With luck, this won't take more than a few days.''

"It's not that simple. I do share an office with another therapist, but she's in the process of easing into maternity leave. She can't take on any extra at the moment."

"Surely just for two or three days—"

"*No*, T.J." The words came out sounding just the way she felt, adamant and slightly alarmed. "A woman needs lots of rest, extra rest, when she's expecting a child. And I've spent months telling Patricia that she's already doing too much work. If you think I'm going to call her up now and dump a lot of my own work on her—"

"All right." T.J. seemed to have picked up on the urgent tone of her voice. "It was just a suggestion, sugar."

"It was a rotten one. And I don't like having to cancel on my clients, either. There are some people who depend on me at the moment, T.J., and I hate to let them down. Unlike you, I've never been good at just walking away from people."

There was a very long silence this time. "Are you trying to tell me something, Jenny?" T.J. asked finally.

Should she explain her words, and the reason for the bitterness behind them? Jenny thought hard about it, wondering what T.J.'s reaction would be if she told him what had really happened to her eight years ago.

She realized she had no idea how he might react. She knew him so well in so many ways, but she couldn't begin to predict whether finding out her unhappy secret would make him run or stay.

She needed to find out, she thought suddenly. She was going to have to tell him, sooner or later. But something deep inside her kept saying, *Not yet.* She couldn't stop thinking about the fierce hunger she had given in to last night, or the healing sweetness of sleeping in T.J.'s strong embrace. There were plenty of rough edges to their relationship. Surely, just for one day, they were entitled to do what they could to smooth some of them out, before they got down to the dangerous business of sorting out the future.

She looked into T.J.'s dark eyes and saw that he was puzzled by her silence. It was her turn to wave her hand, trying to dismiss his question for the moment.

"I *am* going to have to make some arrangements about my clients," she said. "But that's my problem, not yours. And you're right—I can hardly go back to Charlotte until I know it's safe."

"Which leaves us—"

"It leaves us filling up the rest of the day until we can call Sunny and Creed and get hold of that diary, I suppose."

T.J. had reclined onto one elbow. The sexy awareness in his eyes made her pulse start to race all over again. "Got any ideas on how we might fill up the day?" he asked.

"I hadn't thought about it."

"I had." There was a very faint grin on his face again. "My friend Peter—the guy who runs the inn—has a little twelve-foot sloop that he keeps around for guests to use. And the wind is offshore, and about as steady as it gets around here. I thought—"

Jenny couldn't help laughing. "You're going to have to translate that into English," she said. "You know I was always the complete landlubber."

His grin widened, telling her he hadn't forgotten. "What it means," he said, "is that if we waited for a year we wouldn't get a more perfect day to go sailing. And there's an island not far offshore that's worth seeing. Are you interested?"

She leveled her brows and looked hard at him. "The one other time I went sailing with you, I ended up treading water in the Potomac River," she said. "Is that going to happen again?"

He shook his head. "We're a long way from the Potomac," he said.

"That wasn't what I meant, T.J."

"I know." His white teeth showed against his tanned skin, and Jenny felt her heart turn over. "Hell, Jenny, I think I was showing off the one time I took you sailing. I dumped us over because I was trying to go like the dickens, that's all."

"I always had a sneaking suspicion you did it because you knew I was scared and you wanted to loosen me up," Jenny said.

T.J. raised one dark eyebrow. "It's a possibility," he admitted. "It *did* loosen you up, didn't it?"

It had. That was the annoying thing. She'd been seventeen years old, worried and disapproving and not sure she really wanted to be in an unstable open boat with her daredevil guardian at the helm. But after he'd dunked them, and they'd splashed around a bit and then gotten the boat righted and running ahead of the wind again, she'd discovered that she was having far more fun than she'd realized. T.J. had always been able to make her laugh when he put his mind to it.

She'd missed laughing with him, she thought suddenly. Missed it far more than she'd admitted until just this moment.

"All right," she said. "Let's go sailing. Can we take the rest of the breakfast with us?"

"Hey, it's your birthday, sugar." T.J. got up again quickly, she noticed, as though he wanted to get going before they could start talking about serious matters again. "You can do whatever in the world you want to."

Jenny's heart tugged at her as she followed his lead and got out of the bed. What *did* she want to do most in the world? she asked herself.

The answers were painfully clear. She wanted a family, to make up for the fact that she'd felt alone most of her life.

She wanted children, to replace the child she'd lost. She wanted that desperately, constantly, achingly.

And she wanted T.J. Madison to be much more than just an occasional colorful presence in her world. She wanted the passion and certainty she'd felt in the darkness of the last night to be strong enough that it could survive into the daylight this time.

She wanted all those things, but she was far from believing she could have them. T.J. had promised lightheartedly that whatever she wanted was hers simply because it was her birthday, but T.J. had promised her other things, too, and he hadn't been around to deliver on his word.

Jenny sighed as she headed into the bathroom to take a shower. There was no one in the world like T.J. for being able to lighten the mood when he wanted to. He'd done it just now, and she'd gone along with it gladly.

In fact, there was no one in the world like T.J. at all. But that didn't mean this momentary happiness would last. She had to remember that, before she let herself be seduced into loving him all over again.

The rest of the day made it very difficult to recall that she was supposed to be keeping her heart in reserve. T.J. had been right: the weather was perfect—balmy and clear—and the blue sky reflected in the endless ocean seemed to offer an eternity of happy chances.

When they rowed out to the small sailboat in the harbor, Jenny saw that it hadn't been just roses and croissants that T.J. had been busy procuring so far this morning. There was a wicker picnic hamper already on board, and a couple of plaid wool blankets.

"It almost looks like you knew I would say yes to this expedition," she said.

T.J. shrugged. "Why not plan for success?" he said.

Jenny paused as she was climbing from the little rowboat into the larger craft. "Is that how you operate?" she asked. "Assuming things will go your way, I mean?"

"Usually. The trick is to have a bunch of ideas up your sleeve for *making* things go your way."

"What have you got up your sleeve about this business of getting Gen. Haviland Ross off our backs?" she asked him.

He looked at her, pausing in the mysterious process of getting the sailboat ready to go. "Rule number one is to plan for success," he said finally. "Rule number two is not to plan too far ahead. I really don't know what we're going to do, until we see that diary of your father's. And rule number three is never to let yourself get sidetracked by shoptalk when you're out sailing with a beautiful woman on a beautiful day. Hand me that oar, would you, sugar?"

As the day unfolded, Jenny felt her spirits lifting as though they were being carried on the sea breezes. She had carefully strapped on her life jacket, as T.J. had requested, but it soon became apparent that the chances of needing it today were slim. T.J. handled the boat with an offhanded certainty that was graceful to watch, and there was none of the breakneck speed that he'd been shooting for the last time they'd sailed together.

Instead, they set a leisurely course for the island he'd mentioned to her, and within minutes Jenny felt herself relaxing, enjoying the spring sunshine on her face and the easy camaraderie that she and T.J. had slipped back into.

"I think that sea gull is following us," she said, leaning back against the edge of the boat and looking up into the blue sky.

"He sees the picnic basket," T.J. said. "They have sharp eyes."

"Where is your own boat now, T.J.?" she asked, shading her eyes against the sun as she looked over at him.

He looked as if he had been made to be on the sea, she thought. His whole face changed, lighted up, came alive to the challenge of the wind and the waves. She'd seen him looking this satisfied only two other times: when they'd been making love. The thought was both arousing and disturbing.

"It's at a marina just outside D.C.," he said, and Jenny had to work to remember what she'd just asked him. "I live on it in the warmer months and move to Dad's old place in the winters."

"Did you really sail all the way around the world by yourself, eight years ago?"

There was no way to avoid the troubled overtones of her question completely. But for the moment Jenny was content to put them to the back of her mind, and after a moment's hesitation, T.J. seemed ready to do the same.

"I really did," he said. "Took me a while. I kept getting sidetracked along the way."

His stories about that marathon trip—which included jobs piloting charter trips in Bali and Singapore, an inland jaunt in Australia, and a lengthy and very nearly permanent stay in Tahiti—filled the rest of their crossing to the island. By the time they got there, they were conversing with their old familiarity, all their unresolved difficulties temporarily forgotten. When they beached the sailboat and T.J. slung an arm around Jenny's shoulders as they walked up the beach together, it was almost impossible to remember that those difficulties even existed.

They picnicked on sandwiches from the bakery where T.J. had gotten their breakfast, washed down by a thermos of lemonade packed by T.J.'s friend at the inn. Dessert was a small chocolate cake that T.J. advertised as being "far more chocolate than cake."

"You remembered," Jenny said.

"How could I forget? Especially after the year you ate your entire Easter rabbit in one sitting."

"He wasn't a *huge* Easter rabbit."

"He was half a pound of pure chocolate, Jenny, and the really amazing thing is that you weren't any sicker."

"Well, it didn't cure me. I still have chocolate cravings."

"Somehow I knew that." T.J. seemed to be having trouble getting the little cake out of its box. "Well, you can share this with me if you want to, but if you don't want to, I'll stand back and let you at it. I don't particularly want to end up like the Easter rabbit."

When he finally produced the cake, it had a single candle flickering in the middle of it. T.J. was sheltering it from the mild breeze with his palm, and something about the gesture—the homeyness of it, Jenny thought, or maybe the sight of T.J.'s big hand cupped so protectively around the small flame—brought sudden tears to her eyes.

"Happy birthday, sugar," he said gently.

"Oh, T.J...." On an impulse that she didn't even try to deny, Jenny leaned forward and put her hands on his shoulders. She'd wanted this so badly, she thought—wanted this closeness and the familiar sight of T.J.'s grin, the familiar strength of his presence. Even if it was only for the moment, she was deeply grateful for the sense of family that he was giving her.

All of that spilled over into her spontaneous embrace. When she felt his broad shoulders under her hands, something relaxed and dissolved inside her, and she let go of the last barriers she had been keeping around her heart. As naturally as if they'd been together forever, she kissed T.J. on the lips, quickly, softly, with a tenderness that didn't quite mask the desire that the gesture woke in her.

"Thank you, T.J.," she whispered. She couldn't stop herself from adding, "I've missed you more than I realized—more than I let myself realize."

His gold-flecked eyes had glittered at her touch, and she saw the single candle flicker precariously as he moved his shielding hand away from it and brought it up to cup Jenny's face. "It sounds crazy," he said, "but I almost feel as though we've never been apart."

So he was sharing that sense of closeness, she thought. They moved away from each other again, concentrating—

at least on the surface—on blowing out the candle before the wind did it for them, and then on digging into the sinfully dark chocolate cake. But something important had happened in that instant of silent communication. Neither one of them could deny the strength of the old bonds that tied them to each other.

They spent the early part of the afternoon walking on the beach, hand in hand, talking about nothing in particular. They climbed over the sandy ridge that ran along the center of the island, and explored its outer shore, gazing out at the wide blue ocean in silence for a long while.

"Ever think of just setting sail, Jenny?" T.J. asked the question suddenly, casually, it seemed.

"To where?"

"It doesn't matter. I'm talking about just picking up and going, and figuring out your destination when you get there."

"It sounds very... uncertain."

"It is. That's the best part."

"Do *you* ever think of settling down?" She turned the question around on him. "Having a home that's more permanent than a boat?"

He didn't really answer her, any more than she had answered him. "I've lived like this for a long time" was all he would say, and both of them dropped the subject, as though they didn't want to stray any closer to harsh realities on this magic afternoon.

The magic drew to a close all too soon as it was. By mid-afternoon there were clouds starting to form on the horizon, and T.J. was casting an experienced eye at the wind and the tide. "We should probably get back," he said. "And by the time we do, it'll be time to call those folks in Memphis and see about your father's diary. We've been out long enough that you're starting to show a little tan, though. It looks good on you."

Jenny had just been thinking that T.J.'s own dark complexion was pleasingly enhanced by the gloss of the sun's rays. His grin seemed whiter, and the glint in his eyes was even sexier against his tanned skin.

They were quiet on the trip back. The clouds had thickened by the time they reached the small harbor and rowed back to the pier. When they were in their room at the inn again, T.J. finally voiced what they'd both been thinking.

"Time to go back to work," he said. "Do you want to call these people in Memphis, or shall I?"

"I'll do it." Jenny got Sunny and Creed's home number from telephone information and sat down on the bed she'd shared with T.J. last night, cradling the phone against her shoulder.

The real world came back with a jolt the moment Creed answered the phone. "Jenny." The deep rumble of his voice sounded both welcoming and apprehensive. "Take down this number, all right? And call me there in about five minutes. Somebody's been trying to track you down, and I have a feeling they haven't given up yet."

Chapter 9

Pete Alvarez's Diary

She is too beautiful to be mine. All wide eyes and asking questions, three she is now, maybe four. How can I be with her like this? Not remembering, not how old she is or whether to take her to school in the mornings or the afternoons?

She wants to know so much. Why isn't mommy coming back? Why did I forget the things I promised her? Can't even remember what they were. Why am I sick like this?

Tried to tell her once. The devil came and made your daddy sick. I scared her, made her eyes even wider. Made her cry. That was when I decided. I hated making her cry. Talking about the devil to a little girl, maybe I am crazy. Maybe they were right.

She'll cry when I leave. But then she'll stop. If I don't leave, she'll never stop. I can't make her happy. But at least I can make her safe.

Some things I'll never forget. I was there, the night she was born. Even then, those wide eyes, asking questions. A beautiful baby, everybody said. Too beautiful to belong to me. .

"I honestly never realized how long five minutes could be." T.J. completed his tenth circuit of the big room, hands shoved deep into the pockets of his jeans.

"You're going to wear a track in that carpet, T.J.," Jenny told him, looking at her watch for what felt like the hundredth time.

This time it showed her what she'd been waiting for. Quickly, she dialed the number Creed had given her. His deep voice started speaking as soon as she'd identified herself.

"We have to do this fast," he said. "I suspect there may be a tap on our home phone, and that means they may have heard me giving you the number of this pay phone. But they can't trace it, if we talk fast enough."

"They?" Jenny's mind was still too shocked to take in what he was saying.

"I don't know who they are, darlin'. That's your end. I only know a couple of official-looking gentlemen showed up here just after Sunny and I got home, asking if you'd been in touch with us. Look, we've got under a minute here. What's wrong, Jenny?"

She marshaled her wits and decided she would have to figure out the details later. "I need your copy of my father's diary," she told Creed. "And I need it absolutely as fast as you can get it to me."

"Right. Where are you?"

She'd already gotten T.J. to write the address of the inn for her, and she read it to Creed now. "I'll make a spare copy, just in case," he said, "and get a courier on this right away. Are you okay, darlin'?"

"I'm fine." The question almost made her laugh. Okay? With her life threatened and her heart completely turned upside down by the handsome man who was glaring at her from across the room, like a tiger getting ready to spring? *Okay* wasn't exactly the right term for how she was at the moment.

But there wasn't time now to convey any of that to Creed. "We should wrap this up," he said. "Take care of yourself, all right?"

He had hung up before she could answer. For a moment Jenny just sat there looking at the receiver in her hand, and then she realized that T.J. was firing questions at her.

"What the hell was that all about?" he wanted to know. "Is he going to help us or not?"

"He'll help us. He's going to photocopy the diary and send it out by a courier right away. But, T.J.—" Her voice faltered slightly. The threat surrounding them was more far-reaching than she'd realized, and the thought of it chilled her. "He said two men came to their apartment this afternoon, wanting to know if Sunny or Creed had heard from me. Creed said...he thought their phone had been bugged. That's why we had to keep the conversation short, so nobody could trace the call to this number."

T.J. slammed an open fist against the tabletop on his way by and spit out a couple of furious expletives.

"How did they do that, T.J.?" Jenny got off the bed and joined T.J. by the big window overlooking the sea. The sun was getting lower behind the inn, casting everything in a dim light that made it hard to see clearly. "How did they find Sunny and Creed's number?"

"You said you called them that first time from the lobby of the motel in the mountains, right?"

Realization dawned on Jenny. "And somehow they got access to the phone records for the motel," she said.

"I told you the military has resources that nobody else can come close to."

Whoever was chasing them must have worked through all the phone numbers that had been called from the Night o' Rest Motel while T.J. and Jenny were there, Jenny thought. "How did they know when they'd found the right one?" she wondered out loud.

"Easy. It's a trick I've used myself, on occasion. You just call people and say you're delivering an important message from Jenny Alvarez. The wrong numbers all say, 'Who's Jenny Alvarez?' When you find the one that doesn't, you've got what you're looking for."

"So they traced Sunny and Creed's address from their phone number and went visiting."

"And probably tapped their phone. Which is why your friend Creed didn't want to talk to you from home. A smart man, I'd say."

"He is." The idea that she might be putting her friends at any kind of risk—especially since she'd heard the news of Sunny's pregnancy—made Jenny feel sick inside. The calm happiness of the afternoon all but vanished when she thought of the forces that she and T.J. were up against.

"T.J., what are we going to do?" she asked.

"Correction, sugar." He turned away from the window now, pulling the sheer inner curtain closed as though he, too, was suddenly feeling exposed and more vulnerable than he liked. "*I* am going to make a few arrangements, and *you* are going to sit tight until I've gotten things sorted out once and for all."

"If you're thinking of leaving me here—"

"Of *course* I'm thinking of it! Jenny, do you imagine for one instant that I'd drag you with me into this mess?"

He was walking away from her now, as if he wanted to put physical distance between them. Jenny took three rapid steps after him and put her hand on his arm.

He turned, startled, as she said, "I'm already *in* this mess, T.J. It's too late to talk about leaving me behind, when I've come with you this far."

He was already shaking his dark head as she spoke. "The next step I take is going to have to be closer to General Ross, not farther away. And General Ross is where the danger is, I'm certain of that. I can't head in his direction if you're with me."

"Why not?"

"Jenny, for heaven's sake—"

She cut him off, tightening her hold on his arm. She knew exactly what that look in his eyes meant, and she didn't like it. "In case you'd forgotten, I've already helped you out," she said. "You would have had a much harder time getting out of Charlotte if we hadn't been able to take my car. And when that policewoman wanted to know what we were up to on that side street—"

She felt herself color slightly at the memory of their kiss, so impersonal at first, and then suddenly so intimate. The lid had been blown off Jenny's emotional world in that confused, sensual moment. And that was why she was being so blunt with T.J. now. There was no use pretending they could go back to the way they'd been only a few days ago.

"Just don't imagine I'm going to sit passively while you walk away on me this time," she said firmly.

T.J. looked startled by her tone. They were frowning at each other now, locked in a silent battle of wills. "This is my business, Jenny," he said. "I need to handle it my own way."

"You made it my business when you showed up on my doorstep. Besides, if my father's diary can help sort this out—well, that gives me some kind of connection to what's going on, too." Jenny thought of how she'd felt while she and Sunny and Creed had been sorting out the old mystery her father had left unsolved in Memphis. She'd had the strong sense then that she was making a belated contact with Pete Alvarez, and she had the same sense again now.

In Memphis, though, she'd been dealing with strangers. Having T.J. Madison around made things much, much more personal. Her voice was a little bit husky as she pointed that out to him. "Anyway, this business with General Ross is hardly the only thing between us at the moment, T.J.," she said.

At least he didn't try to deny it. But he didn't exactly address it, either. For a moment he looked over her head toward the curtained window, and then, to her surprise, he pulled her gently into his arms. There was simple affection in the embrace, and she had to admit it felt good to be surrounded by his warm, breathing strength. She nestled against his chest and felt his steady heartbeat at her ear, close and reassuring.

She was in danger of letting herself start to count on T.J. Madison's presence in her life again, she knew. And at the moment she almost didn't care. She only knew that she needed to be in his arms like this, accepting the silent support he was offering her.

"Have I mentioned to you," he murmured, "that I like the woman you've turned into?"

She tilted her head back, startled. "No," she said. "You haven't mentioned it."

"Well, it's true. Let's not talk about General Ross anymore until after the diary gets here. All right, sugar?"

"All right." She had heard the slightest quaver in his voice when he'd said he liked the way she'd grown up, but it was already gone again, as if he found this kind of openness too uncomfortable to sustain for long.

T.J. was as infuriating as they came, she thought, as they slowly stepped apart again. On the one hand, he was brash, candid, maddeningly direct. And yet there were places in him that could be achingly vulnerable, places that she'd only caught sight of fleetingly.

He knew how to seal those places off in a hurry when he wanted to, she thought. He was doing it now, turning the conversation to what they were going to do about dinner and how soon they could reasonably expect a courier from

Memphis to get to the coast with Pete Alvarez's diary. Jenny sighed and went along with the new direction, wishing there were some way to get past the walls that T.J. had built around the deepest levels of his heart.

Jenny's eyelids were drooping by eleven o'clock. She wasn't accustomed to spending most of the day in the open sea air, and it had left her pleasantly tired.

T.J. had been restless all evening, repeatedly ducking out of the room to talk to his friend at the front desk. Jenny didn't know if he was avoiding being alone with her, or making arrangements that he was keeping to himself, or whether—as he said—he was just keeping an eagle eye out for the courier Creed had promised to send. She only knew that by eleven, she was having trouble staying awake, so she got into her white T-shirt and climbed into the bed she had shared with T.J. last night.

She was just on the edge of sleep when she heard him come back into the room. She listened to him turning off the lights, leaving the room warmed by a single lamp next to the bed. Then there was silence, and when Jenny raised her heavy eyelids, she saw him standing at the foot of the bed, hands deep in his pockets, watching her.

In the soft light his eyes looked very dark, and there was a yearning in them that echoed immediately inside herself. There was something almost sad in T.J.'s eyes, too, that surprised and puzzled her.

"Are you coming to bed?" Her voice was groggy, already saturated with sleep.

For a long moment he didn't answer. Jenny sensed that he was debating with himself about something, but whatever it was, he wasn't letting her in on it.

And suddenly she didn't want to know. She didn't want to get back into one of those wordy wrangles that were inevitable whenever they tried to talk about their shared past or their difficult association with each other now. All she wanted was T.J.'s strong body next to hers, uncomplicated and loving.

She reached a hand out to him, shifting slightly under the covers, and saw him shake himself, seemingly jolted out of whatever thoughts had been bothering him. "Yeah," he said, his voice almost as husky as hers had been. "Yeah, I'm coming to bed."

Jenny had folded her clothes neatly on the other double bed. T.J. didn't bother; his new jeans and green shirt ended up in a pile on top of his sneakers in less than a minute. And then he was crawling under the covers with her, wrapping her in his arms, whispering in her ear that having her invite him into bed in that throaty tone of voice had been one of his most persistent fantasies for years.

Jenny was awake enough now to have noticed that he had shed every piece of his clothing. His skin still felt warmed by the sun, and suddenly she needed to feel her own skin against his, with nothing between them. She pulled her T-shirt over her head and dropped it on the floor next to the bed.

"Part of me wants tomorrow to get here quickly, so I can get back to my real life," she whispered. "And part of me wants to stay this way forever."

"I know." T.J. kissed her forehead, her cheek, and then, very softly, her lips. "There's a lot to be said for living out your dreams."

Dreams didn't answer all the questions of day-to-day life, Jenny knew. You couldn't raise a family or build a long-term relationship if you were busy living out your fantasies, tossing caution to the winds whenever it suited you.

But just for now, while T.J. was in her arms and they were rediscovering the closeness they'd always shared—just for now, Jenny thought, what was the harm in admitting that this was one of her own most cherished dreams? She had longed for this man so inescapably, and now he was with her, murmuring to her that no woman had ever aroused him the way she did.

Dreams could be shattered all too easily. Jenny was aware of that. But she was also coming to realize that a life without them felt incomplete, unfinished. And her dreams came very close to reality when T.J. was holding her like this.

She met his kisses with a fierce hunger of her own and heard him groan as her mouth merged erotically with his. Jenny's whole body came alive at the touch of his hands on her skin, at the knowing, intimate way he explored every inch of her.

She cried his name out as he teased and caressed her, and heard him whisper, "Ah, Jenny" in return. Last night they had given in to a furious hunger for each other, but now they seemed to share a sense that this moment should be made to last, that tomorrow would bring new dangers and they should draw this sweet exploration out to its utmost.

Jenny felt light-headed, half-dissolved with pleasure, by the time T.J. finally drove inside her. He filled her deeply and completely, and they moved together as if they heard the same pounding cadence, the same spiraling cry of need and longing and love. They had never spoken the word *love* between them. But somehow it didn't matter tonight. As she eased back into awareness after a shuddering climax that had left them slick and sated and clinging fiercely to each other, Jenny felt as though something had changed, something powerful and profound. She was sure that T.J. shared her sense of belonging, of completion. It was too strong—too inevitable—to deny.

She didn't know where that left them. She only knew, as she drifted back into sleep, that for the first time in many years she was able to think of the past without pain, and to look forward to the future with the dawning of hope.

T.J. wasn't in the bed when she woke up. At first Jenny wasn't alarmed; he hadn't been there yesterday morning either, but only because he'd been out getting breakfast for them.

She opened her eyes. The big bouquet of pink roses was still on the bedside table, with yesterday's happy-birthday note still propped up against them. There was no new addition to it, in T.J.'s blunt dark handwriting. And there was no coffee burbling in the pot, either. Jenny frowned and sat up.

The room felt empty, except for herself. T.J.'s clothes were gone, even the jacket that had been hanging on the hook next to the door. If he'd just gone down to the front desk to check on the courier, would he have taken his jacket?

She knew he wouldn't have. And somehow the empty coffeepot made her think he hadn't just gone out to get breakfast, either. Quickly, Jenny got out of bed and back into her own clothes, wishing she didn't feel so cold all of a sudden.

A quick survey of the room showed no evidence that T.J. had ever been there at all. There was no note, not one scrap of his clothing or anything else. Even the drugstore bag with the gauze and tape in it was gone, and that seemed most conclusive of all. Without even bothering to comb her hair, Jenny slipped into her own jacket and headed out into the hallway.

She could hear his voice just before she got to the main desk. He was speaking quietly, as though he wanted to keep his words private.

She soon figured out why. The hallway took a sharp turn just before it met the lobby, and she stayed out of sight, moving just close enough to hear what T.J. was saying.

"She's not going to like the idea, so if you can break it to her gently, I'd appreciate it." The words caught her like an unexpected blow. "By the time she wakes up, I should be far enough away that following me won't be an option."

"You better get going, then." That was T.J.'s friend, his sailing buddy, Jenny thought. Did the friend, too, subscribe to the philosophy that the best thing a man could do in a sticky situation was to head for the open sea as soon as humanly possible? She could hear the two of them moving now, going into the office, she thought. She was still absorbing the shock of the fact that T.J. was on the verge of walking out on her again, and part of her wanted to stay hidden, immobile, until she had a better command over her emotions.

But if she did that, she might be losing her one and only opportunity to confront him, to make him understand that taking off into the wide blue yonder only created more problems than it solved. She'd been too young, too hurt, too scared, to do it last time. This time, she had eight years of anger and determination stored up inside her, and she was tired of keeping all of that to herself.

She slipped back along the silent hallway and took an exit door that led out to the beach. By the time T.J. and his friend emerged from the main entrance, she was already clear of the building, watching carefully to see where they were headed next.

For the first time in his life, T.J. felt ambivalent about setting out to sea.

This had always been the thing he'd looked forward to most: the moment he felt the sails fill and the boat leap forward along with the wind. He loved the feel of the tiller under his hand, and the sharp humming sound of the sails stretched taut.

This morning, though, the familiar excitement seemed dimmed. He should be enjoying this, in spite of—or maybe because of—the danger he would be facing at the other end of this trip. The weather was clear again, and the breeze steady. The sailboat he had borrowed from his buddy was a real gem, superbly crafted and responsive as a woman's body.

That was the problem, he thought, as he turned the boat's nose slightly farther out toward open water. Every thought that came into his mind was somehow connected with Jenny, with the superheated satisfaction of their lovemaking last night, or the perfect beauty of her skin and eyes, or the easy laughter they'd shared only yesterday.

Leaving her sleeping in that bed this morning had been one of the hardest things he'd ever done. Every nerve ending in his body had screamed at him to slide back down against her, to waken her gently with a kiss and move on from there, into the accepting softness of her body and the feminine passion of her heart.

Instead, he'd slid silently out of the bed and gotten dressed as quickly as he could, before meeting his friend at the front desk and collecting the copy of Pete Alvarez's diary that had arrived by courier just after midnight. The two men had gone out to buy provisions, and T.J. had stocked the sailboat and set sail by himself shortly after seven.

He'd navigated the waterway along this coast many times. Once he was well away from the Wanderers' Rest and his own treacherous thoughts of Jenny, he would travel more sedately, he told himself, sticking to the Intracoastal Waterway that threaded along the east coast. He would probably use the motor after a while, although to T.J.'s way of thinking, powering a sailboat with a gasoline motor came close to blasphemy.

He was going to need some time to study Pete Alvarez's diary and decide what his next move should be. He couldn't do that if he was ripping along at top speed in open water. But first, he needed to go as fast as he could, to put some distance between himself and the seductive memory of Jenny's warm, sleeping form.

It was nearly noon by the time he felt himself start to calm down, to get into the rhythm of sailing and away from the thought of Jenny beckoning him to join her in bed last night. He knew his concentration was still split, but at least he was able to think about piloting the boat into the Intracoastal Waterway and toward calmer waters.

He had provisioned the boat for several days, not knowing how long it might take him to wrap up his investigation. He ducked down into the galley now and heated up a can of soup as the sailboat bobbed gently in a sheltered inlet. When the soup was hot, he carried the bowl and Pete Alvarez's diary back up to the cockpit. He started the small motor and set a leisurely course northward, while he ate his lunch and began to read the thick stack of paper that Jenny's friends had sent.

She'd been charitable in describing it as incoherent, he quickly realized. A lot of what Pete had written was simply gibberish, obviously scribbled while he was under the influence of one substance or another.

Here and there, though, a paragraph or a page would stand out in sudden clarity, and T.J. began to concentrate on those, getting a picture of a haunted, unstable man who had been tormented by demons he had long since given up trying to fight.

"Too bad," T.J. said out loud, more than once. He often talked to himself when he sailed. He'd gotten into the habit during his solitary trip around the globe, when he sometimes hadn't seen another human being for weeks and had needed to hear the sound of a voice, even if it was his own.

Now he found himself commenting on what Pete Alvarez had written, gradually coming to a sense of what the man had been like. A deeply troubled character, T.J. thought. Talented, but dogged by some kind of bad luck that might—if he was reading the diary correctly—have begun while Pete was in Vietnam.

It was hard not to get sidetracked by the occasional mention of Jenny, and harder still to stop picturing her as she'd been when Pete had first delivered her to T.J.'s home. T.J. hadn't been around to see Pete Alvarez, but he had a crystal-clear memory of four-year-old Jenny, with her wide, dark eyes and her determined stance. She'd been scared to death and trying not to show it, and T.J. had fallen instantly for that combination of vulnerability and courage.

"You're not going to do her—or anybody—much good if you can't concentrate on this case, Madison," he muttered to himself, when his attention had been snagged yet again by Pete Alvarez's description of his small daughter. "It's Pete you're supposed to be interested in, not Jenny."

"You've already proved you're not interested in her." The voice seemed to answer him out of his own thoughts. "Walking out on her again was hardly an expression of interest, was it?"

For a moment T.J. accepted the words as a product of his imagination. He had slipped back into his usual solitary habits, he told himself. It was true that until now he had never heard answers when he'd talked to himself. Maybe it was just a predictable result of the emotional turmoil of the past few days.

But the words echoed on the salt air in an exceptionally realistic way. And he'd conjured up Jenny's voice many times in his lonely travels, but it had never sounded so close.

It had never sounded so irritated, either. It was the angry edge to the sound that finally made T.J. turn in his seat.

Jenny was sitting on the top step of the staircase that ran down into the cabin, arms folded tightly against her chest. The breeze ruffled her hair, but her eyes stayed firmly fixed on T.J.'s face. He had never seen her looking less pleased.

Chapter 10

At first he was far too startled to speak. And Jenny, too, stayed silent, watching him with that steady, dark-eyed glare.

When he got over being astonished, T.J.'s mind was overrun by a lot of things. Fury was right at the top of the list, and fear was just underneath it.

"Jenny!" He stood up abruptly, glaring back at her now. "You're not supposed to be anywhere *near* here. What the hell are you trying to pull?"

Jenny stood, too. Her stare never wavered. "I'm just trying to keep you from doing the same thing to me you did the last time," she said.

"The last time—" T.J. couldn't believe this was really happening. One moment he'd been cruising along, concentrating on his work, independent and sure that Jenny was safe. He hadn't expected that she would be exactly thrilled to find out he'd left her at the Wanderers' Rest, but at least he'd hoped she would understand the reasons for it. And he'd made sure she would have a comfortable, congenial place to stay until he could get back to her. Now he discovered that she was square in the middle of whatever danger he was headed toward. The thought made him crazy.

"I'm putting you ashore," he said bluntly. "At the very first possible opportunity."

"And then what?" she demanded.

T.J. didn't have a good answer. He still had money left, but it wasn't enough to get Jenny far. And she'd fled Charlotte without her purse. Without a driver's license, she couldn't even rent a car to get herself back to the haven of the Wanderers' Rest, assuming she would agree to go there in the first place. From the stubborn set of her lips, that didn't seem very likely.

He favored the sea air with a couple of distinctly sailorlike curses and then looked back at her. Her expression hadn't changed. She seemed to be waiting for him to arrive at the inevitable conclusion that he was stuck with her.

That didn't mean he had to do it gracefully. "This is all wrong, Jenny," he told her. "I had a good reason to take off the last time we got ... close. And I had an even better reason this morning."

"It was for my own good, right?"

He didn't miss the challenge in her tone. She was forcing him to take a hard line, he thought, backing him into the situation he'd hated so much when he'd been her guardian. He had never liked telling Jenny what to do. But damn it, *one* of them had to think ahead.

"Of course it was for your own good," he said tightly. "If you can't see that—"

"T.J." She was pointing now. "The diary."

In his shock at the sight of Jenny, he'd put down the pile of loose papers he'd been reading, and they were starting to ruffle in the breeze now, in danger of blowing away. T.J. slammed a palm down on top of them, scowling at Jenny as though she'd caused the problem, and gathered them into some kind of order again. He killed the motor, letting the boat drift for the moment.

"Excuse me," he said, moving toward the staircase. "Since my investigation is the original purpose for all of this, maybe I'd better pay closer attention to my evidence."

He hoped his message was clear. Jenny moved aside, onto the deck, and T.J. stalked past her. He put Pete Alvarez's diary onto the small table in the galley and anchored the pages with a heavy book of charts for good measure. When he turned around, Jenny was at the bottom of the small staircase.

"So that's it?" she said. "This is still just a simple investigation, and nothing more?"

"At the moment," he said, "yes. That's all it is."

"And last night? And the night before?"

He didn't want to be reminded about last night and the night before. And at the same time, he hadn't really stopped thinking about them since setting sail early this morning. Just standing this close to Jenny in the confined space of the cabin was making him ache for her all over again, making him remember in exquisite detail how good it felt to hold her close to him, how her mouth melted under his, inviting him in to a softer world than the one he usually inhabited.

That softer world enticed him and scared the starch out of him, all at the same time. He didn't know—had never really known—what to do with sweet Jenny and her dreams.

His buried fears—and the hopes that went with them—made him very blunt with her. "This is the wrong time to be pulling this stunt, sugar," he said. "If you'd just stayed put—"

"It's too late for that, T.J. I'm here now."

She was, and T.J. wasn't getting any happier about it. He growled, pacing into the main cabin, wishing the room was larger. Usually he loved the confined spaces of a boat's interior, but today he felt claustrophobic.

He knew it was because Jenny was following him into it, still looking at him with that somber gaze that made him think she wasn't sharing all of her thoughts with him. He remembered that expression well. In general Jenny had been the most agreeable child in the world, but every once in a long while, when she really wanted something, T.J. recalled her mustering up a quiet determination that never wavered, no matter what.

Well, he could be determined, too. And he *was* determined to get the ground rules straight before they traveled another nautical mile.

"Short of turning around and going back," he said bluntly, "I don't see any good way of getting out of this situation. So I guess I'm going to have to accept it. But from here on, I'm running this show, Jenny. That's got to be understood."

"T.J., this is all more complicated than you realize."

"What is? The investigation?"

Her face looked troubled. "No, not the investigation," she said, with an impatience that T.J. couldn't quite account for. "I'm talking about us. About you and me."

"This is bad timing, sugar. Believe me."

"Believe you?" Her words were tinged with astonishment now. "Why should I believe a man who's disappeared into the night the two times we've even come close to saying how we feel about each other?"

"*Damn* it, Jenny." He paced to the far end of the cabin and then turned. They were still too close together, he thought. With two long steps he could pull her into his arms again and feel her soft curves molding themselves to him, seducing him, easing him . . .

Distracting him. That was the main point here, and he was crazy to forget it even for a moment. "Why do we have to say how we feel about each other? We shared things when we were young that made us as close as any two people I know. And we're…obviously attracted to each other. Why do we have to go beyond that?''

She tilted her chin up challengingly. ''Because if we're as close as you say, you have a very strange way of showing it,'' she said. ''Sneaking out on me like that—again—''

He could hear hurt and anger in her tone, and for a moment he wondered if he should have handled things differently. And then he reminded himself that if he *hadn't* snuck out, they would just have had this argument earlier, in a different venue. The basic facts were still the same.

''Keeping you safe is my first priority,'' he said. ''If you can't see that that's more important than anything else at the moment—''

Jenny made an inarticulate noise and raised her hands in the air. ''Stop it, T.J.,'' she said. ''We've been around and around in this circle too many times already.''

''And you still don't get it!'' T.J.'s own frustration got the better of him, and he covered the distance between them in two giant strides. He had a half-formed idea about shaking some sense into Jenny's beautiful head, somehow physically impressing her with the depth of his concern for her safety.

But the moment his hands closed around her shoulders, he knew that shaking her was the last thing he really wanted to do. He felt her muscles tensing and saw her eyes widen, as if he had startled her badly.

He started to frame a sentence about how she was going to have to let him call the shots from here on, but the words got away on him. She felt so soft in his grip, and so slender. And the yielding openness of her responses when they'd made love last night was still making T.J.'s blood sing with remembered passion. But the stubborn strength in her eyes never faltered as she looked up at him.

''This won't help,'' she said quietly.

''It can't hurt.'' He wasn't exactly sure what he meant. He only knew that he couldn't stand to be this close to those rose-petal lips and not touch them with his own. He'd been trying to tell himself that it was fear for her safety that was making him act this way. But the moment he clasped her to him, he knew it was desire, pure and unadulterated.

He could feel it pounding in his temples as Jenny raised a hand to his chest. Was she trying to push him away? T.J. wasn't sure he had the strength of will to let her go again. And then Jenny caught her breath, and he could hear the hunger in the quiet gasp she gave. They had plenty to argue about, he thought. But neither of them could argue against the power that kept drawing them together.

T.J. felt Jenny's body relaxing into his own as he kissed her. Her mouth was warm and welcoming, her tongue slick and erotic against his own. He tried to hold at least a part of himself in check, to remember why this shouldn't be happening, but when he felt Jenny's soft moan vibrating in his own throat, he knew he was lost. The only thing that really mattered, when they held each other like this, was to go on, to demand more, to satisfy the rolling wave of need inside both of them.

He pressed her back against the wooden cabin wall and felt her reaching her hands up to his tangled hair, pulling the two of them even closer together. T.J. groaned, capturing her mouth with a strength and possessiveness that had all his rage and fear and desire wrapped up in it.

There was nothing subtle about the way they were clinging to each other this time. It was a statement of unchecked passion, and T.J. knew he wasn't going to be able to stand it for very long. The small bedroom was three feet to his left. He was already fantasizing about gathering Jenny up into his arms and carrying her in there, laying her down on the built-in double bed and stripping away all the clothes he'd bought her. He could feel the roundness of her breasts under the loose sweater, and the memory of how he had caressed them only last night, coaxing them into arousal, came back to him with an almost physical jolt. He closed his eyes tightly, running his hands over Jenny's breasts now, anticipating the sweet pleasure of stirring her whole body again....

The physical jolt this time was stronger. T.J. closed his eyes, trying to ignore it. Part of him didn't give a damn what had caused the sudden shuddering in the boat's hull. All he really wanted at the moment was to lose himself further in Jenny's kiss, in all of her body.

But something was definitely happening to the boat, and Jenny had noticed it now, too. "T.J.?" Her voice was ragged and breathless, her eyes nearly black, questioning him.

"I know." T.J. struggled for some kind of sanity, some way to get clear of the undertow he'd been swept into. He swallowed a couple of curses and pulled away from her, intending to head for the staircase as soon as his knees would let him. And then, with a sudden sickening lurch, the boat leaned over, tossing him into the empty space of the cabin.

He slammed hard against the far wall, completely unprepared for the fall. He heard Jenny's startled cry and reached out for her as she came careening down after him. T.J. was an experienced enough sailor that nearly everything in the boat had been safely stowed away, but there were a few loose items in the kitchen, and he heard them crashing around now and felt the whole craft shudder as it came to a halt.

For a few stunned seconds he couldn't move, still half-lost in the taste and feel of Jenny's body, wishing his head would stop spinning. He was lying against the cabin wall, and through the small porthole next to his head, he could see water. And sand.

"Damn," he said, struggling to get to his feet. It was like being at the site of an earthquake, he thought, and trying to absorb the fact that things weren't at the same angle as before. He was aware of Jenny following close beside him as he slithered his way over the tilted floor, working hard to stay upright. Every few seconds the boat gave another slight lurch, and by this time T.J. had figured out why.

"We're hung up on a sandbar," he said, as they emerged into the afternoon light. "This is a legendarily bad spot for them."

He let out a whole string of curses when he saw how deeply the keel had driven into the sandy bottom. This was exactly what he deserved for letting his attention be captured so completely by Jenny Alvarez, he told himself. This was what happened when he let his own longings for this sweet, sexy woman get out of hand.

He knew now that he was lonelier than he'd been admitting to himself. He knew Jenny was perhaps the one person on the face of the earth who had ever seen beneath his own rough-and-tumble surface to what was underneath. But that still didn't change things.

The damned sandbar was a warning, he thought. With luck, and some muscle, he'd be able to get them clear of it before long. But the sandbar was only a minor danger, compared with what they were heading toward. If he let his feelings for Jenny take him over again the way they just had—

T.J. didn't even want to think about what the result might be. He was already stripping off his jacket and shoes, telling Jenny she was going to have to handle the motor.

"T.J., that water is freezing," she said, looking apprehensively over the side. "Are you sure—"

"Listen to me, sugar." He paused just long enough to take her by the shoulders again, firmly this time, dispassionately. The scent and familiarity of her were driving him crazy, but he managed to hold on to the main point, which was that he couldn't let her interfere with his powers of concentration just at the moment.

"I've done this before, more times than I can tell you," he said. "I've done all of this before." *Except losing myself in a woman's softness the way I just did with you,* he almost added. "So you're going to have to trust me and just do what I tell you. And the first thing I'm telling you is to sit at that motor and keep it in reverse until I get us clear. Got it?''

Her full mouth was set in that stubborn, sexy line again as he let her go, but she didn't argue. "Good," T.J. said, as he started the motor for her and showed her how to shift it from neutral to reverse. Then he lowered himself over the side, into chest-high water that was just as cold as Jenny had foreseen.

Good, he said again, silently this time. A cold plunge was exactly what he needed to combat the longing that was still racing around in his veins. Being cooped up with Jenny Alvarez on a sailboat was going to be the ultimate test of his willpower, he thought grimly, as he started to rock the hull gently. He didn't know how long they might be stuck with each other, but it seemed likely that this wouldn't be the first cold bath he would need to take.

Fortunately, it was taking all his strength and concentration to ease the boat off the sandbar. T.J. set up a steady rocking motion, synchronized with the waves that were washing over the shallow spot. He dug his toes into the cold sand under his feet and called out to Jenny to open the throttle a little more. Just at the point where the muscles in his arms were beginning to tell him this had gone on long enough, he felt the big hull start to shift on its own, pulling away from the obstacle it had run into.

"All right!" T.J. gave a final push and judged that he'd done enough. As the boat eased itself free and started to move backward in the salty water, righting itself as it went, T.J. launched himself off the sandy bottom and quickly swam the distance to the stern, where Jenny sat.

"Throttle it back!" he called, and heard the motor become quieter. "Now put it in neutral."

By the time she'd done it, T.J. was hauling himself over the side, dripping wet but triumphant. "I'll take over from here," he said. "If you want to help, you can go below and see if anything broke when we ran aground."

She was on her feet now, letting him take over from her at the motor, staring at him as though he'd gone crazy. "T.J.," she said, "you're soaking wet. And it's cold. Don't you want to dry off?"

T.J. gritted his teeth. This was exactly what he was going to have to fight against, he told himself: this temptation to let Jenny's concern wash over him, softening up his judgment and eroding his reaction time.

"What I want to do," he said, "is get back underway again. We've lost some time, and I want to make it up. You can help by picking up the stuff that got slung around down there, or you can just stay out of the way, but whichever one you choose, it needs to be soon."

She still wore that astonished look, as though she couldn't believe what she was hearing. "You're treating me like some cabin boy who's misbehaved," she told him. "T.J.—"

"I'm treating you like a stowaway, which is exactly what you are," he said, cutting her off. He was shivering now, reaching for his shirt and jacket, heading the boat's nose back toward the open water. "The rules are tighter on the water, Jenny. This time it was a sandbar, next time it could be a reef, if we're not more careful. And when we get to Washington, it could be more guys with loaded weapons. Neither one of us can afford to take chances right now. You've got to understand that."

And letting Jenny back into his heart was the biggest chance of all, he thought. Reefs and sandbars and loaded weapons aside, the gentle passion of her loving represented changes T.J. couldn't imagine making in his life. It whispered to him of homes and families and stability and a lot of other nearly mythical things that he had never really had and knew he couldn't offer a woman like Jenny.

So it was safer to invoke his status as a sea captain and hers as a stowaway, and to hope that eventually he would get over the little stab of desire that went through him every damned time he met her gaze. She was lingering for a moment now, looking thoughtfully at him, but finally—mercifully—she turned and headed back down into the cabin. T.J. was cursing under his breath again as he watched her go.

It had sounded as though the entire contents of the kitchen went crashing to the floor when the boat had hit the sandbar, but when Jenny investigated, she found only a few cans that had rolled into the corners, and some utensils scattered around. Her father's diary, though, had slid off the galley table, and the loose sheets were all over the place now.

Luckily, she had numbered the pages when she'd begun her campaign to reopen the three-year-old mystery Pete Alvarez had been involved in in Memphis. It wasn't a big job now to put the diary back in order. After she'd done it, and cleaned up the galley and main cabin, she decided she might as well use the time to reread what her father had written, searching this time for anything that might be a clue about Gen. Haviland Ross.

At first she sat on a built-in bench in the main cabin, feeling surprisingly sheltered and at home in the wood-paneled, red-carpeted room. After about an hour, though, she heard the boat's motor cut out, and she was aware of T.J. moving overhead, hauling up the sails and getting the boat under the power of the wind again.

After that, the world tilted to a forty-five-degree angle that was almost as unsettling as running into the sandbar. It wasn't so much the humming of the sails above the cabin that unnerved her. It was the way she would just get settled in one position and then the boat would tilt very slightly, making her feel as though the whole world had come unhinged from its axis.

She considered going back up on deck. Maybe the sudden adjustments to the wind might be easier to take if she could see T.J. making them. But that would have meant confronting T.J. again, and she wasn't quite ready to do that.

It wasn't that she intended to take his follow-my-orders routine completely to heart. But she had snuck on board early this morning with every intention of confronting him immediately with the story of their daughter's birth and death eight years ago, and now she was no longer so certain that that was the best plan. There were so many questions still unanswered between them: questions of love and lifestyle and their very different dreams of the future and memories of the past.

With all of that unresolved—not to mention the question of the investigation that was still dogging them—was this the time to look into the deepest layers of their own hearts? Jenny wasn't so sure anymore.

So she'd stayed below, exploring the boat and discovering that in the small bedroom there was a built-in seat where she could pull her feet up and feel a little more secure despite the fact that they were careening along through the water at a rate that felt alarmingly fast to her. The image of T.J., wet and wind-torn and sitting at the tiller, determinedly coaxing a punishing rate of speed out of the big sailboat, was a disturbing one, especially when she knew that if she went up to the deck and offered to help, he would probably just snarl at her again as he'd done before.

"Fine," she said out loud, as she curled up in the cozy seat with the pages of the diary on her lap. T.J. had refused her help—more than one kind of help, if she counted the way he had kissed her and then announced that the feelings they'd called up in each other were something to be avoided.

She hadn't given up on reaching the part of him that he was trying so hard to push aside. And she hadn't given up on helping him in other ways, either. So she settled herself in the chair, trying hard to ignore the way the boat moved with the ocean swell, and turned her attention to her father's diary.

Chapter 11

Pete Alvarez's Diary

Can those bastards find her? He said they could. She kept my name, in spite of everything. That was my one condition, when I gave her up. Maybe they can find her. Maybe she's married now. Maybe she has another name. Maybe they can't find her.

He said they would. The world is full of devils, devils in white, devils in green. Devils with long faces that laugh at you.

How many more, like me? I was going to be a doctor, once. Have a family, like other men have families. It all got taken away, so long ago. He laughed at me when he did it. Bad for business, son, he said.

Laying on a table, can't do a thing about it. I heard him laughing. Saw him with the needle in his hand. I wanted to tell him, doctors should heal. Should help. Like I was going to do, once.

But all they see is money, all of them. The devil would sell anybody's soul for a dollar. Mine was pric-

ier than that. Save a man's life, lose a man's soul.
Might call it a fair bargain, unless you were the one
losing his soul, like I was.

It shouldn't have happened this way. The man with
the stars, he had the power to take my soul away. The
only power I had was to keep her safe, and I used it,
when I had to. He knew I wouldn't tell, because I was
scared for her life. So nobody knows the truth, how I
lost my soul, my family, everything. Nobody knows
how it happened. How it still happens. Every day, every
war, every time there's a buck to be made.

How many more came home like me?

It was well after nightfall before the boat stopped.

She had actually made some progress in her quest through
the diary by the time she felt the boat angle back close to
upright again. There were no portholes in the bedroom, but
when she glanced out at the small round windows in the
main room, she could see that the world outside was dark.

"Thank goodness," she muttered. She'd wondered
whether T.J. had intended to career along through the night
at that same breakneck speed, or whether he would have the
sense to slow down once the sunlight was gone. She realized she had no idea what the limits of his recklessness really were, or whether there *were* limits to it.

She'd seen in his tiger's eyes this afternoon that he was no
closer than he'd ever been to changing his wandering ways.
It was a relief to discover now that even though he was as
bullheaded as he'd ever been, at least he apparently didn't
intend to set sail clear across the Atlantic by night.

Not long after the boat righted itself, she heard the quiet
chug-chug of its motor start up and guessed that T.J. was
steering them back into the more sheltered waters of the Intracoastal Waterway. They cruised along at a sedate speed
for what felt like about an hour, and then the motor cut out,

and Jenny could hear the sound of the anchor line unwinding.

She'd been dog-earing the pages of her father's diary that seemed significant to her, and she gathered the sheets together again in order now. When T.J. came down the steps into the galley, Jenny was on her feet, holding the diary against her chest. His oversize frame filled the cabin immediately. His hair was snarled by the wind, and his tan seemed a shade darker. And no wonder, Jenny thought. He'd been up there for hours, keeping the boat at racing speed.

His jeans had long since dried, and he had his sneakers and jacket on. But somehow she still felt the urge to warm him if she could, to smooth out the tangles in his dark brown hair and ease the fearsome sense of responsibility that he felt for their mutual safety.

Apparently, though, warming, smoothing and easing were not on the evening's agenda. T.J. strode into the galley and opened a cupboard without really looking at Jenny.

"There's soup," he said brusquely.

Jenny was conscious of the disappointment welling inside her. So he was going to stick with his tough-guy stance, was he? Well, she'd known it was a possibility.

"Soup sounds good to me," she said. "Want a hand?"

"There isn't room for two people in the galley."

And that seemed to be that. He might be treating her like an unwelcome stowaway and nothing more, but at least he didn't seem to consider her to be a galley slave, as well. Jenny was inclined to take that as a small, positive sign.

She watched him heat the can of soup over the small propane stove, and slid into place opposite him at the table when it was ready. She was still holding her father's diary, and she put it on the table next to her. At least they had *that* to talk about, she thought.

"I've been going through the diary again," she said, as she waited for the first spoonful of her soup to cool.

"And?"

"Well, the first few times I read it, I was mostly trying to come to terms with who my father had been. And then I got hooked on the mystery he had been involved in in Memphis, the mystery Sunny and Creed helped me clear up."

"I saw some notes in the margins about that." T.J.'s voice was neutral. He was being cautious, Jenny thought, not wanting to let them stray into deep waters again. His keep-your-distance air saddened her, but she wasn't ready to try to push past it quite yet.

"Some of the notes were mine, some were Creed's," she said. T.J. would have recognized her handwriting; he'd helped her with her homework enough when she was a child. "The business in Memphis had to do with a crooked doctor my father was trying to expose, and I thought that explained all the references to being helpless on an operating table, and being drugged so that he didn't know what was going on."

"Makes sense to me." T.J. was eating his soup steadily, but Jenny could feel his watchful gaze on her face the whole time. Whenever she glanced up from the diary, those gold flecks were dancing just at the edge of her vision.

"It turned out that the doctor in Memphis was performing illegal operations on homeless people, including my father." Jenny flipped to one of the pages she had dog-eared. "But there are other places—here's one of them—that are making me wonder now if there was some other incident, something besides the one in Memphis, that he's talking about. It all gets jumbled together. If you've looked at this, you'll realize his sense of time was pretty hazy. But here, on this page, he talks about 'devils in white, devils in green.'"

"The devils in white would presumably be doctors who take advantage of their patients."

"Right. But who are the devils in green, then?"

"Operating room attendants, maybe. You know, surgical green."

"Or military green?" Jenny tapped the page she was referring to. "Here, and in other places, too, he mentions 'the man with the stars.' I thought that was just a hallucination at first, but what if it refers to—"

"A general's stars." For the first time since he'd come down into the cabin, T.J.'s heavy-lidded stare lightened up with new interest. "That's good, Jenny. I'd looked at that part, but I didn't think of that."

Jenny pushed her soup bowl aside and read directly from the photocopied pages. " 'He knew I wouldn't tell, because I was scared for her life,' " she said. "He meant *my* life, presumably. 'So nobody knows the truth, how I lost my soul, my family, everything.' "

Every time she read the uneven scribbled words, her heart went out to the unhappy, lost man who had been her father. None of the people she cared most about in her life had stayed around for long, she thought, with a surge of remembered childhood helplessness. First her parents, and then Colonel Madison—they had all disappeared from her world suddenly, too suddenly. T.J. had been the one fixture in it, staying in contact with her even when he'd been living alone on his boat, even when he'd enrolled her in boarding school after becoming her guardian. But finally he had left her, too, and it had been the most painful loss of all.

His tone sounded different now, crisper and almost businesslike. He was relieved that she had started talking about Pete's diary, Jenny thought. He was glad that the roiling emotions of their kiss earlier this afternoon could be put aside for the moment.

She swallowed past a stubborn lump in her throat, and wondered if she was crazy even to imagine that she and T.J. Madison could ever be more than very different ships passing in the night.

"There was something else, right around there," T.J. was saying, waving one big hand in the air. "Let me look."

He scanned the page she half turned on the table, and plunked a broad fingertip down on the paragraph. "Here," he said. "'Nobody knows how it happened. How it still happens. Every day, every war, every time there's a buck to be made. How many more came home like me?' I've been wondering what he meant by that."

"He came home with serious substance abuse problems," Jenny said. "And he wasn't the only one."

"I know. But what if—" It was T.J.'s turn to flip through the pages, looking for something. "Back here," he said finally. "When he talks about his 'day in court.' It sounds like he was pretty out of it at the time."

Jenny remembered the description, and the image it had conjured up in her mind, of her semiconscious father being propped up between two military police guards. But T.J. was obviously thinking of something quite different.

"That struck me as odd," he said. "Usually, if you're going to stand trial in the military, you're locked up for a while first."

"He *was* locked up," Jenny said. "He talks about the guards coming and getting him."

"Right. But unless I'm very mistaken about this, it's hardly usual for military prisoners to have access to drugs while they're awaiting trial."

"I don't get it."

"I don't, either, not completely. But I'm wondering if there's a chance that your father was deliberately drugged— maybe deliberately made dependent on drugs—to keep him from spilling some secret that he knew. And if Haviland Ross was in on the secret..."

T.J. was on his feet now, beginning to pace around the main cabin. Jenny listened to his footsteps on the carpeted floor and felt them echoing in her chest, where all her feelings about her unknown father seemed to have gathered suddenly. *Deliberately* drugged, deliberately turned into an addict... How on earth could T.J. talk about these things as though they were just pieces of some puzzle he had to solve? She wanted to cry out against the very possibility of it, just to stop the pacing that told her he was hot on the trail of something that intrigued him.

"A lot of servicemen came back from Vietnam with drug problems," he said. "You're dead right about that."

Jenny winced at the phrase. T.J. didn't seem to notice.

"And a few Americans got rich cashing in on the heroin trade, too," he continued. "Not many, but a few. And some of those were in the military. I never heard of anybody as high up as a general being involved before, but—" He stopped suddenly, thinking hard, his eyes glittering. "Hell," he said at last. "I wish your father had included a few dates in that diary. I just had a hell of a brainstorm, but without specific dates, I'm going to need to check it against some military records before I know if it means anything or not."

Jenny suddenly couldn't stand it anymore. She remembered the way he'd retreated far into himself when she'd gotten close to him this afternoon. Contrasting it with his animated interest now was too hard to watch. And the thought that it was her own tormented father that T.J. was talking about so objectively was the final straw.

"It's too bad he's not still around, so he could just hand you the evidence you need, T.J." The sudden bite in her voice caught him off guard, he could see. *Good,* she almost said out loud.

Instead, she went on. "Of course, he'd probably still be in pretty bad shape if he *was* around, but that's not the main consideration, is it? The only thing that really matters to you—more than me, or my father, or anything that's happened between us—is solving this case of yours. How can you look at that diary and be annoyed that my father didn't think to date everything as though it was a high school notebook? How can you read it and not care that he was an unhappy and unlucky human being?"

She was on her feet now, too, glaring at him. T.J. halted by the bedroom door, hands at his sides as though he wanted to shove them into his pockets but was resisting the gesture for some reason.

"What makes you say I don't care?" he asked slowly.

"Everything about you. Your manner, your tone of voice. The fact that every time—every single time, T.J.—every time something in your life threatens to get too messy and emotional and out of control, you shut it off and go running in some other direction. And if you're stuck on a boat and can't run, then you take off into another subject and shut off the parts you don't want to think about."

She saw that his breathing had quickened, and realized hers had done the same thing. These were things she'd wanted to say to him for a long, long time, she thought. And something in his handsome face made her think they were things that he didn't really want to hear.

"You don't want to face what's happening between you and me, so now you're back at work on General Ross," she said. "Is it easy for you, T.J.? Do you really believe you can just leave trouble behind you?"

The boat was virtually still in the calm evening water where T.J. had moored it, but he was swaying slightly now, as though rocked by unseen waves. "I'm not running," he said stubbornly, defensively. "I'm not running at the moment."

Jenny shook her head at him, exasperated and angry. "Believe me," she said, "you're running. You're just doing it without moving your feet, that's all."

He gave a short laugh, although it didn't hold much amusement. He looked at the floor under his feet, as though to confirm what she'd said, and then he looked right into her eyes for the first time since that turbulent kiss this afternoon.

"This isn't *just* a case to me, Jenny," he said. "Far from it."

"You could have fooled me."

He shook his dark, unruly head. "I didn't get a chance to read the diary very thoroughly before you sprang yourself on me this morning, but I saw enough to make me think there are all kinds of answers buried in there—answers that you and I have both wondered about for a lot of years."

Jenny moved to the bench in the main cabin and sat down on it. Slowly, T.J. followed her example, lowering his big frame into a chair against the end wall of the room.

"What are you talking about?" Jenny asked.

"Give me the diary, and I'll show you."

She reached it over to him and felt her fingertips brush his as he took the unwieldy pile of paper. Even that brief contact was enough to make Jenny's pulse hammer in her veins.

She had a feeling that T.J. was just as affected as she was by the touch of her skin against his. His voice was even gruffer than usual as he said, "First of all, I think we should read this with the question in mind of how your father met mine in the first place."

"We already know that. They were in the military together. They both served in Vietnam."

"My father was a full colonel in the marines. Yours was a medic in the army. The chances of the two of them knowing each other very well are pretty slim."

"Then how did they get close enough that your father would agree to adopt me when my own father...didn't want me?"

T.J. had been riffling through the stack of paper, but now his head came up quickly, as though something in her tone had caught his ear.

"It still hurts, doesn't it?" he said. "Even after all this time."

"Of course it hurts. I'm not saying it affects me every day of my life, but it's always there, in the back of my mind, that the family I grew up in wasn't really my own."

T.J.'s brows came together in the bearlike frown she remembered so well. He was getting ready to defend her, she thought, to argue on her behalf. "I always felt as though you belonged in our family," he said.

"I know you did. I don't know what I would have done if you hadn't been there." And then he *hadn't* been there, she reminded herself. He'd done the same thing he'd done this morning: simply pulled up anchor and gone, when she'd needed him most. Since she wasn't quite ready yet to tell him her side of that momentous event, she switched quickly back to their original subject. "But I still don't know why your father agreed to take me."

"I'm wondering if it was because your father saved my father's life."

That was enough to get Jenny's full attention. T.J. was still cruising through the loose pile of paper, finally stopping with one blunt fingertip on a smeared, scribbled paragraph.

"'I saved him, and it cost me,'" he read out loud. "'But he was a good man, and if I had to save one man and make an enemy of the other one again, I would still do the same thing.'"

"There are a lot of passages like that," Jenny said. "His medical experiences in the war stayed with him. I think he hated the suffering more than anything else that ever happened to him."

"I got the same impression. And—" He paused, and she saw that same serious frown on his face. It wasn't the warmest expression she'd ever seen there, but at least it was open, and he was actually speaking to her again, instead of just issuing angry orders. "I'm really not treating your father as though I don't give a damn about him," he finished. "It's just . . . I feel as though maybe we can serve his memory best by sorting out what really happened to him, that's all. And to do that, I need to be analytical about it, not emotional."

"It's possible to be both, you know." Jenny spoke softly, simply, wishing there was some way to make him understand that running from his emotions wasn't going to take him any further away from them, in the long run.

His frown deepened, and she could sense him resisting the idea. "It isn't possible for *me* to do both," he corrected her. "Now, if we look at this page as meaning that your father saved mine, it opens up all kinds of possibilities. For instance, I always assumed my father's gunshot wound was something he got in the line of duty. But what if your father's diary means that it was an *American* who shot my father?"

In spite of her frustration with T.J., this was a subject that Jenny couldn't help but be fascinated by. She got off the bench and went to crouch beside his chair, studying the page he had turned up. *"An American, in uniform,"* Pete Alvarez had written about the shooting victim he'd helped. *"I had another feeling, like he was still in danger, lying there in the street. I got him into an alleyway, him trying not to make a noise, and then I saw the other man."*

"He doesn't identify the man with the gun," she pointed out. "He just describes him as evil."

"But the description sounds as though Pete actually knew the guy," T.J. said. "Here, where he says, 'I never knew a more evil human being.' That sounds as though he had other dealings with the same man."

"Then maybe all those references to 'the devil,' later on..." It was Jenny's turn to shuffle through the pages, leaning on the arm of T.J.'s chair. She didn't notice at first how still he became as she leaned closer to him. When he spoke again, his voice was a little gruffer than it had been before.

"I thought of the same thing," he said. "It's 'the devil' who seems to be involved in drugging your father—if he really was drugged against his will. And the same man seems to have been involved in the court case against Pete."

"Haviland Ross..." Jenny was beginning to see where he was headed with this.

He nodded. "Right," he said. "Gen. Haviland Ross initiated a disciplinary hearing in Vietnam, in which your father's name came up. That's the end of things that I started with. And now I find a military court appearance mentioned in your father's diary. It's not too great a leap to think they might be the same."

"Then if Haviland Ross was trying to cover up the fact that he'd shot your father—"

"Because my father knew that Ross was up to something illegal," T.J. cut in.

"Knew, or maybe just suspected," Jenny said. "Ross seems to have let your father alone after he came home from Vietnam. Whatever the crime was, it must have been something Ross kept carefully covered up."

"Makes sense," T.J. said. "And Pete was another threat to be gotten out of the way, because he knew that Ross had shot my father. I wonder if Pete actually knew what Ross was up to, or if he just suspected, as well."

"What *was* Ross up to?" Jenny paused and looked up at T.J.

"My guess is that Ross was making big money trafficking in illegal drugs," T.J. said. "That would explain his method of neutralizing your father—by drugging him."

"And sending him home an addict, which meant that no one would take his 'fantasies' seriously." Jenny couldn't believe the cruelty of it.

"I'm afraid that's how it looks to me. But your father obviously had his act together enough to realize that he wasn't in any shape to provide a home for you, after your mother had died. So he contacted *my* father—"

"Who owed him a favor."

"A *big* favor. And my father agreed to adopt you and look after you."

"Why wouldn't your father have exposed what Haviland Ross was up to?" Jenny wondered out loud.

"He may not have known the whole story. He may just have been nosing around, and Ross got panicky and shot him. Or my father may not have felt up to it. He was in bad shape when he first got back from the war. And even after he recovered from his wound, you remember how frail he was. He seemed content not to go beyond the house and the garden most of the time."

Jenny remembered the colonel's reclusiveness all too well. Colonel Madison had been a kindly guardian, but distant, and often unwell. T.J. had been literally the only flame of life in her early days.

She couldn't think about it without experiencing the old feelings of loss and longing that had colored her childhood. "You know, it's funny," she said, hearing the slight choking in her own voice. "I guess I always hoped that your father adopted me because he wanted me. It's amazing how much it hurts to know that he only did it to repay a favor."

"Hey, Jenny." T.J.'s voice was concerned. "Saving somebody's life isn't exactly in the same category as loaning them ten bucks, you know. My father must have had strong feelings about yours. You know he must have. And my dad wasn't the kind of man to do something he really didn't want to do, especially a big thing like adopting a child."

It had always been this way, Jenny thought, with a twist of bittersweet memory. She had always had these secret doubts, gnawing at her heart whenever she thought of how she'd been abandoned by her family. And T.J. had always had the power to ease her past those doubts, helping her see things another way.

Almost always, she corrected herself. She still couldn't get past the fact that he had abandoned her once, too.

"Thanks, T.J.," she said, a bit tartly. "But I really have worked through all of this on my own. It's just...*disturbing* to be reminded of it again, that's all."

He didn't answer, and that surprised her into looking up at him. He was still strangely tense, holding his big body stiffly in the chair.

"We seem to keep getting into these deep waters," he said finally.

"I don't see any way for us to avoid them," Jenny said. "There's just too much history between us." *Even more than you know,* she almost added. Soon, she thought, she was going to have to tell him the rest of it. It was just that the closer they got to each other, the more afraid she was that he would bolt on her again. She didn't want to share her painful secret with him until she felt more certain that it wouldn't simply drive him off on the high seas without her.

Again he wasn't answering right away. Jenny was suddenly very conscious of his breathing, which was hurried and unsteady. Hers matched it, she thought, as she let her gaze travel over the familiar planes of his face, his strong jaw, those high, uncompromising cheekbones, the startled glitter of his eyes.

She saw his lips part slightly, and the memory of this afternoon's kiss came rolling back through her body. There had been unfettered passion in that embrace, undisguised need. And T.J. was trying to deny all of that now.

From the tormented look in his eyes, he wasn't succeeding as well as he would have liked. They looked into each other's eyes at close range, exchanging silent messages that were full of questions and uncertainties.

Then T.J. lifted one big hand and rested it on the back of Jenny's neck, burrowing past her hair to the soft skin underneath. She could feel his heartbeat in his fingertips, and the powerful warmth of him seemed to flow into every part of her body.

She couldn't tell if his touch was intended to be soothing, or possessive, or erotic. She only knew that it connected with places inside her that no one else had ever reached. Physical desire was a part of it, but there was more, too. There was a sense that the bond between them was strong and instinctive and not to be trifled with.

The hungry look in his eyes told him he felt the same way. But he still wasn't letting himself give in to it. They stayed locked together in this moment of silent contact for what felt to Jenny like an agonizingly long time. And then T.J. broke away, growling a little at himself, or at her, getting to his feet and leaving her kneeling on the carpet and aching with the loss of his persuasive touch.

"I'm going to make coffee," he announced, as he headed into the galley. "You want some?"

"No, thanks. It keeps me from sleeping at night."

"Me, too. That's why I'm making it."

Jenny had deliberately introduced the subject of sleeping, wondering how her presence here would affect the sleeping arrangements in the small cabin. What T.J. was telling her now was that it wouldn't be a problem.

"I'm going to try to cover some more distance tonight," he said. "We can't move very fast at night, with just the motor, but it beats sitting here doing nothing at all. To my mind, we've figured out enough of this mess with Haviland Ross to get on to the next stage of things."

Jenny recalled the desperate passion of their lovemaking last night and repressed a sigh at his brusque tone now. "What *is* the next stage of things?" she asked, watching him put the kettle on the stove and start pulling down the coffee-making supplies from the small cupboards.

"The next stage is to contact a guy I know at the DEA." That made sense, Jenny supposed. If Gen. Haviland Ross had been—or perhaps still was—involved in the illegal narcotics trade, getting in touch with drug enforcement officials was a good plan. "With luck, he'll be able to help us.

But I don't want to waste any more time sitting around down here. We need to get to Washington as soon as we can."

At least he was saying *we* now, Jenny thought. He seemed to have accepted that she was here, whether he liked it or not. But the fact that he was planning on spending the night on deck rather than in the cabin was dispiriting.

"Are you going to stay up all night?" she asked.

"Hey, I've done it before. Don't worry, sugar. If I get drowsy, I'll just let the anchor down for a while and catch a nap on the bench in here."

In other words, he had no intention of getting too close to her again, Jenny thought. T.J. was back in action, pouring water through the coffee filter, showing her where the extra blankets were stored. He slipped back into this full-steam-ahead mode like slipping on a comfortable old pair of shoes, she thought. But even the hint of any long-term romantic involvement seemed to affect him as though it were a straitjacket.

She was still sitting with her father's jumbled diary on her lap when T.J. went back up on deck and gunned the motor to life again, and the sailboat started to move slowly through the night.

Chapter 12

According to the clock, T.J. knew he had gotten at least four hours' worth of scattered sleep during the night. According to his body—especially his eyelids, which felt as though there was sand under them—he hadn't rested at all.

He knew it wasn't just the fact that the bench in the main cabin room was too narrow for his broad frame or that his left shoulder still hurt him when he rolled over on it. He tried to blame his uneasiness on the question of how he was going to wrap up this business with General Ross, when General Ross seemed to have connections even within T.J.'s own agency. But he knew that wasn't really the problem, either.

It was the thought of Jenny Alvarez just one small room away, soft and warm under the blankets on the double bed. Memories of holding her, of losing himself in the magic of making love with her, kept invading the sleep he did manage to grab. Waking up, after those graphically erotic dream images of Jenny, left T.J. feeling even more restless than before.

He turned that restless energy straight into action, as he was in the habit of doing. By just after daybreak, he had the boat under sail again, and by the time the sun was warm enough to have chased off the morning chill, they had cleared the Chesapeake Bay Bridge and were cruising up the bay itself, heading toward the capital.

Jenny joined him on deck with two mugs of hot coffee at about eight. At first T.J. prided himself on the fact that exhaustion or strength of will or something else was keeping him from reacting to the sight of her as potently as he had yesterday.

And then her warm fingertips glanced over his chilled ones as she handed him the mug, and T.J. bit back an involuntary groan at the way her touch went straight through him. It always had, he thought. He was beginning to think it probably always would. It didn't make his thoughts about the future any clearer.

"So," she said, seating herself on the high side of the boat and scanning the low-lying shore that looked so pristine and clear in the morning sunlight. "Where are we, T.J.?"

He told her, and added that he hoped to reach Washington by midafternoon. "I'll call this guy at the DEA from someplace along the river," he said, "and we'll try to find a slip at a marina near the city."

"And then?" Jenny hesitated for a moment before asking the question.

T.J. didn't hesitate at all in replying. "And then I think it's time to pay a visit to Gen. Haviland Ross," he said. He didn't miss the startled look in her eyes. "There's no point to waiting, Jenny," he told her. "Ross already knows I've been looking into his past. He obviously feels pretty certain that I've found something he'd rather keep hidden. The longer we give him, the more time he'll have to cover whatever tracks he may have left. I want to get to him before that happens."

Jenny sighed. He could tell she wasn't happy about it. But then, she never *had* been thrilled by the risks he took. He remembered, very clearly, Jenny at eight years old, telling him in an unnaturally solemn voice that she was going to have a heart attack if he went through with his plan of buying an old wrecker motorcycle from a high school friend.

As it turned out, he hadn't bought the bike, only because he'd gotten a chance to go in on a sailboat instead. Jenny hadn't been much more pleased about that, he recalled. But she had eventually come around, prodded by T.J.'s good-natured teasing. She would come around this time, too, he felt confident. She would come to see that, sometimes, facing the lion in his den was the best and simplest way to get results.

He placed his call to the DEA from a pay phone at a marina just outside the city and arranged a meeting for early evening, with the agent he'd met and a few of his associates. "We'll pick you up," the DEA agent said. "Where are you going to be?"

T.J. didn't know exactly where he was going to be, and he didn't want anybody else knowing it, either. "I'll meet you downtown," he said. "I'm kind of on the move right now."

On the move with a woman whose safety was more important to him than anything else on earth, he added to himself. He needed to know that Jenny would be all right before he could begin to think about confronting Haviland Ross.

There were a couple of marinas near Washington that T.J. occasionally used to moor his own boat in. The boat was in one of those marinas now, and he had no intention of going anywhere near it, or of turning up in any of the places he usually went. He scouted around, hauling down the sails and using the motor again, until he found a quiet spot, close enough to the city that he could operate from there, and secluded enough that it wasn't an obvious choice to anyone searching the major marinas in the area. T.J. paid for a slip for one night and told Jenny he would probably be gone for a few hours.

"And I don't want you even to think about setting foot off this boat until I get back," he added. "This is serious business—and it's a business that I know a lot better than you do. So you have to promise me you'll stay put."

"You know I've never liked watching you put yourself in danger, T.J. In fact, it's always been one of my least favorite forms of activity."

"Hey, I've always come back more or less in one piece, haven't I?"

His breezy confidence—and Jenny's grudging promise to stay on the sailboat until he returned—lasted T.J. through what turned out to be a long evening. He wasn't the kind of man who took well to sitting in meetings with government officials, waiting for them to come to a consensus. His job required a certain amount of it, and it always made him crazy.

At least he had some backup at last, he told himself, as the DEA personnel argued back and forth to put together the kind of plan that T.J. could have hammered out for them in half an hour. And backup was going to be necessary if he was going up against a man who had access to the kind of firepower that Haviland Ross had already proved he had.

The meeting broke up at about nine, and by then T.J.'s jaw was aching from simultaneously biting his tongue and trying not to yawn. His nearly sleepless night was catching up with him, and his brain was numbed by the incessant nitpicking of the men and women at the table with him.

If he hadn't been so tired, and so numb, he thought afterward, he probably would have switched taxis partway across town, to ensure that he wasn't being followed. But at the moment all he could think about was getting back to Jenny, making sure she was all right. And at the back of his mind there was the feeling that it wasn't only her safety he was craving at this point. It was Jenny herself—her intelligent, beautiful eyes, her familiar presence in his life. She occupied his thoughts all the way back to the small marina.

He found her sitting up on deck when he arrived, hands clasped around her knees, obviously enjoying the unseasonably balmy evening. She turned her face to meet him as he loped along the floating dock, and her quick smile made him feel better than he probably had any right to.

"You just missed the show," she told him. "There were fireworks over the Tidal Basin. I've been sitting here watching. They just finished a few minutes ago."

T.J. swung a leg over the railing and tried to remember all the good reasons why he shouldn't give in to the temptation to sit down next to her on the deck, sharing the momentary pleasure he could see in her oval face.

He couldn't come up with even one good reason. And that worried him.

He paused at the stern of the boat, badly tempted to let Jenny's innocent, inviting smile seduce him into forgetting everything else but her. Something inside him, though, made him hesitate.

"Turns out it's Presidents' Day," he said. "I didn't realize it myself until the DEA people I was meeting with started griping about having to come out on a holiday evening." He looked out over the wide Potomac River, where the lights from the shore were reflecting off the water like stars on a clear night far out on the ocean.

"Do you ever take holidays, T.J.?" She was looking thoughtfully at him now, with that kissable pout to her bottom lip that made him want to feel her mouth against his own.

He had to work at concentrating on her words. And because he was working at it, he took in the peripheral fact that a car was pulling into the marina's parking lot, just out of T.J.'s field of vision.

Jenny's soft voice was continuing, asking him whether he ever got together with family friends—Colonel Madison had always stayed in touch with a few friends from his days in the marines—or whether T.J. insisted on spending his holidays alone.

"I remember you always used to arrive just in time for Thanksgiving, and Christmas," she said. "I never knew where you had been or whether you were really going to make it, until the moment you walked in the door."

T.J. could hear a car door slamming now, and then another one. It might be nothing, he told himself. Or it might be bad news.

"Mostly I spend those days alone," he told Jenny, only half paying attention to what he was saying. "Some of Dad's old cronies and I get together occasionally. Look, sugar, there's an outside chance that we might have to get out of here in a hurry. Can you get to the bow without standing up?"

"What on earth are you—"

He saw her eyes widen, and he wished he had a little time to break this to her more gradually. By then, though, there were footsteps coming their way. Quiet, purposeful footsteps. T.J. didn't like the sound.

"Just do it," he said, and swore softly when he saw her start to get to her feet. "Don't get up!" he told her sharply. "Come on, sugar, just move, all right?"

He couldn't tell if her expression meant she was frightened or just annoyed. But at least she was moving, crouched over as T.J. was himself, heading for the nose of the boat.

T.J. was cursing continuously now, berating himself for not having foreseen this possibility. He'd scouted out the marina thoroughly before leaving for his meeting, of course—it was a habit that had become ingrained over his years of working for the CID. But he'd expected any danger, if it came, to happen *after* he'd contacted Haviland Ross. If the approaching footsteps meant what he was increasingly afraid they meant, then he and Jenny were in an even worse bind than he'd imagined.

"Would you stop swearing long enough to tell me what's going on?" Jenny's voice sounded indignant. She was more angry than scared, he realized. And that wasn't good. Much as he hated the idea, he needed her frightened, and badly, so she would do exactly what he told her to do.

He spoke quickly, with as much urgency as he could cram into his voice. "Someone's on their way toward us. I don't know who it is, but there's an outside chance that someone at the DEA is in league with General Ross, and that they followed me back here."

Her startled intake of breath coincided with a quiet click that told T.J. all he needed to know. There wasn't time to go into detail—he reached out and took hold of Jenny's arm, urging her over the side rail of the boat.

"We've got to hit the water," he told her in a fierce whisper. "Hold your breath, sweetheart, and keep a grip on my coat if you can."

At the same moment as they lowered themselves into the frigid water of the Potomac, T.J. could hear the first bullets ripping through the side of the boat they'd just left. There wasn't time now to curse or plan or do anything but just plain get out of the way. Thank God he'd checked this place out already, he thought, as he felt the icy water closing over his head. If he hadn't, surviving would have been even chancier than it already was.

The shooters must have seen T.J. and Jenny slipping over the side of the boat. They must have spotted T.J.—that was how they'd known which sailboat to aim at. Their only real hope now was that the gunfire would raise enough of a ruckus in this quiet marina that someone would call the cops. He didn't dare hope that anyone would come out and get a good look at the car or the gunmen. Gunfire in the environs of Washington, D.C., wasn't something that spectators tended to flock to. No, the cops were the best bet. Failing that—

He didn't want to think about the alternative. And at the moment there wasn't really time. He and Jenny had surfaced underneath one of the floating docks, but T.J. knew they couldn't stay there long.

"There's a dinghy on the other side of the marina," he said, barely daring to whisper. "If we dive and then surface under the next dock, we can start heading for it."

With her black hair plastered to her head, Jenny's dark eyes looked bigger than ever, and utterly terrified. But she nodded wordlessly, telling him she understood, and they took in a gulp of air at the same time before diving into the cold, inky water again.

When they came up for air under the next dock, T.J. could hear footsteps on the dock they'd just left. Too damn close for comfort, he thought furiously, and motioned to Jenny that they should dive again. The more distance they put between themselves and the gunmen, the better their chances.

He didn't hear any more gunfire. No doubt the shooters had checked out the inside of the sailboat by now and confirmed that T.J. and Jenny had managed to get away. Now they were searching, and unfortunately there was a limited number of places to hide. T.J.'s lungs were starting to ache from the effort of holding his breath every time they dived and swam toward the next section of floating dock, and he was sure Jenny's must feel the same, burning with the need for more air. But if they didn't keep moving, they might be literally dead in the water.

The faint sound of sirens was the sweetest thing T.J. had ever heard. He was beginning to feel light-headed now, and Jenny's grip on his arm was shakier every time they surfaced for air. But the police sirens were definitely getting closer to the marina, and that gave him a new surge of strength.

"Hang on," he mouthed to Jenny. "This may scare them off."

It did. Even if the police were heading for some other emergency, T.J. had a feeling these particular gunmen wouldn't want to take a chance on being questioned.

Instead of diving again, he held Jenny's arm steady as he listened to the sounds above them. There was the quick patter of footsteps heading back to the car, and then doors slamming, and finally the screech of tires, overlapping with the police sirens screaming into the marina's quiet yard.

Jenny didn't even bother to suggest that they reveal themselves to the police this time. She had grasped, he thought, just how big a problem they were up against, and she'd finally come to share his own view that the fewer official records they ended up in, the safer they would be.

He saw the growing fear in her dripping, shadowed face, and felt a momentary pang at the thought that only a few days ago, she'd been sheltered, secure and happy. It was T.J.'s fault that she was in this situation in the first place. And it was her own fault, too, he reminded himself, for stowing away when she could have stayed safe in the Wanderers' Rest.

"Hell," he said softly, wishing he had some idea where this was all leading.

For right now, it had to lead away from the sailboat, away from the marina. "One more dive," he whispered to Jenny, "and then we're at the dinghy."

He knew they didn't have a lot of time before the police would start poking around the marina, looking for clues or witnesses or dead bodies. T.J. didn't want to be around when that happened, glad though he was for the presence of the police in the first place.

They reached the dinghy without being noticed, and hauled themselves into it with muscles chilled nearly to uselessness by the water. "Keep your head down," T.J. muttered, as he seized the small oars and guided them as silently as he could away from the dock.

His hands were almost too cold to keep a grip on the oar handles, and his back felt the strain of having to row while keeping his head down as far as he could. But the shoreline was mercifully sheltered, with clumps of tall grasses and little inlets that cut T.J. and Jenny off from the view of anyone looking for them from the dock. In under two minutes, T.J. felt sure they were out of sight.

That didn't mean they were out of danger. The gunmen were still around somewhere, and it was entirely possible that they would be searching the shore, checking the probable escape routes. That seemed to have occurred to Jenny, too.

"What can we do now?" she asked him, keeping her voice quiet. "We obviously can't go back to the sailboat."

"I know."

"T.J.—" Her dark eyes were achingly wide, and she had her arms wrapped around herself in a vain effort to restore some warmth to her body. "The diary's in the boat, T.J. They must have seen it."

"I know that, too. Thank God your friend photocopied it before he sent it to us."

"But won't it tip them off—"

"They're already tipped off, sugar." He couldn't keep the grim overtones out of his voice. "And they're going to be hunting for us with everything they've got. We've got to figure something out, and damn soon."

Jenny didn't say anything else, and T.J. focused all his energy on urging the little boat forward, heading downstream with the current. It was hard to do when his muscles were shuddering with the cold, and he kept wanting to take a break to scoop Jenny up in his arms and let their bodies warm and reassure each other.

He knew, though, that any reassurance he could offer her at this point wouldn't be the genuine article. As he'd said, they needed to plan their next move, and not waste any time doing it.

Getting out of the dinghy and off the river seemed like a good place to start. T.J. kept his eyes on the shoreline and finally saw what he was looking for: a landing place not far from a small strip of stores. With luck, there would be a pay phone there. He could call a cab to take them to a motel, which seemed like a good second step.

He could feel Jenny shaking with cold—and maybe with fear, as well—as he ran the dinghy up against the shore and gave her a hand getting out. He pushed the little boat back into the current, not wanting to leave it around as a clue to their whereabouts, and muttered an apology to whoever owned the thing.

"If we keep moving," he said, wishing his back teeth weren't clacking together, "maybe we'll get warm sooner."

He put an arm around Jenny's shoulders as they headed quickly across the riverside street toward the stores. They hit pay dirt on their second try: a pizza place on a corner had a phone near the door. T.J. dug some change out of his pocket, noticing that his roll of bills had dwindled over the last few days but at least it had stayed put during their un-planned swim in the river. It should be enough to buy them a night in a motel and a little time to lay a plan.

"I don't think—I've ever been so cold in my life." Jenny's teeth were chattering, too, as she watched him hang up after calling a cab company.

"I'm sorry, sugar. If there'd been any other way..."

In spite of her obvious anxiety, she had enough spunk left to glare at him. T.J. felt slightly warmed already by the di-rectness of her gaze. "I wasn't looking for an apology, T.J.," she said. "All I'm really looking for at the moment is a hot bath, preferably one that lasts for about a year."

"Sounds—good to me." T.J. was trying to hang on to the remnants of his tough-guy persona, but it was harder and harder to do, when he was so damned cold he could barely move, and was badly disconcerted by what had happened at the marina.

Haviland Ross must have contacts at the DEA, he thought. The only way the two gunmen could have tracked T.J. down so quickly was to have followed him from his meeting downtown. He was inclined to trust the man he'd contacted—the name had come from a reliable source—but there had been half a dozen other people at the meeting. If Ross *did* have friends in the Drug Enforcement Agency, he could have put the word out that he wanted to know if any-one named T.J. Madison came nosing around in the im-mediate future.

The result was that the immediate future, as far as T.J. was concerned, looked bleaker than ever. He and Jenny were virtually cut off from nearly all the sources of support T.J. should have been able to count on. He had some money left, but not a lot. And both of them were very, very cold.

Taking care of the cold was the first order of business. When the cab arrived, T.J. ignored the driver's curious looks at the two sopping-wet, shivering passengers, and asked to be taken to the nearest reasonable motel. With a shrug, the cabbie named a chain motel not far away, and T.J. nodded his agreement because his teeth were chatter-ing so hard that speaking was getting to be a real problem.

The motel was small and reassuringly quiet. T.J. asked for a room at the end of the hall, thinking that at least they'd have access to a stairway, but he knew the chances of them having been tracked here were virtually nil.

Jenny seemed to have come to that conclusion already. The instant they had locked and bolted the door behind them, she was heading for the bathroom. "You can share my bath," she said, "or you can share my shower. I don't care, but I need to get warm before my teeth clatter right out of my head, and you do, too."

He knew she was right. It wasn't the time to think about sex or modesty or anything else. They weren't about to die from hypothermia, now that they'd reached a heated room and cranked the wall unit's setting up to High. But they were both so badly chilled that sitting around in their wet clothes any longer would be pure foolishness. Telling himself he was far too close to frozen even to think about sex, anyway, T.J. stripped off his jacket and shoes and followed Jenny into the bathroom.

She had turned on the heat lamp in the ceiling already and was busy getting the water going in the big, glass-enclosed tub. By the time they had shed the rest of their sodden clothing, the small room was already filled with steam, and T.J. had to grope to find the shower curtain.

The first blast of water was so hot it hurt. T.J. swore loudly and heard Jenny's gasp as the hot water hit her cold skin.

"I never felt anything that hurt so good," she moaned.

"Maybe we should stay in here for *two* years," T.J. agreed.

They were standing very close together, both trying to soak up as much of the blessedly hot water as they could. At first T.J. told himself he was putting his arms around Jenny's waist because it was a way of maximizing the warmth. And if she was feeling as dizzy as he was from the sudden hot flood of water, a little mutual support probably wasn't a bad idea. So he clasped his hands tight around her, pulling her against him and letting the slow warmth seep into his frozen veins.

It didn't take very long before something else started seeping in, too.

Jenny seemed aware of it even before he was. She'd been making rapturous noises about the steamy shower, and he'd felt her quivering muscles gradually stop shaking, as she turned slightly from one side to the other, luxuriating in the heavenly heat. And then, suddenly, she was very quiet.

"You all right, sugar?"

He didn't realize until he heard the huskiness in his own voice that their simple embrace had already turned into much, much more. He tightened his hold on her and felt her now-warm skin slick and smooth under his palms.

"I'm all right." Her voice was as throaty as his own. "But I'm just not sure—"

She didn't finish the sentence. T.J. had lowered his face to her neck, nestling against the soft hollow of her throat. He could feel her pulse pounding close to his lips, and the sudden need to kiss her there was too powerful to resist. His mouth caressed her under the steamy waterfall of the hot shower, and he felt both of them shudder with a shared awakening that went far beyond the reasons they'd stepped in here in the first place.

I'm not sure this is the time for this. T.J. was virtually certain that had been what Jenny had started to say. His conscious mind was telling him the same thing, but it wasn't making much headway against his growing arousal, and the primitive and glorious and utterly consuming sensations of their wet bodies moving against each other under the shower.

It was more than just a physical excitement. It was the sense of having cheated death, of having survived that cold and risky plunge into the river. It was the realization that they were stranded, endangered, on their own, but by God, they were still alive—and together. That in itself was a triumph that made T.J.'s blood race. The sinuous curves of Jenny's naked body only added another layer to the excitement that was quickly building inside him.

He ran his hands upward, over her full breasts, feeling her heartbeat in his fingertips. And then he moved them down again, across her belly, along her thighs.

"Oh God, T.J. . . ."

He paused, trembling. He could feel the muscles in her legs quivering now, too, and he knew it was no longer from the cold. For an agonizingly long time he held himself still, breathing hard, trying to tell himself that now, in this light-headed and unprotected moment, making love would be a crazy thing to do.

He had a feeling Jenny was trying to tell herself the same thing. They stayed locked together under the steaming water, breathing faster with every passing second. And then Jenny gave a small moan that told him she was as deeply, as hopelessly aroused as he was. When he heard that soft, tantalizing sound, T.J. gave up even trying to pretend that he didn't want to follow this where it was leading them.

He slid his hands upward again, finding the pulsing core of her, discovering that she was as slick and wet on the inside as both of them were on the outside. The discovery made him weak in the knees. Jenny's openness, the unmistakable hunger in her responses, had always astonished him, and startled him a little, too.

He didn't find it startling now. For the first time he felt himself accepting the strength of Jenny's passion as a natural partner to his own. Maybe it was the experiences they'd shared these last few days, or the sense that they had only each other as allies now.

Whatever it was, it was shattering what was left of T.J.'s self-control. And Jenny's gasps of pleasure told him she loved what he was doing to her. Her own hands were holding him close, and her hips rocked seductively against him as he probed deeper inside her. The mutual need that cascaded through them was so strong T.J. thought it might lift the top of his head right off.

"If we're going to stop," he said, grabbing at the last shreds of sanity, "we'd better do it damn soon."

"I know." Jenny's words came out on a long indrawn breath, made shaky by desire. "But if we stop—I think—I might go crazy."

He knew exactly what she meant. The force that was pounding through them was demanding to be satisfied, refusing to be denied. And when Jenny turned in his grasp and fit herself against him, T.J. couldn't have denied it if he'd tried. He shuddered with the pure delight of her body sliding over his, and it was his turn to gasp out a wordless plea for more as she outlined his torso with her hands, surrounding the hard maleness of him with her soft, strong grip, and finally guiding him inside her, gathering him into the sweet haven of her loving.

T.J. stopped thinking, stopped doing anything at all but riding this cresting wave to its final destination. He wrapped his arms tightly around Jenny, lifting her to him, cradling her in the hot embrace of the water that was still tumbling over them.

Her arms circled his neck, her lips whispered at his ear, telling him this felt right, that they were meant to be moving together like this. T.J. turned slightly, leaning on the shower wall for support because he suddenly didn't trust his knees anymore. The erotic certainty of making love with Jenny Alvarez was surging through him like a riptide, opening him to new possibilities that were almost frightening.

Jenny's fingers bit into his shoulders, and he felt her body starting to tighten around him. He dove deeper, wanting to possess this moment with her. Everything in their two bodies quivered on the brink of an unbearable need, and then it all flared into a climax at the same instant, leaving them holding on to each other as if for life itself.

The moment drew itself out, slowly subsiding into reality again. Jenny's face was still hidden against T.J.'s shoulder. He couldn't see her expression, but if what she had felt was anything like his own response, he was pretty sure she must be sharing his own look of satisfied wonder.

Even after she had shifted her position and regained her footing on the floor of the tub again, he still couldn't see her face. He felt himself wince slightly as they separated, hating to lose the intimate contact with her. And it was only then, as he reached to pull her back into his arms, that he realized something was wrong.

There was no look of wonder on Jenny's oval face. In fact, she had her hands over it, covering her features tightly, and when he saw her shoulders shaking in spite of her obvious efforts to hold them still, he realized to his utter astonishment that she was crying.

Chapter 13

"Jenny?" He spoke cautiously, still too caught up in his own skyrocketing feelings to be able to guess what was going on. "Jenny, sugar, what's wrong?"

She shook her head. He saw the knuckles on her hands whiten and realized how tensely she was holding herself. He frowned, hauling in a deep breath, and felt doubt replacing the passion that had been filling his whole body just a moment ago.

With one arm still around Jenny, he reached out and cranked the shower control to Off. There was a pile of thick white towels within reach, and he slid the glass door open, grabbing one of them. He wrapped Jenny's quivering form in it and saw her nod slightly, as though she appreciated the gesture. Her hair was slicked back from her face, and as she finally took her hands away and tucked the towel more securely around herself, he saw that her eyes looked very wide, and achingly vulnerable.

Maybe she was just having a delayed reaction to the shock of being shot at this evening, T.J. thought fleetingly. But he rejected the idea almost immediately. There was something in her face that told him this went far beyond physical danger, far beyond the circumstances of the moment.

It obviously had something to do with him. And making love had triggered it, for some reason he didn't understand. All of a sudden he was both desperate and terrified to know what was wrong.

"Will you tell me about it, sugar?" His voice was low, but it sounded loud in the stillness of the steam-filled room.

Jenny nodded, but added huskily, "Just . . . give me two minutes, all right?"

It was T.J.'s turn to nod. He scooped up a towel for himself and grabbed their wet clothes from the floor for good measure as he headed out into the bedroom.

The heater had done its work—the place was nearly tropical in temperature by now. But in spite of the warmth, T.J. felt a growing chill deep down inside. He caught himself grumbling out loud as he laid their clothes out on the windowsill and the sofa to dry.

"I should have known better," he told himself. "I shouldn't have let any of this happen in the first place."

Something inside him was answering back, though, reminding him that just a few minutes ago he'd been reveling in the certainty that he and Jenny were made to be together. Their undeniable hunger for each other seemed to prove it. Then why, at the moment when neither of them had been able to hold back, was Jenny reacting this way?

"Damn it, hasn't it been two minutes already?" he muttered, savagely resettling the towel around his hips. He was on the point of charging back into the bathroom and demanding some answers when Jenny finally came out. Her hair was combed back and there was a slightly steadier, more determined look on her face.

T.J. sat on the edge of one of the double beds. Jenny sat on the edge of the other one. He wasn't exactly reassured by the fact that she seemed to be deliberately putting some distance between them.

Her first words weren't any more encouraging. "I've been trying to figure out how to tell you this ever since you showed up at my apartment," she said. "I guess maybe there isn't ever going to be a perfect time to do it, so I might as well just tell you now."

"Tell me *what?* For God's sake, Jenny—"

"T.J." She held up a hand. It was shaking slightly. "This is hard enough as it is. You've got to let me do it my own way, because heaven knows—" For the first time he caught a flash of buried bitterness in her voice, and in her eyes. "Heaven knows I've heard your side of things enough times already. But there's another whole side to our relationship, T.J., that you don't know anything about."

That was sobering enough to shut him up in a hurry. T.J. lowered his brows even farther as he waited for her to go on.

"What you need to be filled in on," she said, "is what really happened the last time we ... let ourselves admit how we felt about each other." She raised her chin slightly. "The time you walked out on me," she added. She seemed to be deliberately making the words blunt. "You said you disappeared because you weren't the right man for me."

"I still say that. You were sheltered, inexperienced, you weren't even out of college yet—"

She cut him off in midsentence. "I was also head over heels in love with you," she said. "I think I had been for years. You always seemed to understand how I felt, in ways that nobody else ever did. I don't know if it was because we'd both lost our mothers so young, or because we were so close when we were growing up, or—or what. All I know is that when we made love the night I turned twenty-one, it felt to me like the next natural step for us to take."

T.J. closed his eyes. He could picture so clearly how she'd looked that evening. He'd searched every women's clothing store he could find in greater D.C., until he'd come up with a dress that he knew was perfect for her. It had been deep blue velvet, almost iridescent, like moonlight on a midnight sea, and he'd been sure the moment he set eyes on it that it would make Jenny's dark eyes into pools of mystery and magic.

Seeing her in the dress had done unimaginable things to T.J. Helping her out of it, when they were alone in her apartment, had been even more agonizingly sweet.

He clenched his teeth, not wanting to think about the wave of blame and regret that had swamped him when he'd wakened next to her in the morning. He had spent a lot of effort holding that memory at bay, but Jenny was forcing him to relive it again now.

"I had no regrets about what we'd done," she said pointedly. "I didn't know where it might lead us, but I *did* know it felt right to me. And then you told me it was impossible, that we'd made a mistake, that you didn't want to go any further with what we'd started."

"It was true, damn it." T.J. muttered the words almost to himself.

"Was it?" There was that challenging tone again, as if Jenny was finally voicing thoughts she'd kept hidden deep inside for a long time. "Were you really just concerned about me, T.J., or were you scared that letting me get too close to you would threaten that precious independence of yours?"

"Jenny, for God's sake—"

Again she cut in on his words. "For *my* sake, let me finish telling you this," she said. "It doesn't really matter what your real motives were in clearing out so completely. It only matters that when I went looking for you, you were gone."

They'd been over this already, too many times, it seemed to T.J. Then why was Jenny's face so set and pale now, and her voice so tight?

"I said I didn't consider our lovemaking to have been a mistake," she said. "But we *did* make a mistake that night.

We made love without stopping to think what the consequences might be—just like we did tonight.'' For a moment she seemed to be on the verge of losing the control she was working so hard at, but with a visible effort, she hung on, and added, ''The reason I went looking for you a couple of months later was that those consequences had become... uncomfortably real.''

''Consequences?'' He repeated the word stupidly, unable to imagine what she meant.

And then, suddenly, he could.

Jenny's face told him it was true. T.J. felt his jaw slacken with shock, as though the news had physically jolted him. *We made love without stopping to think what the consequences might be—just like we did tonight....* For a moment, all he could remember clearly was that instant at the Wanderers' Rest, when he'd reached into the drawer of the bedside table to pull out the protection he'd thought to buy.

He recalled being puzzled by her silence, and the serious look on her face when he told her he didn't want to be as careless as they'd been last time. And she had said, with a sadness he hadn't understood, that she didn't want things to be the way they had been before, either.

He knew they'd been careless, that first time they'd made love. But the idea that they hadn't gotten away with the chance they'd taken—that *Jenny* hadn't gotten away with it—

''Jenny...my God....'' He had gotten to his feet without realizing he was doing it. He was staring at her now, unable to take his eyes from hers. ''Are you telling me you got pregnant?''

She nodded.

T.J. turned away, and then back again. His mind still only half comprehended what was going on. ''And I was gone,'' he said.

''Long gone.'' There was no hint of emotion in her voice.

T.J. looked up at the ceiling, at the walls, at the ridiculous spectacle of their sodden, wrinkled clothes spread out all over the motel room. None of it offered him any answers to the sudden turmoil in his mind. He felt himself gripped by an insane urge to cut loose, to get out of here, to go away by himself until he could come to terms with what Jenny had just told him.

The need to clear out was a powerful one, but he couldn't do it until he knew more about what had happened. "There isn't...any eight-year-old child in your life now," he said haltingly. "What—"

He didn't even know how to frame the sentence. This was so completely unexpected, and yet so appalling plausible. He recalled Jenny's bitter comments about how he'd walked out on his responsibilities.

And he recalled, too, her immediate reaction when he'd suggested having her pregnant colleague take over some of Jenny's workload while Jenny was away. *A woman needs lots of rest, extra rest, when she's expecting a child,* she'd said. She'd been more than just concerned in a friendly way, he thought. She'd been edgy about the subject, almost panicky.

How much rest had Jenny had during her own pregnancy? T.J. had been the only person in the world she considered family, and he had cut and run, making sure she wouldn't find him. And she'd been a shy college senior, hardly a woman of the world. None of that made T.J. any more eager to hear what she had to say next.

But he had to know. He forced himself to sit back down on the bed and clenched his jaw hard in the silence between them.

Jenny's voice had that same almost neutral quality when she finally spoke. "I didn't have a good pregnancy," she said, confirming his fears. "I had to drop out of school, because I was sick so much. I had some money—thank God—from the trust fund your father left me. But it wasn't much, and I had to get another place to live, which left me pretty strapped for funds.''

"Why did you have to get another place to live?"

"My two roommates were studying for their senior year," she said. "They weren't really close friends of mine, and they couldn't cope with a sick, pregnant dropout in an apartment that was already too small."

He remembered the apartment in detail, although he'd only been there once. Jenny's two roommates had been gone for spring break the one time he'd visited. At the time, he'd seen it as providential.

"I figured I would have the baby in the fall and try to pick up my last three courses again in the spring," Jenny said. "I thought I could look after her—the ultrasound had showed it was a girl—and still finish my degree."

For the first time she hesitated, and her steady gaze wavered a little. T.J. wondered how many times she had rehearsed saying these words out loud to him. He wondered if she'd ever said them out loud to anyone else. He wondered what would happen if he invited Jenny to take a swing at him right now, because it was only the very beginning of what he deserved.

"It turned out that I didn't have to worry about long-range plans," she said at last. T.J.'s jawbone ached from the way he was holding it, but he managed to keep himself silent, waiting, letting Jenny tell this at her own speed. Her words had gaps in them now, and he could hear the emotion showing through.

"The baby was born too early, in August. She wasn't impossibly premature, but because I hadn't been healthy, she wasn't, either."

T.J. could hear a lot of things she wasn't telling him: the anguish of going through with the pregnancy alone; the stress of trying to find him, only to discover he'd taken off for Timbuktu and points east; the shock of losing the one person she'd always counted on, the man she'd come to

love, the father of her child, at the moment when she'd
needed him most—

It didn't take a genius to figure out why she'd had a difficult pregnancy. Or why the baby had been born early, and
not strong. T.J. closed his eyes and said grimly, "What
happened to her, Jenny?"

"She died. In December."

He wasn't as prepared as he'd thought for the words. He
closed his eyes again and fought against the agony that was
suddenly rocking him from inside.

Five short months of life, T.J. thought. He'd started a
new life and then walked—no, run—away from it. Jenny
wasn't coming right out and saying so, but he knew with
absolute certainty that if he'd stayed around, the story she
was telling him might very well have had a happier ending.

As it was, it was the story of a life cut pitifully short, and
another life—Jenny's—shadowed by a tragedy that didn't
need to have happened. T.J. thought of the two years he'd
spent sailing from one exotic port to the next, telling himself over and over that he'd done the right thing in breaking
things off. She would find another man, one who could give
her the kind of steady domestic life she deserved. That had
been his consolation for the lonely nights he'd spent, thinking about her, longing to be with her.

Lonely! He almost laughed at the idea now. What right
had he had to feel noble and self-sacrificing—and lonely—
when back at home, Jenny had been living with the consequences of what the two of them had started together?

"I named her Joy." Jenny seemed to be finishing her story
now. Her voice was definitely shaking, but she managed to
keep it under control as she added, "She was a beautiful
baby, T.J. She had the biggest dark eyes. After she died, I
went on doing things in a kind of fog for a long time. I finished my degree, without really noticing that I was doing it.
I worked in a law office for a while, and eventually I started
to...come to terms with what had happened. Finally I went

back to grad school and got qualified as a psychotherapist. I've worked a lot with bereavement counselling—I guess it's been a way of putting my own experience to use.''

All of a sudden T.J. couldn't stand it anymore. He could see in her eyes that despite the pain she obviously still felt, she *had* come to terms with the birth and death of their daughter. That explained the poised maturity that had struck him the moment he'd set eyes on her, back in Charlotte.

The problem was, it was all too new to him. He couldn't even begin to come to terms with something as raw as the news that he'd fathered a child and left Jenny to deal with its arrival and its painful departure, all on her own. He felt like the most complete and utter bastard on the face of the earth, and suddenly he needed to be somewhere—anywhere—away from here, away from the wounded look in Jenny's dark eyes.

He stood up again, even though he knew there was nowhere for him to go. His feet felt restless—hell, *all* of him felt restless. He knew the feeling only too well. It was what had propelled him out of Jenny's life once before.

If he'd stayed, their daughter might not have died. Or at least Jenny would have had his help in coping with the grief and loss of it.

He fought against the idea, but it kept coming back at him. All his life he had tried to stay as mobile as he could, had tried to write his own rules. He had always felt stronger, more capable when he was on his own.

Jenny's words made him question every rule he'd ever made for himself. He'd seen himself as so strong, leaving her the way he had. Now it seemed that *she* had been the strong one, not T.J. It made him wonder how many other things about his life might not be as solid as he'd always thought.

Suddenly he couldn't stand it. He was used to action, damn it. Standing around questioning the fundamentals of his life made him want to climb the walls.

He looked around the room again. His clothes were still soaking wet. It would take an hour, at least, before they were dry enough to wear. And even if he *did* have dry clothes, he asked himself, where the hell was he planning to go? He had no means of transportation, a rapidly dwindling supply of cash, and bad guys in at least two powerful government agencies doing their level best to kill him. And then there was Jenny to consider—Jenny, and the fact that in those few sweet moments of passion in the shower just a little while ago, they had been courting exactly the same kind of consequences that she had just spelled out for him now.

"You want to take off, don't you?"

Her voice was surprisingly level. He wondered if she'd gotten used to pushing past the emotional flash points in her life, used to coping in spite of the pain. He wondered how long it took before one *could* get used to something like that.

The hell of it was, she was right. He did want to take off. And he couldn't. For the first time in his adult life, he was absolutely rooted in one spot, physically and otherwise, and he was going to have to figure out a way to deal with it.

"Being on the move is like a reflex action with me," he said, not sure if he was explaining this to Jenny or to himself. "It always has been."

"I know that, T.J."

"I always thought it gave me breathing room and flexibility. And options. Good things like that."

"And now?" She paused. "What do you think now?"

He could feel himself getting mad, because he was boxed in and he didn't know what to think. "I don't know," he admitted gruffly. "Saying 'I'm sorry' just seems so damned inadequate. And I don't know what else to say. Not yet."

"I understand that, T.J. I've had years to absorb it. I didn't expect you to do it in ten minutes." She looked down at his hands, clenched into fists, and T.J. wondered if she was thinking suddenly of the erotic caresses they'd shared just half an hour before. Things had seemed so simple, only that short time ago, he thought savagely.

"I need some time to think this through." He didn't mean the words to come out so abruptly, but the truth was that he was at a complete loss and had no idea what his next move was going to be.

Jenny looked disappointed—or was it his own sudden contempt for himself that made him think that was what her expression meant? Whatever she was really thinking, she seemed content to give him the time he'd asked for—no, demanded. Her apparent understanding only made him feel like more of a prize heel.

"There isn't a lot of breathing room in here," she pointed out.

"No kidding." He growled the two words.

"But I'm willing to let the subject drop, if you really want to."

She definitely did sound disappointed. And she was tossing the ball clearly into his court, which he supposed she had every right to do. It didn't do anything to calm the hellish sense of responsibility inside him.

Everything in his bones and his blood was telling him that the best thing he could do for her now was to get out of her way. And the story she'd just told him proved beyond any possible doubt that taking off had been the worst possible response the last time they'd made love. And this time—

He couldn't stand it. He needed to absorb this shock, and to rearrange his personal universe around it. He couldn't do that while he was just a few feet away from Jenny and her steady, questioning stare.

He put a hand on her elbow and pulled her up until she was standing facing him. Even that small contact made his body ache for her, but this time he had no difficulty clamping down on his instinctive response.

"If it happens again—" How the hell did one say this gracefully? he wondered. Maybe there was no graceful way to do it. Maybe it was time to stop feeling as though he ought to be anything but the rough-and-tumble wanderer he really was.

"If there are... consequences to our making love just now," he finally managed to say, "I won't walk out on you again, Jenny. I promise you that."

He'd meant the words to reassure her. The hurt that passed across her face startled and dismayed him.

"Don't promise me things, all right, T.J.?" There was real anguish in her voice now, in spite of its softness. "You always used to tell me that everything would work out fine, when I was little. And I believed you. And then, when things *didn't* work out... you were gone."

T.J. ground his back molars together and tightened his grip on Jenny's elbow. There was no good answer to what she'd just said, so he didn't try to offer one.

"If something happens this time, and you stick around, then I'll be able to believe you," she went on. "But until then—please don't make promises. I wanted to tell you about the baby, and I'm glad you know about her now. But what you do with that is your decision, not mine."

T.J. let her go abruptly and moved toward the window. He didn't know what to say. He didn't know what he was going to do now. He wished he knew some way to force his wet clothes to dry faster so he could hit the streets and walk off some of the excess energy that was crowding in on him. He wished he could rewind the last eight years and get it right this time.

He didn't have a single answer, damn it. And he was naked except for this damned bath towel, and trapped in a motel room with a woman whose beauty and honesty and unhappiness were beginning to scare the stuffing out of him. T.J. growled and turned back to face her.

"When the clothes are dry, maybe we can go out and get something to eat," he said. The words sounded ridiculously ordinary, coming out of the emotional turmoil in side him. But at least he was offering her something—some small assurance that at least for the moment, he wasn't running true to form, walking out on her when things got difficult.

"All right." Her voice was small, and neutral again now. "Until then, I need to think."

"Me, too. And I'm feeling . . . cold again, for some reason. I think I'll run a bath and soak for a while."

What she really meant, T.J. thought, was that being cooped up together in the same room was too difficult for both of them. He listened to the sound of water splashing into the tub, and tried not to think of their two bodies so passionately entwined under the shower, and cursed himself for being three different kinds of a fool all at the same time.

By the time Jenny had soaked in the tub for an hour, she felt almost restored to calm again. In fact, there was a sense of relief that finally, after all these years, she had shared her secret with the most important person in her life.

But that only opened up new questions. The power of their lovemaking, and the intensity of the bond that still existed between them, only proved beyond any doubt that T.J. *was* still important in her life—even more important than she'd been letting herself admit. And she had no idea where they were headed after this dangerous adventure was over—assuming they both walked away from it unscathed.

Would the story of Joy's birth and death bind them more closely together? Or would it be an even more pressing reason for T.J. to clear out of her life again? She sighed as she toweled herself dry, wishing she could look into the future.

The immediate future seemed to hold the prospect of food. She could smell it as she stepped out of the bathroom, and she recalled hearing voices at the door not long ago. T.J. had obviously ordered out, and Jenny was suddenly glad he had. Not only was she ravenous, but the simple domestic act of sitting down and eating a meal together would be a welcome change from the highly charged emotional moments they'd just shared.

Better yet, their clothes seemed to be dry, or mostly dry. T.J. had put on his jeans and shirt, and Jenny gladly climbed into her own clothes, not minding their slight dampness. She wasn't sure how much more time she could have stood being cooped up with T.J. with both of them wearing nothing but bath towels, especially after the scalding passion of their lovemaking in the shower. Clothing wasn't much of a barrier to the feelings they stirred in one another, but it was better than nothing at all.

"At least we're back in a part of the world where I know how to find the decent Chinese restaurants." T.J. was busy setting out the food as Jenny dressed. He was being deliberately casual now, she thought. And he was very deliberately not looking her way as she dropped the bath towel and wriggled into her jeans.

Well, they'd both agreed that he would need some time to come to terms with what she'd just told him. She acknowledged the little bubble of disappointment that welled up in her chest when she saw him focusing so fixedly on the containers of Chinese food rather than on her. And then she set it aside, telling herself firmly that it wouldn't help to let their feelings race out of control again so soon. And besides, she was hungry.

"I've been thinking," T.J. said, as he served some rice onto a paper plate and handed it to Jenny. "It's clear that Haviland Ross has some kind of contact within the DEA, and that somebody tipped him off about my being here."

"I wondered if that was what happened."

"It seems pretty conclusive. And that means I don't dare contact them again. Which leads to the obvious question—who in this whole wide world can I really trust enough to ask for help in nailing General Ross?"

"I suppose you—we—have to nail him, if we're going to put an end to this."

"I don't fancy spending the rest of my life hiding out, sugar, any more than you do. And the money supply is running low, anyway. As soon as I have to get access to more money, they'll be able to pick up my trail again. I—we—need to do something before that happens."

"Have you come up with anything?"

"I think so. You remember me mentioning James Wilder?"

James Wilder, Jenny recalled, was the old friend of Colonel Madison who had gotten T.J. his job with military intelligence in the first place. She remembered him visiting the Madison house once or twice a year, although she'd never known him well.

"Slightly," she said. "I assume he's one of the people you really trust in this whole wide world."

T.J. stopped with a bite of beef and noodles halfway to his lips. He put his fork down again and looked searchingly at her for the first time since she'd come out of the bathroom. "He's one of the very few," he said slowly. "Wilder, and a couple of other older guys who knew my father. And you, of course."

He wasn't going to reopen the subject of their lost child tonight, Jenny thought. He'd been serious about wanting some time to rearrange his thoughts about their shared past. But the steady directness of his gaze was telling her wordlessly that she still played an important role in his life, just as he did in hers. She put a hand over his briefly and squeezed, and his dark brows lowered a little.

"We're in this together, this time," he said gruffly.

"Good. I want to see this through, T.J. I want to see . . . what comes next."

He nodded once and turned his attention back to his dinner and his plans for tomorrow. "I called Jim Wilder while you were in the bath," he said. "He's already agreed to help, and to line us up some support. I think—and Wilder agrees—that we're only going to have one shot at surprising Haviland Ross. So here's the way I figure it's going to have to go..."

Chapter 14

The sun was still high enough to light the February sky, but as it got closer to the horizon, the warmth of the afternoon was fading. Jenny burrowed into her jacket in the front seat of the rental car and wished they could turn the heater on.

They couldn't, of course. Two people sitting in a car on this pleasant suburban street were already courting neighborhood observation. To have kept the car idling would only have called more attention to their presence here. "We don't want any more cops taking notice of us, if we can help it," T.J. had said, reminding Jenny inescapably of that first kiss they'd shared the night they'd fled Charlotte in her car.

It was clear from his manner that there was no chance of his attention straying toward sensuality this evening. He'd been resolutely businesslike all day, and now that they were actually sitting one street away from where General Ross lived, she could feel T.J. gearing up to a pitch of concentration that told her only too clearly how critical the next hour was likely to be.

"Ross is a widower," he'd told her, as he'd outlined his plan last night. "Lives by himself in a nice house in the suburbs. He rides the train in to the Pentagon every day and tends to show up at home at around the same time every evening."

It was almost that time now. Jenny shivered a little, watching the sun inch closer to the rooftops of the neatly kept single-family bungalows. General Ross's neighbors took care in tending their lawns and gardens, just as Colonel Madison had once done. It was hard to imagine the pleasant cul-de-sac as the home base of a man powerful and desperate enough to have called out the cold-blooded assassins who had been tracking T.J. and Jenny for days now.

They had rented the car at the airport this morning and had used it to drive casually around Haviland Ross's neighborhood. There was no protected place to sit on Ross's own street, but the next street over was slightly higher, and a convenient gap between two houses gave a view of the general's house, slightly obscured by the branches of a budding apple tree.

T.J. had declared the spot perfect for their purposes. "You won't really need to see the house itself, anyway," he said. "Mostly you'll be monitoring me by listening."

After visiting the car rental agency, they had stopped at an electronics store in a mall and bought the rest of the supplies T.J. had decided they needed: a microcassette tape recorder and a tiny, voice-actuated walkie-talkie transmitter and receiver. The tape recorder was in T.J.'s shirt pocket now, under his jacket, loaded with a brand-new cassette and ready to go. The transmitter was in his jacket. The receiver was already in James Wilder's car.

T.J. had a gun with him, too. Wilder had produced it for him from somewhere, and it was tucked into a shoulder holster against his body. Jenny knew it was a sensible precaution. But she still hated the idea of it.

"I still think you would take somebody else in with you," she said to T.J. now. "What if Ross takes one look at you and pulls a gun?"

"I don't think that'll happen." It could, Jenny knew. And T.J. knew it, too. She hated to watch the deliberate way he calculated the risk and decided it was worth taking. "And, anyway, I plan to get the first word in. Once I do, Ross should be interested enough in knowing what kind of proof I've got that he'll at least want to keep me talking for a while."

And the plan was that in talking, Haviland Ross would let slip something that would confirm what T.J. and Jenny had already figured out about his criminal activities. "It doesn't have to stand up in a court of law," T.J. was saying. "It just has to be enough to get the military to start a full-scale investigation, one that Ross won't be able to pull strings to stop. He can't have covered his trail completely, all these years. One slip is all we need."

It was still a risk, and Jenny knew it. But she also knew that T.J. was probably right to force the issue now, to get this settled once and for all. She'd wakened in the motel bed this morning thinking she was home in her own bedroom. When she'd realized she wasn't—and that T.J. had spent the night in the other double bed, carefully keeping his distance—she'd been filled with an overwhelming longing to be done with this and to go back to her old life, or ahead to a new one.

Whichever it was going to be, it couldn't happen until something was done about Haviland Ross. And much as Jenny hated to admit it, anything they did was likely to involve some risk. At least T.J. wasn't trying to operate completely on his own this time.

She heard the sound of a car's engine behind them and half turned in her seat to see the sight she'd expected: an inconspicuous brown sedan pulling alongside them. It didn't stop. T.J. and James Wilder had decided that two cars sitting doing nothing would be even more likely to attract attention than one. The brown sedan cruised sedately past, with the barest flick of T.J.'s index finger to indicate he'd seen them. The other car, and the three men in it, would be there when T.J. radioed them that Haviland Ross had arrived home.

The face in the driver's window was familiar to Jenny. She remembered James Wilder, and the two marine officers with him, visiting Colonel Madison from time to time. Generally the men would spend their time reminiscing in Colonel Madison's study, so they hadn't been a big part of Jenny's early life. But she was sure T.J. was right to trust these men, and it felt reassuring to see them now.

People were starting to come home to their houses, she noticed. Lights were going on in the attractive bungalows. Cars passed them more frequently. If things went according to plan, it wouldn't be long before Haviland Ross, too, would arrive home from work to find T.J. waiting for him.

Just as he'd been waiting for Jenny, only a few days ago. She felt as though her entire world had been overturned since then. And the worst of it was that she simply couldn't imagine how she would face it if T.J. went out of her life again, if he told her he couldn't, after all, see any way her need for a home and family could fit with his restless spirit.

Impulsively, she turned to him, wanting to share her thoughts before Haviland Ross showed up. If something went wrong—if this was her last chance to tell T.J. how she really felt—

The possibility was almost too appalling to be faced. But she felt its urgency inside her as she put a hand on T.J.'s arm and said, "T.J., if this...goes well—if Ross does incriminate himself somehow and you manage to get him off your back—"

He turned to her sharply, obviously making an effort to drag his attention away from the front door of Haviland Ross's house, which he had been watching like a hawk. "It isn't a good time for this, Jenny," he said.

"It might be the only time we have." Something might go wrong with his plan, she thought. Or he might, when it was over, simply pull up the tentative roots he'd started to put down with her, and sail off over the horizon again. Suddenly she couldn't stand not knowing if that was a possibility.

"If things work out, what are you going to do next?" she asked. She had felt herself shaking inside ever since they'd stopped the car here, thinking of how close they were to the source of so much danger. The shaking intensified a little as she waited for T.J.'s answer to her question.

His eyes were back on Ross's front door as he replied. "I never know what I'm going to do next," he said shortly. "I told you, the CID tends to hand me one crazy job after another."

"Then you're definitely planning on staying with the CID." She phrased it as a statement, not a question.

His brows lowered, and he drummed his broad fingertips against the steering wheel. "Do we have to decide right now?" he asked.

Jenny took a deep breath. "Something could very easily go wrong with this plan of yours, T.J.," she said. "You know it could. And if it does—"

"Hey, sugar." He turned back to her, and the sudden, brilliant grin he gave her made her heart turn over. She loved this man, she thought suddenly. She loved him more than she'd ever loved another human being. Just a glance from his gold-speckled eyes could make her spirits soar and her blood race.

And he was only looking at her that way now because he was trying to convince her that he could walk into a poten-

tially explosive situation and come out of it again un-
harmed. As though that were the only kind of danger she
was worried about.

Before he could offer the kind of familiar, cavalier comment that she just knew was rising to his lips, Jenny leaned
over and kissed him, briefly. She could tell that the gesture
startled him. His eyes darkened suddenly, and she thought
he almost moved to pull her into his arms and continue what
she'd started, only to catch himself at the last instant.

"I know this isn't the time to talk about the future," she
said quickly, urgently. "But if something happens to you in
there, T.J., I want to know that I've at least said this to
you."

"Said what?" His breathing was more rapid now, and his
gaze wasn't getting any less dark. Those seductive gold
flecks were crowded right to the very edges of his eyes,
making them glitter even more intensely.

"You were the first man I ever loved. I'm beginning to
realize that, for all practical purposes, you've really been the
only one. I don't know how that fits into your view of your
own life, T.J., but I have to be honest with you. If you disappear again after this is over—if you try to tell me we don't
belong together, after everything we've been through—"

She wasn't exactly sure where her words were headed.
What she really wanted to say was *If you leave me again,
don't bother to come back next time.* But the bluntness of
it almost frightened her, and so did the thunder in T.J.'s
darkened gaze.

He was silent for a few seconds, nearly glaring at her.
Then he looked up at the roof of the car, and finally straight
ahead out the windshield. "What the hell kind of a father
would I have been for that little girl?" he asked.

She couldn't tell if he expected an answer, or if he was
speaking to her or to himself. She thought hard and quickly,

and then said, "Nobody ever knows what kind of a parent they'll be until they plunge in and try it, T.J."

"Most people plunge in deliberately. They at least have some idea they're going to *be* parents."

"Not everyone. Accidents happen."

"Accidents!" He said the word bitterly. He'd been thinking this over, Jenny realized. But she couldn't tell what he'd decided. And maybe he hadn't decided anything at all. She saw uncertainty in his eyes as he met her gaze again. "I don't know how to be part of a family, Jenny," he said. She could hear just a hint of vulnerability in his tone, a glimmer of that softness he tried so hard to hide. "I never did. You know that."

"You could learn," she said. "Or you could make the kind of family you want to be a part of. There are lots of different ways to look at it, T.J."

He swiveled his gaze to the windshield again. "I wouldn't have the first damn idea how to be anybody's father," he said. Once again, he was almost muttering, speaking his thoughts out loud experimentally, she thought. "My own father—well, hell, you remember, sugar. His idea of parenting was to discipline me for what I'd done wrong and leave me pretty much alone the rest of the time."

"I remember." Jenny remembered, too, T.J.'s pitched battles with his father over Colonel Madison's very strict ideas of what was right and wrong. Had T.J.'s own rebellious past soured him permanently on the whole idea of family life? It was beginning to sound as though it had.

"I had the same upbringing you did," she reminded him gently. "And somehow I came out of it believing that it should be possible to have a very different kind of family. And somehow—" She had to work at keeping her voice level. "Somehow that was always tied up in my mind with the thought of you. T.J.—"

She saw him start, as though her words had shaken him. A moment later, though, she realized that it was something outside the car that had caught his attention.

"We're going to have to talk about this later, sugar. Old Haviland Ross just showed up."

He was on the move already, reaching for the door handle and automatically checking his pockets for the equipment he'd stowed there. Jenny winced when she saw his big palm glance over the spot where the shoulder holster was. It looked like a gesture he'd used many times before.

"Just make sure there *is* a later so we can talk about it, all right?"

She felt compelled to say the words, but she wasn't sure T.J. really heard them. He leaned over very briefly and touched her lips with his own, but at the same time he was reaching for the small microphone that would let him transmit his words to the listening men in the other car. Jenny watched him install it in his collar and check in the rearview mirror to make sure his slightly shaggy dark brown hair covered any sign of it.

And then he was out the car door, sparing her one quick wave of his hand. Jenny felt her throat tighten with anxiety as she watched him striding down the slope between the two houses they were parked in front of, heading for the home of Haviland Ross.

He would be radioing to James Wilder that the general was here, she knew. And sure enough, even before T.J. had reached Ross's front door, the brown sedan with the three men in it came cruising along the street. It stopped just ahead of the rental car, and Jenny wasted no time in joining the men in the other vehicle. Their greetings were brief; all of them were already concentrating on whatever sounds might come out of the small receiver that sat on James Wilder's dashboard.

"I'm ringing the front doorbell." T.J.'s voice sounded loud and sudden. Jenny didn't need to be told that he was ringing Haviland Ross's doorbell; from her vantage point in the back seat, she could see him through the screening branches of the apple tree. A moment later, she watched the door open and wondered if the three men in the car with her were all holding their breath the way she was. This was the moment the rest of the scene depended on, they all realized.

And T.J. played it like the pro Jenny knew he was. "General Ross," his voice said, slightly tinny through the little receiver. "I'm T.J. Madison. I believe you've been looking for me." Without giving the general time to answer, he added, "I've got some pretty convincing proof of how you've been feathering your nest all these years, General, but before I do anything with it, I thought it might be wise for us to talk."

Jenny could see the uniformed general over T.J.'s right shoulder now. He was in his sixties, she judged, patrician and white-haired, and a good three inches taller than T.J. He was hesitating at the door as though he suspected he wasn't getting the whole story.

The little transmitter T.J. had bought was designed only to relay the words of the person wearing it. Jenny and the others wouldn't be able to hear what General Ross said, and she found it frustrating now to see the general speaking and not to know what he was saying.

T.J.'s reply, though, made it clear. "You can see I'm alone," he said, gesturing over his shoulder at the street. Jenny saw Ross's eyes rake the nearby surroundings, but fortunately he didn't seem to notice the brown sedan behind the sheltering branches of the tree one street over. She let out a sigh of mingled tension and relief as the general opened the door wider and invited T.J. in.

"So far, so good," James Wilder said.

"Now for the *really* tricky part," one of the other men agreed.

They had already discussed their plan in detail. T.J. would engage the general in conversation, trying to get Ross to compromise himself somehow. Once that had been accomplished, or if T.J. felt the situation was growing dangerous somehow, he would signal to the listeners in the car to back him up. Ross might be prepared to shoot T.J. himself, they had reasoned, but a backup team of three credible marine officers, plus Jenny, would—with luck—be enough to convince Haviland Ross that violence wasn't going to work in his favor this time.

Jenny hadn't anticipated just how torturous it would be to sit in the surveillance car knowing that T.J. was striding into Haviland Ross's living room. And listening to his casual tone of voice, when she knew the danger he was in, only made it worse.

"I guess you've collected both copies of Pete Alvarez's diary by now," he was saying, through the receiver. "One in his daughter's apartment, one off my boat." There was a pause while the general spoke, and then T.J. said, "No, of course I know that. No court in the country is going to convict on the basis of what Pete wrote, poor bastard. You made sure nobody would take him seriously, didn't you?"

General Ross didn't seem to have an answer for that one. T.J. went on almost immediately, "The diary was enough to point me in the right direction, though. And once I started looking around, I turned up another witness who'll be a lot more believable in the witness stand."

He was saying *I* and *me* again, as though he'd done this all on his own, Jenny noticed. It made her angry to think about it, especially when she'd been beside him every step of the way, helping him out as much as he'd helped her.

And it had been Jenny, not T.J., who'd placed the call to her colleague Patricia in Charlotte this morning. A lot of

Patricia's clients were Vietnam vets who'd come home addicted to one substance or another, and Jenny had wanted to know—within the limits of confidentiality, of course—whether any of these men had ever mentioned to Patricia that American army personnel might be involved in the trafficking of narcotics.

"As a matter of fact," Patricia had said slowly, "there was a guy I worked with a few years ago. I always thought he was being paranoid, insisting that there were high-level military officers getting rich off the heroin trade. This guy is completely straightened around now, as far as I know. Let me call him and see if he's willing to tell me anything." And she'd wanted to know, before hanging up, "Jenny, are you all right? Where in heaven's name *are* you, anyway? And when are you coming back?"

Jenny had reassured her friend as thoroughly as she could, and added, "How are *you*? Are you feeling okay?"

"Surprisingly, I am. I think I'm finally getting the hang of this pregnancy business. You just put your feet up and keep them there, and the rest of the world rushes to do things for you."

"See? I told you that was how it was supposed to work."

Jenny's voice had been light as she said goodbye to Patricia, but her heart had ached at the contrast between Patricia's experience of pregnancy and her own as she'd described it to T.J. last night.

All of that was still churning around inside her as she sat in James Wilder's car and listened to T.J. telling Haviland Ross what Patricia's client had said.

"Turns out Pete and my father weren't the only ones with their suspicions about you," he was saying. "We've got at least one other witness who's pretty bitter about the years it took him to get cleaned up after his Vietnam experience. He'll be more than happy to testify to what he knows about the officers who were running the heroin traffic. Or should I say, the officers who are *still* running it?''

There was a very long pause this time. Jenny wished desperately that she knew whether Haviland Ross was speaking, or just reacting silently to what T.J. had said.

''Is that true?'' one of the men in the car wanted to know. ''Is Ross still involved in the drug trade?''

''He seems to be,'' James Wilder muttered. ''Apparently the DEA has suspected something like this was going on for some time. But they couldn't track it down, because there's somebody in their own organization who's been passing information along to Ross. And Ross had access to a few military intelligence boys who didn't mind working for him on the sly, because he paid so well out of his heroin profits.''

The other two men shook their heads disgustedly. ''Oughta shoot him right on the spot,'' one of them said. ''The man doesn't deserve the uniform he's wearing.''

''He's not the only one involved,'' Jenny pointed out. ''T.J. wants to make sure they're all stopped.''

T.J.'s voice broke back into their conversation. ''What *kind* of a deal?'' was all he said, but it was enough to make Jenny and the three men with her sit up very straight.

The silence this time was excruciatingly long. Jenny leaned forward slightly in the back seat, as if by getting a little closer to the small receiver on the dashboard she would be able to figure out what was going on.

They'd hoped this might happen. Haviland Ross's career—and his freedom—were at an end if his illegal drug dealings were made public. But right now, he felt he still had leverage. He still had things to offer a potential partner, and he seemed to be offering them to T.J. now. And if he was making a concrete offer, the chances were good that he was incriminating himself in the process.

''You're talking some pretty big money, General,'' T.J. was saying, his voice sounding neutral, perhaps interested, perhaps not. And then, a few seconds later, "I won't say I'm not interested. Problem is, I have this ethical thing about not wanting to cash in on the habits of a lot of desperate people. Or doesn't that bother you, after a while?"

"Careful, T.J.," Jenny murmured. "Don't get him mad too soon."

The small cassette recorder in T.J.'s shirt pocket would be recording both sides of the conversation, she knew. And she prayed that T.J. was savvy enough in this kind of situation that he wouldn't do anything rash until he had some kind of proof on the tape that Ross was, in fact, at the head of the heroin ring. But still—

T.J.'s next words confirmed her lurking fear that his hot head could get him into trouble yet. "Say that again," he said. His voice was still neutral, but there was something in the way he phrased the words that made Jenny think Haviland Ross had just said something that had gotten under T.J.'s skin.

A pause. And then there was a definite challenge in T.J.'s voice as he said, "Are you telling me you offered my father the same deal you just offered me? To shut up in exchange for a share in the profits?"

The pause this time was brief. "So that's why you shot him," T.J. said, tightly now. Another short pause. "What are you talking about?"

What *was* Ross talking about? Jenny's eyes flicked from the distant house to the box on the dashboard, desperately wishing she could fill in the blanks.

"He was a recluse because he wasn't well." T.J.'s voice sounded even tighter now. He hadn't expected what he was hearing, Jenny thought. His words were quieter now, as he said, "And he died because his heart gave out on him. If you expect me to believe otherwise—"

They were talking about Colonel Madison, Jenny realized. All three men in the car with her were leaning forward as intently as she was, puzzling over this reference to their old friend.

"You bastard." T.J.'s voice was nothing more than a whisper. "You smooth-talking bastard. And I just bet you've got an alibi all ready, haven't you?"

"An alibi for what?" Jenny wondered out loud.

"I say we go in," one of the men said. "T.J.'s starting to sound pretty edgy."

"He hasn't given the signal yet," James Wilder pointed out.

The signal was simply Wilder's name. Jenny found herself aching to hear him say it, but what she heard was much, much worse. "You're going down in flames for this, Ross," he said. "I don't know whether you're telling me the truth, but if you can sit there and even hint to me that you caused my father's death—"

A dozen desperate thoughts swirled through Jenny's mind. It was obvious that Ross's hints or revelations about Colonel Madison's death had rattled T.J. Had he let his guard down too far? Jenny felt a powerful urge to burst out of the back seat of the car and head for the house that looked so sedate on the outside and was full of such threat on the inside.

"By God," T.J. was saying now, "if you even think of touching a hair on Jenny's head—"

"T.J., no..." She said the words involuntarily. Haviland Ross must be threatening her now, and if there was any faster way to make T.J. lose his cool, she didn't know what it was.

"Steady, Jenny," James Wilder murmured.

She tried to tell herself she should listen to him, that T.J. had been in tight spots before now and had always come out of them more or less unscathed. But he'd never faced down a man who was intimately bound up with T.J.'s own past. He wasn't used to confronting the darker questions about his own life, as Jenny knew only too well. Faced with emotions he wasn't comfortable with, his overwhelming impulse had always been to clear out, to charge into action, to do something wild and reckless.

What was he doing now, with Haviland Ross obviously dredging up what seemed to be new truths about the past and new threats for the future? She couldn't stand the agony of not knowing.

There was nothing from the receiver for what felt like forever. And then there were two short, taut phrases.

"All right, they're up. Just leave her out of—"

Jenny dug her fingernails into her palms, waiting for the rest of the sentence. It didn't come. The receiver, in fact, suddenly sounded dead. Even the faint background hum they'd been listening to was gone now.

"Sounds like we've lost him." Wilder's voice was as tense as T.J.'s had been a moment ago. "Maybe we should—Jenny, wait!"

Jenny couldn't wait. She had heard anger in T.J.'s tone, and a kind of resignation that startled her. But there had been fear, too, and that was enough to get her out of the back seat of the car and moving fast across the lawn between her and the house where T.J. might be facing death at any moment.

All right, they're up... What could that refer to, except his hands? Jenny's imagination was filling in the gaps in the conversation as she ran, ignoring the shouts of the men behind her, and the three other slamming car doors that followed hers. *Get your hands up where I can see them....* Had those been General Ross's orders, cutting T.J. off from the gun he wore? If T.J. had obeyed the order, it must be because Ross had come up with a weapon of his own. And the sudden silence from the transmitter must mean that it had been disconnected.

If that was the case, it probably meant Ross had found the tape recorder, too. The damning proof T.J. had risked so much to record was in imminent danger of destruction, if Ross had laid his hands on it.

But even that wasn't what was spurring Jenny on to the fastest sprint of her life, across the lawns and the street where Haviland Ross lived. It was the thought of T.J. dying—of the split second it would take for a bullet to end his life.

The front door was unlocked. She pulled it open and threw herself into the front foyer, following the sound of low voices from somewhere in the house.

They weren't in the living room, as she'd expected. The voices seemed to be coming from down a half flight of stairs, and she headed that way, calling out T.J.'s name as she went. She had just rounded the doorway into a book-lined study when she heard a noise she recognized with sickening clarity.

It was a gunshot, muffled by a silencer. She'd heard it too often in the days since T.J. had barreled back into her life, but it had never frightened her more than it did now.

She rocked to a standstill in the door, just in time to see T.J. diving out of the way and the tall, white-haired general looking up, clearly startled, to see who else had invaded his house.

In a second Jenny had taken in the details: the lethal weapon in General Ross's right hand, T.J.'s gun on the desk, the tape recorder and transmitter lying next to it. Ross held all the cards at the moment, she realized. The only thing she had on her side was surprise.

"If you shoot him, you'll have to shoot all of us," she said breathlessly, hoping that James Wilder and his two colleagues would show up in the next few seconds. But they were older men, not in as good shape as they'd once been, and they hadn't had Jenny's gut-level fear to inspire their race toward the house. Would they get here before the murderous rage in Haviland Ross's blue eyes spelled death for T.J. or Jenny or both of them?

"Jenny, get the hell out of here!" There was rage in T.J.'s eyes, too, and it all seemed to be directed at her. He had landed behind a heavy oak desk, nearly spitting the words out in his fury. She shook her head, clamping down against the fear that churned in her stomach and made her wonder if she could trust her own legs at this point.

"It's too late," she said, directing the words at Haviland Ross. The general was standing with his weapon leveled, but he hadn't pulled the trigger again, and that gave Jenny some hope. "We've got help coming. They've called the police." She hoped to God they had followed that part of the plan. "If you shoot him—"

She couldn't finish the sentence. Haviland Ross's gun swerved from T.J.'s direction to hers, and she saw T.J.'s gold-studded eyes following the moving barrel as though it were a snake charmer's pipe.

"Jenny, for God's sake—" His voice was hoarse.

Again she shook her head. "This can't help," she said to General Ross. "Shooting either one of us can't help you now."

She was only barely aware of T.J. moving, of his strong body hurtling through the air between them and his arms catching her around the knees, tackling her with a ferocity that drove her back out into the hallway and into the opposite wall.

In the study, she could hear glass shattering, but she didn't have time to wonder what it meant. There were voices from upstairs now, and T.J. was answering them, telling them to hurry the hell up.

"T.J.—" She struggled to get to her feet, to reassure herself that he was all right. But the look on his face was anything but welcoming.

He shook her, hard, by her upper arms. For a moment it was nearly impossible to catch her breath, between the strength of his grip and the anger in his face. "When I say I don't want you following me," he said furiously, "it's an *order,* damn it."

And then suddenly he had let her go. Jenny pushed herself upright with the wall at her back and heard one of the men shouting that Ross was in the back garden. T.J. was on the move again instantly. Jenny could hear his footsteps thundering down the hallway, and she was dimly aware of a back door opening, and shouts from the yard. At the same time, there was a commotion from the front—neighbors, she thought, and maybe the police. James Wilder must have called them from a neighbor's house, as they'd planned.

All of it seemed to wash over her, leaving her feeling distant and surreal. The only person who really mattered was T.J., and T.J. was alive. And he'd just made it as plain as possible that Jenny's intervention had not been welcome.

"I probably saved your life, you bastard." She was on her feet now, realizing just how shaky she was after her sprint across the street and her confrontation with the man who had been trying to kill T.J. "If it hadn't been for me, you'd probably be dead. And all you can think about is that you'd rather you were on your own."

"Ma'am?"

Jenny was startled by the woman's voice. She turned to see a uniformed police officer coming quickly down the half flight of steps.

"They're in the backyard," Jenny said, suddenly weary of the whole adventure. "General Ross tried to kill a man. I don't know if they've caught him or not."

It wasn't very clear, and the officer looked puzzled as she hurried toward the open back door. But it was all the explanation Jenny felt capable of making at the moment. Her head was still ringing with the force of T.J.'s big body slamming into hers, but it was the body blow of his rejection that really hurt. It was going to take a long time to recover completely from the force of his words and his anger, she thought wearily.

Well, she'd started the day with a lot of things on her mind, but most of them boiled down to just one question. Once this was all over, was T.J. Madison any likelier than he'd ever been to regard her as a partner in his life instead of a problem to be solved, a memory to be put aside, a responsibility to agonize over?

It hurt unbearably to know that when they'd needed each other just now, needed each other for survival itself, he still couldn't see past his own stubbornly independent way of conducting his life. She'd hoped against hope that the day would end differently. But at least it had ended, she thought, listening to the sounds from outside that seemed to indicate Haviland Ross had finally been cornered and caught. The hunt was over, and Jenny had her answer at last.

Chapter 15

Pete Alvarez's diary

I have one wish for her, really. Just one. I had the same wish for me, once. Not anything ambitious, just a wish for a safe home. A happy home. Someone she cares for, someone who cares about her, as much as I care about her.

The devil is greedy about these things. He must be unhappy—what else would make a man do the things he's done? Anyone else's happiness is like an insult to him. He took away mine. I can't let him take hers away, too.

I don't remember when I saw her the last time. I don't know how old she is now. Maybe she's grown, maybe she's married. I remember she looked like me. Dark eyes, just like me.

Nobody can live this kind of life and survive to be an old man. The devil took care of that. But sometimes I think about her dark eyes, looking just like mine. And I think it doesn't matter as much. He is still the devil, but there's something in the world that he can't destroy. Something of me.

If she could just be happy, it would all have been worth it, after all.

"I think that's it." Patricia Nesbitt closed the last file folder in the pile and looked at Jenny across her dining room table. "I know I've been carrying on like Superwoman these past few months, but I have to admit it feels good to be able to stop thinking about work for a little while."

"I should hope so. Even if you weren't pregnant, you still have all that vacation time coming to you. If nothing else, having this baby will force you to take a little time off."

"It's done more than that. It's funny—Steven and I have always said we would get around to having a family someday, but the time just never felt right. And then this happened more or less by accident, and at first we were in a complete panic, as I'm sure you remember." Patricia gave a wry smile. "And now that it's actually happening, I'm starting to see that this is going to change absolutely everything about my life, and I don't even mind anymore. That probably sounds like a pretty slapdash way to be looking at having a baby, but—"

"It sounds fine." Jenny spoke quickly, before her friend's words could prompt the tears that seemed to be just below the surface these last few days. "You and Steven are going to be wonderful parents," she added. "And I doubt the baby is going to think you've been slapdash about things."

"Well, at least his room is done." Patricia eased herself from the depths of the sofa and sat up as straight as she could. "Do you want to see it?"

Jenny, too, had once decorated a baby's room with love and hope in her heart. She had made curtains on a borrowed sewing machine and wished she'd had the strength and energy to put up new wallpaper in the apartment she'd rented for herself. Since she hadn't, she'd made do by hanging posters and painting the room's trim a gentle, robin's-egg blue.

She could still see the exact hue of it when she closed her eyes. But the baby had never come home to her little room. She'd spent the five brief months of her life in the special ward for premature babies, finally giving up her determined struggle as one too many infections attacked her tiny body.

"Jenny?" Patricia's voice sounded startled. "Did I say something to upset you?"

Jenny blinked away the stubborn tears. She was getting tired of them, she told herself fiercely. It was time to stop mourning her lost hopes and get on with life again.

"It's all right," she said. "I've just been...unsettled since I got back."

"I noticed. Do you want to tell me about it?"

Jenny hesitated. It might do some good, she thought, to share the story of the past week with her sympathetic friend. But that meant opening up so many things, from her first sight of T.J. sitting on her front steps, cocky and almost too good-looking to be true, to the moment last Tuesday evening when she'd watched him leading a captured Gen. Haviland Ross into a waiting police car.

T.J. hadn't looked her way, even once. His jaw had been clamped in that grim line that told her he was fighting against something in himself that a court order couldn't have gotten him to admit. And she hadn't seen him since then, although she'd expected to. She had been questioned by a succession of military and law enforcement officials, until the terms CIA and FBI and DEA were all jumbled together in her head like alphabet soup. She'd been asked to stay on in Washington for another day, until an official statement could be taken, and someone—she wasn't sure which agency was behind it—had very kindly rented her an expensive hotel room downtown.

But she hadn't seen T.J., not even fleetingly. The last words she'd had from him had been angry ones, telling her that her help had been unwelcome, even though it had very likely saved his life.

Her eyes started to fill again now, remembering it. *When I say I don't want you following me, it's an order,* he'd barked at her. As though she were still the little sister, much loved but also much too young and sheltered to share in the life he'd made for himself outside his family.

"I don't really want to talk about it," she said to Patricia. "At least, not now. I might at some point. And I want to see the baby's room at some point, too, but not today, all right?"

Patricia nodded, obviously interested, but just as obviously willing to give Jenny the time she was asking for. Patricia accepted her friend's extended hand to help her get to her feet, and the two women walked together through the kitchen toward the door. As Patricia opened it, she asked, "You haven't mentioned what happened with my ex-client, the one you talked to earlier in the week. Was he able to tell you anything?"

"He sure was. It turns out he was a military aide assigned to the same command post as the general who was after T.J. and me." Jenny had given her friend the bare bones of the extraordinary adventure she'd been on, promising to fill in the gaps at a later date.

But Patricia deserved a little more information for having so quickly come up with the man who'd proven to be a damning witness against Haviland Ross. "Your ex-client not only had his own suspicions about the general, but he's been able to put us onto some of his colleagues who've been willing to talk." She'd learned that much before leaving Washington on Thursday morning. "Ross was pretty fiendish about the way he did business. People who were in a position to blow the whistle on him had a habit of becoming addicted to the drugs he was responsible for exporting.''

"Just like your father," Patricia mused.

"Exactly like my father. And once these men were hooked, no one took them seriously as witnesses.''

"Including me." Patricia shook her head, looking disturbed now. "Paranoid delusions are a common result of narcotic abuse. I accepted my client's fantasies without thinking twice, which ought to be a lesson to me.''

"I don't think you can blame yourself too hard," Jenny said. "Ross's victims even ended up doubting their own experiences. My father's diary is full of garbled interpretations of what really happened to him. The general had a good deal—a steady income from the heroin he was continuing to bring into this country from his connections in southeast Asia, and a lot of potential witnesses that nobody would ever listen to.''

"Thank God it's been stopped.''

"I know." As T.J. had suspected, Ross's carefully constructed plot had fallen to bits once his accomplices had started testifying against him. Haviland Ross's personal empire had virtually collapsed by now.

Patricia was reaching around to rub the small of her back, stretching slightly. "If you ever decide to do this," she said, smiling, "make sure you have somebody around to rub your back for you. Even with all Steven's ministrations, it *still* hurts to stand up.''

I'm going to have to get out of here, Jenny thought. There didn't seem to be any subject that wasn't loaded with emotional bombshells, all ticking away dangerously.

She gave her friend a determined smile, and said, "You'd better get off your feet, then. I'll call you if anything comes up after I've read these files, but you've been so organized about getting them ready that I can't imagine I'll have any problems.''

Everyone seemed to be out driving on this first truly balmy Saturday. It was a relief to have to concentrate hard on the traffic, and on handling the still-unfamiliar rental car she'd driven from Washington two days ago. She had kept the car she and T.J. had used while watching Haviland Ross's house, because her own car was still—with luck—in a wooded glade somewhere down the road from the Night o' Rest Motel in the Blue Ridge Mountains. Getting it back was just one of the many loose ends she was going to have to start tying up soon.

But not yet. She'd promised herself the rest of the weekend to come to terms with everything that had gone on in her life since T.J. had shown up in it again. She'd desperately needed the last two nights just to catch up on sleep, for one thing. She felt as though she hadn't had a real night's sleep since T.J. had arrived last Friday night. And the night she'd spent alone in the posh hotel room in Washington, D.C., had been full of wakeful tossing and turning. She'd been half expecting T.J. to call, or to show up in his old sudden and dramatic way.

But there hadn't been so much as a message on her answering machine when she arrived home in Charlotte. She'd gone briskly about the business of ordering a replacement door—the superintendent had had the bullet-riddled original covered with plywood, and it was an all too grisly reminder of how close she and T.J. had come to death several times this past week.

Jenny had carried on from dealing with the door to cleaning up the mess that the two gunmen had made in searching her apartment. Her belongings were thrown all over the place, drawers overturned, piles of paper disturbed. Even getting things back in order hadn't calmed her restlessness, so finally she had decided to turn her excess energy to potting the plants that were wilting from lack of moisture on her balcony.

But just setting foot out the balcony door had been enough to bring back a flood of memories that had overwhelmed her: T.J. sitting grinning at her in her balcony chair, T.J. gathering her into his arms to kiss her, T.J. next to her in bed at night at the Wanderers' Rest, behaving for all the world as though he wanted them to be together forever instead of just for one stolen moment in time....

She'd spent the rest of the evening in tears, unable to fight off the waves of anger and frustration and loss that were rolling over her. And since then she'd been trying, tentatively, to pick up the pieces.

Taking on some of Patricia's work load was a good place to start, she thought. Talking to clients again, getting to know Patricia's cases, remembering that other people, too, had difficult griefs to come to terms with, would be a kind of therapy for Jenny.

She was planning to spend the rest of the day going through Patricia's files in more detail. Her plans altered radically when she opened her apartment door.

She still hadn't quite gotten over the uneasy feeling that danger might be lurking around every corner she turned. She felt the anxiety of it as she turned her key in the lock, and gave a small sigh of relief when she saw that the living room and kitchen were empty.

And then she heard running water.

In her apartment—in her bathroom, to be exact. Jenny froze, instinctively debating with herself whether to run or stand her ground. Was it possible that it *wasn't* over, after all—that all of General Ross's accomplices *hadn't* been caught, and some of them had come to Charlotte for retribution against the woman who'd helped to point the finger at them? In which case, what on earth were they doing in her bathroom?

She didn't have time to come to any definite conclusions. The sound of the running tap ended abruptly, and T.J. Madison appeared in her hallway.

Her astonishment at seeing him was absolute. It made her realize—after the first few seconds of shock—how completely she'd written him off, how utterly certain she'd been that she would never see him again.

He was walking toward her now as though he had every right in the world to be here. For a moment Jenny was disoriented, half wondering whether the dramatic events of the past days had really happened at all, or whether they had come to an ending different from the one she remembered. Had T.J. really shouted those hurtful words of rejection at her in the awful moments after General Ross had fired at him? Or had things ended the way she'd hoped, with T.J. recognizing that they belonged together? Was that why he was here now, sauntering down her hallway and drying his hands on the thighs of his jeans as though he did this *every* Saturday afternoon?

His steady grin only added to her confusion. And then she remembered his skill with locks.

"You picked the lock on my door," she said accusingly. "Doesn't it ever occur to you that you might not be welcome, T.J.?"

She saw his grin falter slightly. He was smiling at her out of pure bravado, she recognized. He was, in fact, unsure of his welcome. And he had good reason to be.

Jenny had spent the last couple of days working hard to come to terms with the fact that T.J. Madison just wasn't the man for her. She loved him, it was true. And she wanted desperately to believe—based on the way passion flared between them whenever they were within touching distance of each other—that T.J. loved her, too, as far as T.J. was really capable of settling down and loving anyone.

But T.J.'s definition of love was obviously very different from her own. And that was the difficult truth she'd been grappling with since coming back to Charlotte. It wasn't going to help to have to tell him so, face-to-face.

But she could do it if she had to. She lifted her chin, and added, "I could call the police and charge you with breaking and entering, you know."

"Please don't."

The simple phrase wasn't what she'd been expecting. T.J. had reached the living room by now, and she could see in the light she'd switched on that he looked as tired as she still felt. His eyes bore the marks of sleepless nights, too, and something in the way he hitched his thumbs into his belt loops and let his strong arms hang slack at his sides made her think that he was fighting off a weariness that was bone-deep, or maybe even deeper.

She knew how that kind of weariness felt. She'd been feeling it herself, ever since T.J. had walked away from her last Tuesday evening. And she wasn't about to let him forget about that.

"Give me one good reason why I *shouldn't* call the police," she said.

"Because I would just tell them I was practicing breaking into a friend's apartment to check the security in this building, which frankly isn't as impressive as I thought the first time I was here." He pulled something out of his back pocket and handed her—of all things—a business card. "I'm just drumming up business, that's all."

"Thomas Jefferson Madison" the raised black ink on the card read. "Security Specialist." There was a toll-free number printed under the words.

There were too many things to be astounded about all at once. "I thought you hated using your full name," she said to him. "You always said you didn't like the feeling that you had to live up to not just one president, but two."

T.J. shrugged. He was wearing a blue-striped flannel shirt, tucked into his jeans, and the masculine slant of his shoulders and hips was making Jenny's pulse rate quicken. Something in the way he shrugged made her think his gunshot wound wasn't entirely healed, and that caught at her, too, making it harder to stay as aloof as she wanted to.

"I thought it sounded more dependable this way," he said. "You know, like the kind of guy you would want to trust to make your home secure."

"What happened to the CID?"

"They're still in business, last I heard."

"T.J." Jenny put the business card down on her hall table and moved into the living room. "Explain yourself."

The phrase was one Colonel Madison had used, usually when his rebellious son had done something even more outrageous than usual. Jenny chose the words deliberately, but even they didn't seem able to chase T.J.'s grin away. It hung on, half defiant, half amused, daring her to make him stop.

He shrugged again. "There's not a whole lot to explain," he said. "I suddenly realized, when Haviland Ross pulled out that cannon he called a handgun, that I was tired of letting people shoot at me in the name of making a living."

He paused. He seemed to be finished, but Jenny motioned to him that she was far from satisfied. "Go on," she said.

"So I quit."

"And now you're going to break into people's houses to convince them they need you to set up security systems for them."

"Well, I wasn't planning on breaking in on a regular basis. This was just a one-time experiment, kind of. Seeing that you're an old friend and all."

"T.J." She shed her jacket and dropped her purse next to the sofa, feeling oddly as though she were rolling up her sleeves to do battle with a tough and unpredictable foe. "Did you really come all the way back down here to try to convince me that I need a better security system in my apartment?"

She was close enough to him now to read the expression in his eyes. His grin might still be in place, but his eyes were telling her he was far from as certain as he looked. *Good,* she thought.

"Well, no," he said. "That's not really why I came."

"I'm glad to hear it. Why don't you tell me the *real* story?"

He eased his big frame into a comfortable chair, and Jenny sat down, just as tentatively, on the sofa. They were both sitting on the edges of their seats, she noticed, as though they expected to have to get up and run at any moment.

T.J. cleared his throat and ran a hand through his hair. It needed a trim, Jenny noticed. And he clearly needed about a week's sleep, as she did. She fought off the difficult, tender feelings that kept creeping in, and frowned at him as he started speaking.

"I thought you might have gotten the wrong impression from the way we left things on Tuesday evening," he said. "At Haviland Ross's house, I mean."

She knew exactly what he meant. He seemed determined to stay casual about this, as though they'd parted after a minor misunderstanding. "What would make you think that?" she demanded tartly. "Was it the fact that immediately after I saved your life—and don't deny it, T.J., because you know Ross would have shot at you again if I hadn't showed up right then—immediately after that, you started yelling at me that I should have followed orders and stayed out of your way?"

T.J. winced. "I wish you wouldn't put it quite like that," he muttered.

"How *should* I put it, then? I thought you were making it perfectly clear that I'd been in your way all along—ever since you decided you didn't want to be in love with me when I was twenty-one. And what happened at General Ross's house was just the final straw."

T.J. was frowning now, too. That rakish grin had gone. "Hell, sugar, it wasn't that I didn't want to be in love with you when you were twenty-one. I *was* in love with you—I never would have made love to you if I hadn't been." She hadn't recovered from the shock of the statement when he went on. "It was just that I didn't want *you* to be in love with *me.*"

She had to puzzle that through. "Is there a difference?" she asked finally.

He waved one broad palm and left her question hanging. "What happened at Ross's place *was* the last straw," he said.

She noticed he'd veered abruptly away from the subject of love. *Same old T.J.,* she thought, and her heart contracted a little, preparing for more hurt to come.

But once again, T.J.'s words surprised her. "Here's how it looked to me, sugar," he was saying. "I kept trying to tell myself all along that this was my case, my adventure, and you were just along for the ride, more or less by accident." She saw the quick glitter of gold in his eyes and realized how deeply this was stirring him up. The thought was disturbing, but not unpleasant.

"And then, the moment we'd cornered Ross and I knew it was all over, I knew you were right when you said that you'd been as much a part of this as I was—maybe even more. And you're absolutely right that if you hadn't shown up in that doorway, Haviland Ross probably would have put me out of the picture for good."

She'd thought she was furious with T.J. She'd thought she could sit here and make him talk and wait until he'd explained himself satisfactorily. But at the idea of how very close he'd come to dying, Jenny felt something inside herself give way, and she said impulsively, "I wasn't thinking when I ran into that house, T.J. I just couldn't stand the idea that you might be killed. I still can't stand it now."

He seemed to catch the emotion in her voice, and he leaned forward, covering her hands with his. In spite of the tiredness in his face, the warmth and vitality of him were pulsating in his touch, and Jenny felt the stirring of something deep inside that she'd thought might be gone forever.

"I can't say I'm wild about the idea myself," he said. He was speaking casually again, but his eyes were very serious. "You know, Ross probably *would* have killed me if you hadn't come slamming through that front door when you did. It distracted him and put his aim off. And it gave me time to dive for cover. They told me at the CID that Ross had the highest target-shooting scores of anybody in his class at West Point. So I'm not just lucky to be alive—I'm *damn* lucky you didn't take my own advice about keeping out of the way."

He'd just admitted that his shouted, angry words of Tuesday evening had been a mistake, and the suddenness of it left Jenny feeling disoriented again. She'd been building her new world around T.J.'s rejection of her, and now it was gone.

"T.J., where have you *been* since Tuesday?" The question seemed suddenly important. "I didn't know how to find you—and I thought you might call, or leave a message, but—"

He made a face. "I've been sitting through more debriefing sessions than should be allowed by law," he told her. "First I had to explain about Haviland Ross. And then I had to explain why I was leaving the CID. And then I wanted to sort out...some things that Ross had said that night. To see if they were really true.''

"Things about your father, you mean."

"Yeah." T.J. reached for his jacket, which, she now noticed, he had slung over the back of a chair. He pulled a small cassette recorder out of an inner pocket. "I had to argue like hell before they would give me a copy of this, but I finally convinced them they owed it to me," he said. "I wanted you to hear it, so you'd know why I lost my head the way I did."

He pushed the Play button with his thumb, and Jenny heard his recorded voice, taut and metallic, coming out of the little machine.

"He was a recluse because he wasn't well." Jenny shuddered, remembering the nearly unbearable tension of hearing him say those words the first time. "And he died because his heart gave out on him. If you expect me to believe otherwise—''

"You can believe it or not, as you like." It was a voice Jenny hadn't heard before—the smooth, confident tone of General Haviland Ross. "All I'm saying is that if you think I was likely to let a threat like your father walk around loose without some assurance of his cooperation, you're more naive than I would have suspected. He died after a reunion with some of his fellow officers, didn't he? And perhaps it wasn't just a coincidence that one of my...associates happened to be at the same dinner. A pity about your father's weak heart, wasn't it?"

Jenny remembered the dinner well, and the shock of finding out that Colonel Madison, her adoptive father, had collapsed during it. The idea that Haviland Ross had engineered the heart attack was an appalling one, and she could see in T.J.'s eyes now that he still hadn't quite absorbed the monstrosity of it.

"You bastard." His recorded voice was faint, reflecting his shock. "You smooth-talking bastard. And I just bet you've got an alibi all ready, haven't you?"

"You may feel quite certain I have."

T.J.'s next words sounded louder, harder. "You're going down in flames for this, Ross," he said. "I don't know whether you're telling me the truth, but if you can sit there and even hint to me that you caused my father's death—"

"It *is* only a hint," the older man said, "so please don't imagine you can turn it against me. But since we're dealing in the realm of hints, I might add that it might have been your safety, and the Alvarez girl's, that kept your father so quiet all those years. When he started appearing in public again, it seemed risky to take the chance that he might talk to someone about it. A pity, really—the threat to harm the girl or yourself had been quite effective in shutting your father up."

Jenny was startled by the sudden change in the general's style. Until those last few moments, he'd been careful not to say anything that might directly incriminate him. But now he'd let slip something that amounted to a confession. And that must have meant—

T.J. had seen her puzzled look, and he nodded as she came to an understanding of what must have happened. "He waited until he saw that I was flummoxed by what he'd said about my father's death," he said, holding the Pause button briefly. "And by the time I realized what was happening, he had the gun out and aimed at me."

He released the button, and his own voice came out, stronger now. "By God," he was saying now, "if you even think of touching a hair on Jenny's head—"

"I've already thought of it, haven't I?" The pleasure in the general's voice made Jenny shiver. Her own father had called this man "the devil" with good reason, she thought. It was clear from the tape that Haviland Ross believed he was above any and all human rules—and human mercy. "Put your hands up, please, Mr. Madison. Let's be as civilized about this as we can."

There was a very long pause. Jenny remembered the agony of waiting in the car, imagining everything that might go wrong. And then the horrible certainty that T.J.'s next phrase had evoked.

"All right, they're up. Just leave her out of—"

The tape ended abruptly. "The bastard figured out I was taping the conversation," T.J. said, switching the machine off and stuffing it back into his jacket. "He pulled the cassette out, but fortunately he hadn't had time to destroy it before you came in. I think he was a bit panicked to find the transmitter, too. The idea that there were other witnesses threw him, which is probably why he shot at me. It was a crazy reaction, really. They've got him for attempted murder on top of everything else, and he's not likely to see the outside world again, even if he lives to be a hundred."

Jenny still couldn't stand the offhanded way he was talking about this. "T.J.," she said, "you are without a doubt the most maddening person I've *ever* met. How much did that shot miss you by?"

He shrugged. "Not much."

"Not much!" Jenny raised her hands and stood up suddenly. She was vaguely aware of T.J. following her lead, but then she was moving, pacing restlessly across the living room and back.

"I don't know how you can come through something like that and carry on as though it was no more important than being stung by a bee," she said. "I don't understand this desperado mentality that said you had to confront Ross by yourself in the first place. And, my God, T.J., you ought to know after all these years that the moment your emotions get caught up in something, your judgment goes right out the window. Remember that older girl down the street from us who used to call me names because I got the part she wanted in the school play?''

He nodded and seemed about to speak, but she went on anyway. ''You scared that poor kid half to death, because you were trying to defend me,'' she said. ''She's probably *still* trying to get over it. You've always been like that—all anybody had to do was upset me, and you were all over them like a wolf pack in hunting season. And then you walk into a situation as volatile as the one with General Ross, and he made some vague threats about my safety, and you completely lost your head. Didn't you?''

It seemed important to hear him admit it. And to her astonishment, he did, although it was little more than an incline of his dark, unruly head.

''When are you going to learn to understand yourself, T.J.?'' The words were pouring out of her now. She couldn't have stopped speaking if she'd wanted to, and suddenly she didn't want to. This was important, she knew. These were things she wished she'd had the maturity and strength to say to him long years ago.

''When are you going to see that you get yourself into more trouble, not less, running away from everything that makes you feel uncomfortable or angry or—or that just makes you *feel* in the first place? Haviland Ross only got the opportunity to shoot at you because he'd found your weak spot first. And you and I only got into this mess with each other because you let your feelings panic you, so you didn't stick around to see whether I might have anything to say on the subject.''

All of a sudden the flood of words ran dry. She turned at the end of her circuit around the room and saw that T.J. was facing her from only a few feet away. She was suddenly aware, too, that her voice had choked up on her, conveying all the anger and love and frustration she'd been struggling with in the last few days.

T.J. put his hands out and took her by the shoulders, in a much gentler version of the grip that had so infuriated her the last time they'd spoken. He didn't pull her closer, although she could feel the tug of attraction between them, beginning to build with the inevitable swell of a rising tide.

"You're right."

The simple phrase brought everything inside Jenny rocking to a halt. "I am?" she said involuntarily.

"Yes. Absolutely and completely." With that same gentleness, he steered her toward the sofa, and the two of them sat down. T.J. slid his wide palms down over her arms, until he was holding her two hands in his.

"You're right about a lot of things." He was trying for the casual air he'd sauntered in here with, Jenny could tell, but his voice, like her own, was suspiciously husky. "A lot of things changed for me when I found myself looking down the barrel of Haviland Ross's gun on Tuesday. And then, when you came barging in—" He looked away briefly, as if troubled by the memory.

"I shouted at you because I couldn't stand the idea that you might have been killed, too," he said, meeting her eyes again. "The shock of that stayed with me until we'd finally gotten General Ross behind bars. And then it hit me—that I was only alive because of you. And you were only alive because of me. And I'd been a damn fool not to realize all along that I'd been protecting myself from my own feelings as much as from anything else."

"T.J.—"

"And you're right that I've always gone off the deep end when it seemed as though you were unhappy, or in any kind of trouble. But it didn't occur to me until Tuesday night that the smartest thing to do, instead of charging off trying to slay dragons you weren't interested in, would be to stick around and see if there might be other ways to make you happy."

Jenny wasn't quite sure she believed what she was hearing. "T.J.," she said, very firmly, "what *have* you been doing since Tuesday night? When did you come to all these conclusions?"

"I told you—just about the time we got Ross to the police station. And then I had to sit and make a lot of long-winded statements to people, and then my boss had to talk to me, and by that time you were already on your way back here. And then I decided, to hell with it, I was going to take off and I didn't care who didn't like it. Except you can't just do that with the military—they have these damned procedures and things. I hustled them along as fast as I could, which wasn't as fast as I would have liked, but at least it gave me a couple of days to think about what I was going to do to support myself, and to get some new wheels and get down here." He stopped and looked at her, clearly waiting for an answer.

Jenny frowned. "I don't think," she said slowly, "that you've explained absolutely everything yet."

"I want to be with you, sugar. I don't want to be anywhere else. What else is there to explain?"

For a moment Jenny's head seemed to spin, and she had to hang on to the image of T.J.'s laughing, gold-specked eyes to keep her bearings. "You want to be with me all the time?" she asked, still feeling slightly dazed.

"Always and forever. You and . . . any children we happen to produce along the way."

There was no way he could keep up that laughing sound in his voice as he mentioned children. They had *happened* to produce a child the last time they'd let themselves love each other, and the experience had shaped Jenny's life in ways that had not been easy to cope with.

The sudden seriousness in T.J.'s eyes and voice now told her that instead of running away from the realization of what had happened, as he once would undoubtedly have done, he was facing up to it, absorbing its pain, refusing to let it deflect him from the main point, which was—

"I love you, sugar." He said the words softly, as if he were trying them out for the first time. Jenny's eyes swam with tears for a moment, and then she blinked them away.

"Are you very sure you're not just doing the same thing you've always done?" She felt compelled to ask the question. She'd hoped for this so long that it seemed impossible it was actually happening now—that T.J. Madison was holding her in his arms and telling her he loved her, that he wanted to be with her, to create a family with her. "Are you sure you're not just escaping from Washington because you don't like the way things turned out up there? Am I going to be more than a way station, T.J.?"

At that, he gave a full-throated laugh that told her beyond a doubt how ridiculous he found the idea. "You're not a way station," he said. "You're my harbor, Jenny. You're my safe haven. You're the only place I want to be. And if I'm pulling up my stakes in Washington, it's only because I want to be completely free to be wherever you are. If you won't have me yet, then I'll go and hang around on the periphery until you change your mind."

"You sound fairly confident that I will."

"Hell," he said. His voice was rich with satisfaction and possibility now. "If *I* can decide I want to put down my anchor for good, I figure anything's possible."

He didn't wait for her answer. Or maybe he saw it in her eyes. Jenny moved toward him in the same instant that he pulled her closer, and his lips closed over her happy acceptance of everything he was offering her.

"I love you, T.J. Madison," she breathed.

She knew, for all his sailor talk about harbors and anchors and safe havens, that he wasn't a man who was about to curl up and spend the rest of his life quietly on shore. She didn't want that—she wanted T.J. as wild and passionate and exhilarating as he'd always been.

But now he would be coming home to her. They would always have a home, whether it was a house in a city or a ship's cabin or the outer edge of an island set in the sea. That was what T.J.'s words had meant, and that was what Jenny was responding to as she met his eager kisses. Together, they would create their own harbor. They would shelter their children in it, as they hadn't been able to shelter baby Joy. They would make for themselves the kind of world Jenny's father had tried so hard to make for her. They had lost one chance, but all the sadness and secrets of the past had, in the end, brought them back to each other again

Together they would sail out beyond the horizon, and meet the challenge of the new day.

*   *   *   *   *

Dark secrets, dangerous desire...

Lovers
**DARK AND
DANGEROUS**

Three spine-tingling tales from the dark side
of love.

This October, enter the world of shadowy
romance as Silhouette presents the third in their
annual tradition of thrilling love stories and
chilling story lines. Written by three of
Silhouette's top names:

LINDSAY McKENNA
LEE KARR
RACHEL LEE

Haunting a store near you this October.

Only from

Silhouette®
TM

...where passion lives.

LDD

The Loops™

Is the future what it's cracked up to be?

This October, Christopher finds out what life's all about in

GETTING REAL: CHRISTOPHER
by Kathryn Jensen

He didn't know where he was going, but he knew where he came from: nowhere. But he was tough. He didn't need anything or anyone—especially not some brainy babe who wasn't his type anyway. Only problem was, she was driving him crazy with her quiet sexy ways! Christopher had learned the hard way that love never lasts, but maybe he was about to learn something new....

The ups and downs of life as you know it continue with

GETTING PERSONAL: BECKY
by Janet Quin Harkin

GETTING ATTACHED: CJ
by Wendy Corsi Staub

Get smart. Get into "The Loop!"

Only from

V *Silhouette*®

where passion lives.

LOOP3

JINGLE BELLS, WEDDING BELLS:
Silhouette's Christmas Collection for 1994

Christmas Wish List

*To beat the crowds at the malls and get the perfect present for *everyone,* even that snoopy Mrs. Smith next door!

*To get through the holiday parties without running my panty hose.

*To bake cookies, decorate the house and serve the perfect Christmas dinner—just like the women in all those magazines.

*To sit down, curl up and read my Silhouette Christmas stories!

Join *New York Times* bestselling author Nora Roberts, along with popular writers Barbara Boswell, Myrna Temte and Elizabeth August, as we celebrate the joys of Christmas—and the magic of marriage—with

JINGLE BELLS, WEDDING BELLS

Silhouette's Christmas Collection for 1994.

JBWB

SILHOUETTE®

Shadows™

MORE GREAT READING FROM
BARBARA FAITH

If you enjoyed Barbara Faith's DESERT MAN, you'll want to join her in November as she visits the dark side of love with DARK, DARK MY LOVER'S EYES, Silhouette Shadows #43.

When tutor Juliana Fleming accepted an assignment in Mexico, she had no idea the turn her life would take. Kico Vega—her solemn, needy student—immediately warmed to her presence, but Kico's father, Rafael, showed her nothing but contempt. Until he took Julie as his bride, ravishing her with his all-consuming desire—yet setting in motion Julie's worst nightmare.

Take a walk on the dark side of love with Barbara Faith—only in **SILHOUETTE SHADOWS**

You can also order Barbara Faith's first Shadows title, *A Silence of Dreams*, SS #13, by sending your name, address, zip or postal code along with a check or money order (please do not send cash) for $3.50, plus 75¢ postage and handling ($1.00 in Canada), payable to Silhouette Books, to:

In the U.S.	In Canada
Silhouette Books	Silhouette Books
3010 Walden Ave.	P. O. Box 636
P. O. Box 9077	Fort Erie, Ontario
Buffalo, NY 14269-9077	L2A 5X3

Please specify book title(s) with your order.
Canadian residents add applicable federal and provincial taxes.

BFSS

And now for something completely different....

**In October, look for
ANNIE AND THE OUTLAW (IM #597)
by Sharon Sala**

Gabriel Donner rode into Annie O'Brien's life like an outlaw—and an angel—saving her from the gang who threatened her safety. Yet the fight of Annie's life had only just begun, and bad-boy Gabe would move heaven and earth to save her again.

**Don't miss ANNIE AND THE OUTLAW,
by Sharon Sala, available this October,
only from**

SPELL5

Premiere

The stars are out in October at Silhouette! Read
captivating love stories by talented *new* authors—
in their very first Silhouette appearance.

Sizzle with Susan Crosby's
THE MATING GAME—Desire #888
...when Iain Mackenzie and Kani Warner are forced
to spend their days—and *nights*—together in *very* close
tropical quarters!

Explore the passion in Sandra Moore's
HIGH COUNTRY COWBOY—Special Edition #918
...where Jake Valiteros tries to control the demons that
haunt him—along with a stubborn woman as wild as the
Wyoming wind.

Cherish the emotion in Kia Cochrane's
MARRIED BY A THREAD—Intimate Moments #600
...as Dusty McKay tries to recapture the love he once
shared with his wife, Tori.

Exhilarate in the power of Christie Clark's
TWO HEARTS TOO LATE—Romance #1041
...as Kirby Anne Gordon and Carl Tannon fight for custody
of a small child...and battle their growing attraction!

Shiver with Val Daniels'
BETWEEN DUSK AND DAWN—Shadows #42
...when a mysterious stranger claims to want to save
Jonna Sanders from a serial killer.

Catch the classics of tomorrow—*premiering* today—
Only from

Silhouette®
™

PREM94

"HOORAY FOR HOLLYWOOD" SWEEPSTAKES

HERE'S HOW THE SWEEPSTAKES WORKS

OFFICIAL RULES — NO PURCHASE NECESSARY

To enter, complete an Official Entry Form or hand print on a 3" x 5" card the words "HOORAY FOR HOLLYWOOD", your name and address and mail your entry in the pre-addressed envelope (if provided) or to: "Hooray for Hollywood" Sweepstakes, P.O. Box 9076, Buffalo, NY 14269-9076 or "Hooray for Hollywood" Sweepstakes, P.O. Box 637, Fort Erie, Ontario L2A 5X3. Entries must be sent via First Class Mail and be received no later than 12/31/94. No liability is assumed for lost, late or misdirected mail.

Winners will be selected in random drawings to be conducted no later than January 31, 1995 from all eligible entries received.

Grand Prize: A 7-day/6-night trip for 2 to Los Angeles, CA including round trip air transportation from commercial airport nearest winner's residence, accommodations at the Regent Beverly Wilshire Hotel, free rental car, and $1,000 spending money. (Approximate prize value which will vary dependent upon winner's residence: $5,400.00 U.S.); 500 Second Prizes: A pair of "Hollywood Star" sunglasses (prize value: $9.95 U.S. each). Winner selection is under the supervision of D.L. Blair, Inc., an independent judging organization, whose decisions are final. Grand Prize travelers must sign and return a release of liability prior to traveling. Trip must be taken by 2/1/96 and is subject to airline schedules and accommodations availability.

Sweepstakes offer is open to residents of the U.S. (except Puerto Rico) and Canada who are 18 years of age or older, except employees and immediate family members of Harlequin Enterprises, Ltd., its affiliates, subsidiaries, and all agencies, entities or persons connected with the use, marketing or conduct of this sweepstakes. All federal, state, provincial, municipal and local laws apply. Offer void wherever prohibited by law. Taxes and/or duties are the sole responsibility of the winners. Any litigation within the province of Quebec respecting the conduct and awarding of prizes may be submitted to the Regie des loteries et courses du Quebec. All prizes will be awarded; winners will be notified by mail. No substitution of prizes are permitted. Odds of winning are dependent upon the number of eligible entries received.

Potential grand prize winner must sign and return an Affidavit of Eligibility within 30 days of notification. In the event of non-compliance within this time period, prize may be awarded to an alternate winner. Prize notification returned as undeliverable may result in the awarding of prize to an alternate winner. By acceptance of their prize, winners consent to use of their names, photographs, or likenesses for purpose of advertising, trade and promotion on behalf of Harlequin Enterprises, Ltd., without further compensation unless prohibited by law. A Canadian winner must correctly answer an arithmetical skill-testing question in order to be awarded the prize.

For a list of winners (available after 2/28/95), send a separate stamped, self-addressed envelope to: Hooray for Hollywood Sweepstakes 3252 Winners, P.O. Box 4200, Blair, NE 68009.

CBSRLS

OFFICIAL ENTRY COUPON

"Hooray for Hollywood"
SWEEPSTAKES!

Yes, I'd love to win the Grand Prize — a vacation in Hollywood — or one of 500 pairs of "sunglasses of the stars"! Please enter me in the sweepstakes!

This entry must be received by December 31, 1994.
Winners will be notified by January 31, 1995.

Name _____

Address _____ Apt. _____

City _____

State/Prov. _____ Zip/Postal Code _____

Daytime phone number _____
(area code)

Account # _____

Return entries with invoice in envelope provided. Each book in this shipment has two entry coupons — and the more coupons you enter, the better your chances of winning!

DIRCBS

OFFICIAL ENTRY COUPON

"Hooray for Hollywood"
SWEEPSTAKES!

Yes, I'd love to win the Grand Prize — a vacation in Hollywood — or one of 500 pairs of "sunglasses of the stars"! Please enter me in the sweepstakes!

This entry must be received by December 31, 1994.
Winners will be notified by January 31, 1995.

Name _____

Address _____ Apt. _____

City _____

State/Prov. _____ Zip/Postal Code _____

Daytime phone number _____
(area code)

Account # _____

Return entries with invoice in envelope provided. Each book in this shipment has two entry coupons — and the more coupons you enter, the better your chances of winning!

DIRCBS